They had the evidence—for a moment—then it was gone and, with it, their best chance to help Curtis Ray…

With a quick motion of her hand, Jayme pulled out a thick volume and let the book fall open. She shook it and a single DVD dropped out. She caught the disk before it hit the floor. Holding the DVD in her hands, she looked triumphant.

The girl had put on a great show, Niki acknowledged. It wasn't hard to guess what really happened. Sometime after their initial fruitless search, Jayme had returned to the library and found the missing DVD. It didn't matter because, by then, Curtis Ray was safely out of the hospital and at Open Palms. The chances were good he wouldn't go to jail for stealing the disk, so Jayme decided to hide the DVD again until it was needed. Now that Shamberg was dead, his secret life could be exposed without putting Curtis Ray in danger. Niki wondered if Jayme came up with this plan, or if it had been hatched by Curtis Ray. Was Curtis Ray on this disk? Was that the reason he felt compelled to break into Shamberg's house?

"Well done, Jayme," Niki told the girl as they reached the door. "We'll hand this over to the police. The FBI will be interested, too."

Jayme's eyes widened. "FBI?"

"They're closing the camp. Curtis Ray and Markey will never have to go back there."

A smile spread across Jayme's face. "For real?"

"Yes, for real."

"Awesome. Can I tell Curtis Ray and Markey?"

"We'll call them when we get back."

Niki pulled open the door and held it for Jayme who stepped out into the bright sunlight. A second later, someone plowed into them with enough force to knock both Niki and Jayme against the wall. He ripped the DVD out of Jayme's hand and raced toward the street.

When two young runaways break into a wealthy man's home, with horrific consequences, ex-cop and teen shelter counselor, Niki Alexander, comes to their defense. She soon discovers their motive had been to uncover a crime more heinous than two children could handle alone, and she is determined to finish what they started…

KUDOS for *A Matter of Revenge*

In *A Matter of Revenge* by Laura Elvebak, Niki Alexander is a former cop and teen counselor who's determined to help a couple of runaway teens. Niki gets involved when the mother of a missing girl calls Niki from prison and begs her to find her daughter. The girl was last seen with another runaway, a twelve-year-old boy, and both have been missing for some time. Fearing the worst, Niki starts investigating, but what she discovers is almost more than she can handle. Learning that the two missing kids have broken into a wealthy man's home, Niki assumes they were looking for valuables to steal for money to survive. She soon finds out that she was wrong. The kids didn't break into the house for valuables, but for evidence of a much worse crime than burglary. The story is well written, fast-paced, and touching, giving you a glimpse into the harsh, difficult, and often tragic life of young runaways and the people who try to protect them from others who would prey on them. I strongly recommend it. ~ *Taylor Jones, Reviewer*

A Matter of Revenge by Laura Elvebak is the story of two young runaways and a woman who will go to the mat to protect them. Our heroine, Niki Alexander, was a detective with the Houston Police Department, but she left to become a teen counselor. She now runs a teen shelter called Open Palms, working with troubled teens. Niki gets a call from someone she knew when she was cop. The woman is calling from prison because she just found out that her eleven-year-old daughter has been missing for a month. Niki agrees to try and find the girl, though she has her doubts that she'll find the daughter alive after all this time. As she attempts to find her, Niki discovers that the girl was an accomplice to a break in of a wealthy man's home in Houston. The girl's partner in crime is a thirteen-year-old boy who is still missing and who engineered the break in, telling the girl that he was there to get evidence of a crime. But the evidence he supposedly took is also missing. Niki needs to find it if she is going to help the two troubled kids, but the girl isn't forthcoming, as she doesn't trust adults. And with good reason. *A Matter of Revenge* tells a chilling story of abuse, greed, and revenge, opening a window on the world of runaway teens that we don't normally see. It's not a pretty picture, but Elvebak handles the subject with compassion and sensitivity. Filled with realistic and well-developed characters, as well as an intriguing mystery, it's a book that all teens and parents should read. ~ *Regan Murphy, Reviewer*

ACKNOWLEDGEMENTS

This book wouldn't have been written without the insight of my critique partners: Kay, Amy, Julie, Bob, Dean, Gene, Clif, and Doug, and the generosity of Charlie, Susie, and Isabella for lending their home to our Wednesday night group. Finally, I will always be grateful for the loyal support and love shown by Shawn, Brian, and Tanya.

A
MATTER
OF
REVENGE

Laura Elvebak

A Black Opal Books Publication

DEDICATION

In remembrance of Tara who brought to my attention
the plight of runaways and throwaways
and introduced me to the street church
where I heard so many stories that needed to be told.

I also dedicate this book to Covenant House in Houston,
the inspiration for Open Palms,
for their unwavering work with troubled teenagers.

CHAPTER 1

In the evening haze under a full moon, the pink house in River Oaks, Houston's wealthiest neighborhood, loomed like a castle among the massive oaks. Bushes shaped like gargoyles lined the stairs leading to the burgundy double doors. Eleven-year-old Jayme Rockland had once seen gargoyles in a scary movie. She was sure the monsters were snarling at her as she inched forward. Better not to look at them. Curtis Ray might read her fear and send her away.

He gave a nervous cough, and then covered it by scowling at the house. She knew him well enough to know he'd rather die than show fear. He told everyone he was thirteen, but she knew better. He'd been only one grade ahead of her, not two, when his folks died and he got sent away. But she let him say whatever. Friends stuck together no matter what.

"This be the right place," he announced in a low tone.

She glanced at him, catching the slight tremor in his voice. Who was he trying to convince? For the first time since they'd left the streets of Montrose, doubt crept in like the ugly cockroaches in Granny's house. Her mom once said fear was as contagious as the flu. Now she knew what that meant. What if they were on the wrong street? What if someone waited for them on the other side of the door?

"Why you whispering?" Her voice quivered. "You said nobody would be home." To hide the itch of fear crawling on her skin, she laughed. Didn't help. She stared at the house and sucked in air. "You sure he's gone?"

"He's supposed to be out of town." He didn't sound so sure.

"Yeah, well, you know supposing don't mean nothing." She picked up a stone from the ground and tossed it into the grass.

"Owner's ain't here," he said in a firm voice. "Nobody's here. What's the matter? You scared?"

"Not." She imagined the castle's ghosts peering at her from the windows. "Just saying."

"Come on, we're going around back. Hurry."

She skipped to catch up. "You sure you know what you're doing?"

"Yeah, now stop asking stupid questions."

She followed him around the side of the house and through an unlocked iron gate. Her eyes widened when a gigantic pool came into sight. Holy crap! And a tennis court? Their home town could fit in this man's backyard. She reached into her pocket and took out the cell phone Curtis Ray had given her and pressed the camera app. Pointed, focused and clicked.

He jerked his head toward the sound, yanked her hand down, and snapped her out of her stardust moment. "Not yet," he whispered.

He led her to a small tool shed by the main house and opened the door. She peered in and recoiled at the darkness, the smell of gasoline and pesticides. Dirt scattered the floor. She imagined creatures, hidden in the corner, waiting to pounce. Rats, maybe. Spiders or snakes, even. She wanted to stay outside, but if he could pretend to be unafraid, so could she.

He took a pen light from his pocket and shined the light around the room. He aimed at a flower pot in the corner. Kneeling next to it, he put his hand inside. He closed his eyes.

What was he doing? She listened for sounds, the scratching of animals or the buzz of insects, but all remained quiet. She turned her attention back to Curtis Ray and watched him pull his hand out of the pot. Empty. He dipped into a second pot next to it. This time he came up with a piece of paper wrapped around a key. He tucked it in his pocket, stood, and turned off the pen light. He motioned to the door and they stepped out under the dwindling light of a darkening blue-gray sky.

He acted like she wasn't there. She had to quicken her steps to keep up with him. To her surprise, they arrived at the back door. The key fit into the lock and the door opened.

She couldn't keep silent. "How did ya know?"

He ignored her and entered. To his immediate left, a pad with numbered buttons flashed red. He flattened the piece of paper against the wall next to the pad and, while squinting at it, pushed a series of buttons. The red light turned green. He turned to her and grinned and then gave her a wink. She clapped her hands and he pounded his fist against his puffed out chest.

"Okay, Superman, you never done this before, I bet," she said with a giggle.

To her disappointment his moment of triumph deflated like a balloon. He scanned the room behind them. "Quiet," he warned.

She followed his gaze and her jaw went slack. Soft overhead lights set into the ceiling came on automatically when they stepped under the archway. The kitchen didn't resemble any other she'd seen, except in Granny's magazines. Steel and chrome so polished she could see her reflection. She ran her hand over black granite countertops, expecting to feel grit, but instead found a cold, smooth surface. The light glinted off the copper bottoms of pans hanging from the ceiling. The air smelled of garlic that hung in wire baskets and yellow roses that sprang from glass vases. She dug out the cell phone and clicked away with feverish urgency.

Curtis Ray noticed and covered the phone with his hand. "Not yet. Come on. His office is upstairs."

She ran to keep up with him. Her worn tennis shoes sank in white carpet as she passed through rooms, catching sight of the rich wood of a dining table, overstuffed chairs, and a sofa in the living room, and a theater screen in the den. She wanted to stay there, try out the food, sit in the chairs, and maybe lay in the beds upstairs. Like Goldilocks.

They were halfway up the stairs when she thought she heard a noise. "Did you hear that?"

He stopped, cocked his head. "I don't hear anything."

"I did, I think. What if he's here now?"

"Won't be home for hours," he said. "If he shows, we go out the window."

Out the window? She tried to swallow but her tongue stuck to the roof of her mouth. A hammering hit behind her eyes. Or was that her heart?

"Hurry, Curtis Ray," she whispered. She imagined ghost eyes following her, evil spirits. Her skin tingled. She felt as if she were balancing on a bouncing tightrope. A burst of nervous laughter broke from her lips.

He whirled on her, the whites of his eyes streaked in red. "What's the matter with you?"

"Nothing," she said, not quite able to smother another giggle. If nobody was home, why did they need to be quiet?

"Out of control," she'd heard Mom say to Grams, over and over. "Girl's plumb out of control." That was funny, coming from Mom. Out of control landed Mom in prison.

She listened again, and when she heard nothing, she caught up with Curtis Ray at the top of the staircase and followed him to the room across from the stairs. He flipped a switch on the wall and two lamps glowed with light.

A big wooden desk, polished and neat, filled the center of the room. File cabinets hugged the wall on her left. Paintings and certificates plastered the wall and framed pictures decorated the desk. One showed a pretty blonde woman in a red suit smiling at the camera. Did she live here, too? Curtis Ray had never mentioned her. The next frame showed a man with his arm around the pretty woman, on the beach.

Didn't look like Galveston where Mom took her once. The scene reminded her of magazine pictures, though if someone asked her, she couldn't explain why. Maybe, on account of their phony smiles, each figure looked like a model. She concentrated on the man's face. He looked straight ahead, eyes cold, lips thin. Something about him made her shiver. She hoped she never had to meet him.

Her shoulder brushed against a world globe mounted on a stand near the window. The movement caused the globe to sway, and she caught it before the stand fell sideways.

"Don't touch anything," Curtis Ray said, glaring at her. He turned to the desk and opened the drawers one at a time. He riffled through each of them. Finally, in an act of desperation, he threw half the contents on the floor.

She stuck her tongue out at him and wandered to the window. The glass still held the heat from the day. Below she saw the pool, shimmering under the moonlight. A long drop if they had to escape. Her stomach growled and she glanced at Curtis Ray. He didn't seem to notice.

She moved to the doorway and glanced at the closed doors lining the hall. Something about them raised Goosebumps on her arms. She'd never live in a house like this. The idea made her want to laugh. A chance to fly to the moon would be more likely. After a moment she tiptoed to the stairs and listened, but still heard nothing. Even the silence gave her the creeps.

She rubbed her arms hard and went back to the study. A bottom drawer swallowed Curtis Ray's arm to his elbow. Concentration deepened the lines around his eyes and mouth. Slowly he pulled out his hand, clasped around a set of gold keys.

"What're they for?" she whispered.

Instead of answering, he went out into the hall. She followed and stopped to watch him try the first closed door. He spread out the keys and stuck one in the lock. Didn't turn, but the next one he tried opened the door with little effort. He disappeared inside the room and came out a few minutes later, shaking his head. He repeated this routine with all the doors. She wanted to ask him why they were locked and how he knew, but he seemed far away like he'd forgotten she was there.

She turned her attention to the camera phone in her hand. Curiosity nagged at her, begging to be satisfied. She glanced down the hall to make sure he was too busy to notice her. With quickened breath, she opened the gallery of photos Curtis Ray had briefly shared with her earlier. He said his friend, Markey, had borrowed the camera, from someone—he didn't know who—to take the pictures, but afterward, got scared and gave the phone to Curtis Ray to hide. Curtis Ray suspected the worst when Markey disappeared.

Nothing had changed since the first time she saw the photos. Her eyes had burned when Curtis Ray let her see the room with its single cot and the large round light focused on it. She wanted to ask him why the room was important to him, but his expression stopped her. His voice turned flat and detached when he told her to turn it off and not to look at it again. Whatever happened in that room, she didn't want to know. She only hoped never to see him look that way again.

She turned off the phone and shoved it in her pocket seconds before Curtis Ray came out of the last room. She could smell his sweat and frustration. He muttered under his breath, "Fuck! Where is it?"

"Were you looking for the room? The one in the camera?" He turned away from her. His back arched. She tried again. "Maybe this is the wrong house." She secretly hoped that was the case.

He didn't pay her any mind. She could have been speaking to herself. Instead, he stared at the keys. He turned toward the far end of the hallway, squinting in concentration. His expression hardened and he broke out into a run. She caught his grim smile as he turned the corner.

She followed him to the end of a short corridor that

didn't go anywhere. At least that's what she thought until she saw Curtis Ray reach for a rope in the ceiling. When he pulled, a ladder clattered to the floor. She looked up to see a black hole.

"Curtis Ray, don't go up there," she warned. Her stomach tightened as if expecting a blow.

Of course he didn't listen to her. Probably didn't even hear her with his mind so closed up to anything but his mission. That's what he called this. A secret mission, like when they used to pretend to be spies. She held her breath when he disappeared into the darkness. The voice in her head whispered monsters might be hiding up there to swallow up her friend. Waging war with the voice, her curiosity won out again. What was hidden up there? She strained to listen for signs that the man had come home.

A light went on, and Curtis Ray's face appeared. He waved her up the ladder. "I think I found them," he said when she poked her head inside the attic.

She glanced around the tiny room. Bare wooden planks with pink cotton stuffing sticking out, which Curtis Ray explained was insulation. Along the walls were more file cabinets and lockers. In one corner, cots were piled on top of each other.

Curtis Ray held a stack of DVDs. "These got to be them," he said, before handing them over to her.

"How do you know?" she asked, staring at the case covers with dates as titles.

"They got to be," he answered, his face so tight his features appeared etched in acid on dark metal. His lips stretched thin as a straight line.

"You all right?" she asked, feeling her mouth sucked dry.

He nodded stiffly.

"Let's go. Now," she urged, wanting them both out of there before they were discovered.

She backed down the ladder with one hand guiding her along the rungs. Her other hand clutched the DVDs next to her chest. When he reached her side, he pushed the trap door up. It rose and closed with a loud bang. His eyes grew round and for a moment he froze. Her stomach hurt as his fear transferred to her. Seconds passed as they stared at each other, listening through the silence that followed. Then he took the DVDs from her and jerked his head toward the hallway.

They raced down the stairs. Curtis Ray led her toward the front door. He skidded to a stop next a small table holding a stack of unopened mail. Two high-back cushioned chairs were pushed against the wall on either side of the table. She heard what stopped him: footsteps coming from outside. Her knees shook like jelly.

"It's him," she said in a hoarse whisper. Her arm jerked out, reflexive, and hit Curtis Ray on the shoulder.

The blow startled him and the DVDs clattered to the floor. He swore and fell to his knees, gathering them up as fast as he could. At the sound of the doorknob turning, he shoved one of the DVDs in her pocket. He steered her behind one of the chairs and crouched next to her.

The door flung open and a man's baritone rang out. "Who's there? Whoever you are, you better come out now." He switched on the entryway light. "You can't hide."

Jayme barely breathed. Tears came to her eyes. She squeezed next to Curtis Ray and felt his body tense. His shoulders bunched to his neck. She jerked when his arm brushed against her and she saw the set of gold keys fly into the air.

The man turned toward the sound of the keys hitting the shiny tile floor, sliding until they crashed against the opposite wall. When the man bent to pick them up, Curtis Ray yanked her to her feet and they raced out the door. Shouts and curses followed them as they fled toward the gargoyle bushes.

Curtis Ray pulled her behind the first bush. He dropped to the ground, taking her with him. Both of them gasped for breath, but she couldn't understand why he had stopped.

They both could run for miles. *What was he waiting for?* The stairs to the street were two feet away.

"Go. Run," he ordered in a hoarse whisper.

"With you," she cried. "Come on, let's go."

"Not the stairs," he cautioned, pulling her to the other side of the bushes. "Use the grass."

The man's footsteps sounded close now. Spurred by a rush of panic and terror, and Curtis Ray's hand slapping her back, she leaped on the grass and flew down the hill, gliding and tumbling down the slick carpet of green.

The ear-shattering shot came as she slid painfully onto the concrete sidewalk. Only then did she realize Curtis Ray wasn't with her.

An awful knowledge gathered in the depths of her stomach. Her knees hammered together and didn't want to hold her up. She grabbed hold of a tree trunk to help her stand. Her breath rasped in and out too fast. Way too fast. *Where's Curtis Ray?* She sneaked a look. A strangled sob broke from her at the sight of Curtis Ray on the ground. The man hovered over him, something shiny in his hand. *A gun.* She saw red spread over her friend's caramel skin.

She wanted to run back to him, even started to scramble back up the slope, but, at that moment, the man looked down, right at her. He raised his gun. He was going to shoot her, too.

She stumbled backward and crawled behind the tree. A car turned the corner, coming toward her. It slowed as the driver craned his head out the window. She waved frantically for him to stop. He turned and faced straight ahead. His car picked up speed and disappeared. Ducking down, she raced across the street and rounded the corner.

She ran until she couldn't run any longer. The big River Oaks mansions loomed huge on either side of her and seemed scarier than the shooter's. Across the street a man walked his dog. He frowned when he saw her. His expression made her keenly aware of her dirty secondhand clothes and the certainty that she didn't belong on this street. Where could she hide until it was late enough and dark enough to get back to the streets of Montrose?

She saw very few cars parked in driveways, but there was one down the block. A shiny black Mercedes Benz, a car she would never find in Granny's neighborhood, but she knew what they looked like from Curtis Ray's tattered car magazines. She felt Curtis Ray's cell phone and the DVD case when she dug in her pocket. Whatever Curtis Ray risked his life for, she must protect with her own. But first she had to get help to him. She hurried down the street of money to the big black car and crouched behind it. Her hands shook as she fumbled with the phone, her fingers barely able to press the nine-one-one keys. When the operator came on, her words stuttered.

"Hurry. A boy's been shot. Please, you gotta hurry."

Address? She didn't know it. Concentrating, she recited the street names. Her name?

She sucked in her breath. When the operator repeated the request, she clicked off. Sobbing, she slumped against the car, barely aware of the pain from her skinned and grass-stained knees.

The fresh horror of seeing him on the ground, that murderer standing over him, brought a flashflood of tears. She choked out a sob, remembering how the shooter had looked at her. She was a witness. He would kill her if he found her.

She struggled painfully to her feet. No lights shone in the windows of the big house. That was good, she thought. She limped up the driveway to the side of the house, kept her back against the rough surface until she came to a wooden gate. A push didn't budge it. She strained to listen for footsteps.

As she had done a million times before with similar gates, she fit one foot against the wood and, with both hands gripping the top, she swung herself over and landed on a brick walkway. Her legs buckled and she fell forward on her knees. Pain registered, paralyzing her for a moment. She stifled a cry and concentrated on her new surroundings. She was inside a large backyard. No sign of tennis courts here. More like the Japanese gardens she'd seen once in the park.

She crawled between two bushes, medium-sized and shapeless. She felt the urge to giggle for no reason. The smell of roses made her sneeze and she muffled the noise with her shirt. Thorns scraped her skin with every move.

After what seemed like hours, sirens wailed. So many, all sounding different. Help was on the way. She hugged her knees and rocked. She kept her head down, barely feeling the bushes claw at her skin. She was so terrified for Curtis Ray. Was he alive? Couldn't think. So tired.

The next time she lifted her head, a pale blue-gray light in the sky glimmered. No sirens, no sound of cars on the road, no sound at all but the wind in the trees. She must have slept through the night.

She crawled out of her hiding place. Lights were still off in the house next to her. Now if her luck would only hold as she faced another hurdle. How to get home? The gate she had jumped over now opened without a creak. Had someone unlocked it while she slept? The car that had been in the driveway was gone. Had the driver seen her? No, they would have done something.

She had to tell a cop what had happened, but what could she say? That they broke into the man's house and tried to steal his DVDs? She had no idea what kind of movies were on them or why they were important to Curtis Ray. She only knew that somehow they were connected to the photos on the camera phone. Her hand touched the DVD in her pocket. Curtis Ray had been willing to get killed to find it. Why?

Her head hurt too much to try to figure it all out. She had more immediate problems.

If I go to the police, will they arrest me?

Damn you, Curtis Ray. Are you alive or dead?

CHAPTER 2

Niki Alexander sat opposite Sharena Rockland on a bench in the overheated visitor's area of Gatesville prison for women. The smell of sweat, cheap perfume, and dirt that permeated the once-white walls made her eyes water.

Behind them, a woman who looked somewhere between forty and sixty-five cried softly. Two benches away, a chair scraped and a man jumped to his feet. His angry voice punched the air. The woman at his table cringed. A female guard appeared within seconds and he settled back down, lips moving with words Niki couldn't hear. She tried to erase all that excess noise from her mind to focus on the young woman she had once counseled as a teenager.

"What's going on, Sharena?" Niki tried to keep the impatience out of her voice.

When Sharena had called earlier that morning, Niki almost hadn't responded to her plea for help. A thousand excuses had risen to Niki's lips before they'd died unspoken. She had anticipated the usual high drama that made up Sharena's life and wanted nothing more than to blow her off, but the rising hysteria and fear in Sharena's voice gave Niki no choice but to come and listen to the latest disaster.

Sharena sat with her back rigid. Not a trace of fat showed on her angular body, only muscles in her upper arms and chest from working in the prison laundry room.

Her wheat-blonde hair hung in limp clumps across her bony shoulders. She thumped the floor with her right heel. "Nothing going on for me. I can fucking take care of myself. It's my Jayme needs help."

Jayme's name brought back a memory of the last time Niki saw Sharena's daughter, a pale child with wispy blonde hair and huge blue eyes. A hint of her mother's rebellious nature already defined her.

"What about Jayme?"

"I called Mom two days ago, said to put my daughter on. She said Jayme run off. I asked when, she says Jayme's been gone a month. *A month.* Why the hell wait so long to tell me? I tried to call her before and the bitch wouldn't accept my calls. I guess I know why."

"Did your mother report Jayme missing?"

Sharena scoffed and looked around the room before meeting Niki's eyes. "She couldn't be bothered. The girl's only eleven, my age when I ran away the first time. You know what happened to me. You think I want that for my kid?"

Déjà vu. Niki didn't have an answer for her. Sharena knew more than anyone what could happen to a child trying to survive on the street. The doomed cycle, repeating.

Niki leaned forward, compelling the woman to look at her. "What do you want me to do?"

Sharena's once vibrant blue eyes looked washed out and sunken below furrowed brows. She spread her hands out, not quite touching Niki's. "Find her."

"I may have to involve the police," Niki said. Seeing Sharena recoil at her words, she added, "Jayme's too young."

Sharena gnawed on her lower lip. She looked away, this time at the door where the guard stood with her legs apart and arms folded.

"Don't let her go to foster care. Do whatever else it takes, but not that," she pleaded. "Even if you have to force her to live with my mom, who really does care about her, even if she don't show it sometimes. I just want her found safe. You can do that. I trust you, Niki."

Niki gritted her teeth. "I can't make any promises, you know that. Damn, Sharena, don't give me that look. Any idea where she could be?"

"How the hell should I know? You're my only contact with the outside."

Niki was surprised for about three seconds. "Your mom hasn't visited?"

"Are you kidding? With her record, she won't go near this place. I wouldn't be surprised if she had warrants."

Niki wondered for the millionth time why a system allowed a child to live with a drug-weary ex-biker and ex-con like Sharena's mother. "You used to be close to Jayme. You knew her friends, her interests."

Sharena uttered a short laugh. "Yeah, all that changes the older they get."

Loud voices interrupted them. A young woman arguing with the older version. Sharena turned an angry face to them, opened her mouth to say something, but stopped. She shrugged and shot a look to Niki that said, "See? Mothers and daughters. What can you do?"

Niki gave her a sympathetic nod. Her own mother had died when she was five, left her to be raised by her grandparents until her father remarried. She always believed her childhood didn't give her the right answers when it came to questions about parenting. What she learned, she experienced vicariously when dealing with troubled teens.

She leaned toward Sharena. "What about Jayme's school?"

"Claymore Middle School. She missed a lot last year. Always complaining of stomach cramps. I wanted to home school her…" Sharena's voice trailed off.

Home school? Niki's nails bit into her palm, and she didn't say the words she would regret later. Instead, she said, "Okay, that's a start. What else? Will your mother talk to me?"

"She damn well better," Sharena said. "Why wouldn't she?"

Niki silently counted to ten. "She didn't go to the police or tell you when Jayme ran away."

"But you ain't the police." Sharena pointed her finger at Niki. "She ain't got nothing against you."

"Fine. I'll talk to her. Anyone else who might help?"

Sharena rubbed her hands together. "A girl from the old neighborhood, maybe. Kaley Blunt. Try her. Mom knows her."

"Not much to go on."

The anger leaked from Sharena's face, leaving her looking tired and drawn. "She's missing. If I knew where to find her, I'd tell you."

Niki wanted to put her arm around Sharena's stiff shoulders. Instead, her fingers brushed the woman's arm. "Your mom still lives in the same house?"

Sharena shrugged. "Far as I know. Gonna talk to her?"

"That's the plan. I'll also put eyes on the street."

Sharena nodded as the guard came forward, indicating the end of visiting hours.

Niki gave Sharena what she hoped was an encouraging smile. "I'll stay in touch."

Sharena bit her lip and stood. "Thanks."

Once outside, Niki breathed in the cool, damp air. A rush of sadness overwhelmed her. She sank in the driver's seat and stared at the purple clouds overhead without really seeing them. Thoughts of the teenage Sharena, who wanted to teach, to help other kids who came from similar backgrounds, made Niki remember the laughter from the old days, Sharena's quick response when a friend got into trouble or just needed someone to listen.

There were also the sad days that outnumbered the good, and the days when rage took over when she couldn't cope, and when alcohol and drugs became her only friends.

Then Sharena ended up here.

Niki's cell phone rang. She glanced at the caller ID and

felt a familiar warmth go through her as she answered her favorite homicide investigator. "Hey, you."

Nelson Spalonetti's strong voice rumbled in her ear. "What's up? You were going to call."

"Couldn't."

"Why? Where are you?" No concern in his voice, only curiosity.

She told him and pictured him rising to his feet.

"Gatesville? Oh, babe, what did you do now?"

She ignored his teasing tone and told him about her visit.

"Sharena Rockland. I remember that case. Didn't she try to turn her boyfriend into a crispy critter?"

Niki made a face at the phone. "Just his house."

Nelson's voice hardened. "I thought you were finished with her."

"Thought so, too. But her eleven-year-old kid is missing."

"And Sharena comes to you instead of the police?"

"What do you think?" She switched on the ignition and the engine turned over. "I told her I'd look into it. You got a reason for calling?"

"Yes, as a matter of fact. Something came up, and I might need your help."

Another kid in trouble, she thought. That was the only reason he would involve her in one of his cases. "I'm on my way. Should make it to Houston in about two hours."

"Don't speed."

"Who me?" She laughed. "Where shall I meet you?"

"Ben Taub."

"County hospital?" Niki gripped the wheel tighter. "Do I know the kid?"

"That's what I'm hoping. We don't have an ID. He was shot two days ago by a homeowner who claims the boy broke into his house."

CHAPTER 3

Niki drove to Ben Taub in less time than Nelson would sanction. Parking on the fifth level of the parking garage ate more minutes. Too impatient for the slow elevator, she ran down the stairs and rushed to the ER, packed with sick and injured indigents, some of whom had probably been waiting for over twelve hours. She stopped, took in the scene, and inhaled the stench of disease, blood, and poverty that clung to worn clothing. Those faces devoid of hope wrought the same reaction of anger and frustration every time she visited. The ER held more misery and pain than the planet should allow. For the majority of walk-ins, the wait could sometimes stretch to days. Without insurance they had no choice. No other hospital would take them. However, for trauma victims, Ben Taub had no equal in medical care.

She found Nelson in front of ICU, talking with a swarthy man in scrubs. Nelson nodded and waved her over.

"Dr. Zafarnia, this is the woman I was telling you about. She's the counselor at Open Palms. Niki, this is the doc who performed the surgery on the boy."

"How bad is it?" Niki asked.

Nelson answered before the doctor could respond. "He was shot in the back, bullet pierced his kidney."

His words hit her like a blow across her chest. Her hand covered her heart. She turned to the doctor.

Dr. Zafarnia's expression was impassive, but his eyes held warmth. "It's not as bad as your cop friend makes it out to be. Surgery went well. The bullet went to his abdomen and we were able to remove it and, more importantly, repair the kidney. He's on a ventilator right now."

"Can I talk to him?"

Dr. Zafarnia shook his head. "He's sedated, with endotracheal tubes through his mouth and into his trachea, so he won't be able to speak for another forty-eight hours. After that, the tubes will be removed and he'll be breathing on his own. I expect a full recovery."

Her hand dropped to her side. "How long will he be in the hospital?"

"He could easily to go home with antibiotics and pain medications in about ten days. He'll have pain in the area for several weeks, but this will gradually resolve and eventually he'll be fully normal."

"Would it be possible to see him for identification purposes?" Niki asked.

Dr. Zafarnia hesitated. Instead of answering, he turned to Nelson. "Have you been able to locate any family members?"

"Not yet. We checked all reports of missing children. Nothing fits."

"What about Mr. Shamberg? Did he know him?"

Nelson chewed vigorously on a wad of gum before answering. "Clayton Shamberg didn't ask questions before he pulled the trigger. It was night, he noted the boy's race and claims he was justified. Look, doc, we've canvassed the neighborhood. Drapes are drawn, doors are locked, and no one saw anything. I called Niki because she knows the street kids from the shelter. If he's a runaway, I hoped she might recognize him."

Dr. Zafarnia frowned. "He can't be more than twelve or thirteen."

Niki looked beyond them to the waiting room. "It happens."

The doctor squinted into the overhead lights. "Nothing surprises me anymore."

"The newspapers and TV news have his description," Nelson said. "Maybe someone will come forward."

Dr. Zafarnia nodded at Niki. "He can have only one visitor at a time."

He gave her a mask, and punched in a code next to the ICU door, which swung open.

The boy lay still with tubes covering most of his face. His eyes were closed, an almost peaceful expression on his light brown face. His black hair was curly. Niki thought the likelihood was good that he had a white parent or grandparent.

As she stared at him, her eyes blurred. She was seeing another boy, an older version of the boy in front of her, but different in other ways, too. Dark hair, barely seventeen, crazed drugged eyes, falling from the bullet Niki had fired to save herself and her partner, Luis Perez. The horror came back to her as she remembered how the twisted grin on his face had dissolved into surprise and then turned into a dead stare. Frank James Miller. Frankie. She would never forget that face. She would never again be a cop.

A voice jolted her. "Are you all right?" The doctor peered at her.

Niki pressed her lips together and dug her nails into her palms. With a shake of her head, she pushed past him out the door.

Nelson's expression changed when he saw her. She didn't need to explain. She took in gulps of air until she relaxed her fists. "Let's get out of here."

They went outside and stood under the overhang next to the ER entrance. She glanced at her watch. Almost three in the afternoon, but the darkening sky made it look later. Clouds the color of charcoal squeezed out large drops of rain. The air thickened with humidity and smelled of wet grass and the occasional gas fumes that belched from a passing truck.

Nelson took her arm. "Talk to me."

She fought to keep her voice under control. "How could anyone look at that small boy and shoot him?" She felt Nelson's eyes grilling her. She turned away. He had a habit of reading her thoughts. Not this time.

"You've never seen him before?"

"Sorry, wish I had." A gust of wind hit her. She huddled against the wall. "Do you think this was an accidental shooting? A warning shot gone bad?" She couldn't see how, but had to ask.

"Doesn't look that way." Nelson spat out his gum and took a cigarette pack from inside his leather jacket. He pulled one out and wet the filter with his tongue. "Crazy kid, breaking into a million dollar River Oaks house. Dumb, really dumb. Shamberg came home, caught the boy, and shot him. Luis took the guy downtown for questioning. All we got so far is his statement stating he didn't realize the burglar was so young. Oh, and how bad he feels."

"Oh, sure. Tell him the boy feels worse." She gritted her teeth in disgust. "What his deal? He thought he was shooting a midget? Don't tell me he claimed self-defense?"

"Hey, I feel the same way you do. What I want to know is what meant so much to the boy that he risked his life to get?" Nelson chewed on the filter of the unlit cigarette.

"Where did the shooting take place?"

"Front of the house," Nelson said. "I suspect he was running away."

"Running?" Niki felt a rush of heat to her cheeks. "I hope you arrest this Shamberger, or whatever his name is, for attempted murder. This kid dies, I want the bastard to fry for it." She turned from Nelson, not wanting him to see the tears forming in her eyes.

His hand grazed her shoulder. "I thought you didn't believe in the death penalty."

"I could make an exception." She paced in front of him, staying clear of the rain that now came down in sheets. Thunder boomed and lightning forked.

Nelson said, "Shamberg lawyered up, of course, and he's back home. I heard he's friends with the chief so there's a chance the DA won't even charge him. He'll say he was protecting his property. In Texas, he's within his rights. You know how the system works."

"No, the system always confuses me, especially when the victims are young and poor. Wait a minute, I thought someone had to be inside the house and the resident feared for his life."

"Not always, not when it happens at night and the burglar is getting away with the goods. I'm not saying I agree with the law, but I'm just a cop."

"So what did the kid steal?"

"That's the question. We didn't find anything on him. We figure he didn't have time to get what he was looking for." Nelson glanced across the parking lot and tensed as he focused on movement to his left. "You got to be kidding me."

A man in a tan raincoat lumbered toward the emergency entrance, his arms swinging in tandem with his long legs. The back of his dark hair stood up like a fan against the wind. The turned-up collar of his London Fog caught drops of rain that ran down his neck. He was minus an umbrella.

"Who is he?" Niki asked.

"It's the fucking shooter, Clayton Shamberg. What the hell is he doing here? He shouldn't be anywhere near this hospital."

Nelson moved and planted himself like a sentry in front of the entrance.

Shamberg drew closer and motioned Nelson aside. "Excuse me."

"Forget it, pal," Nelson said. "Turn your ass around and get back to your car."

Niki stepped next to Nelson, preparing to be his backup. Nelson at six-two had several inches on Shamberg. Nevertheless, all her cop instincts and experience taught her to be ready for the unexpected. Shamberg had not hesitated when he shot a child and, therefore, became sub-human in her eyes.

Shamberg scowled. "You're one of the dicks who came to the house. In case you haven't heard, they let me go. You have a problem with that, speak to your chief. Now get out of my way." He sidestepped Nelson, but Niki predicted he wouldn't go anywhere.

Before the man could take another step, Nelson grabbed Shamberg's right wrist and twisted his arm to his upper back while exerting pressure on Shamberg's hand at a point between the thumb and forefinger. "I guess you didn't get my message the first time," he said in Shamberg's ear.

Shamberg's chest heaved and he angled his head toward Nelson. "I'll sue you and your damn department for this. Your girlfriend's a witness. I didn't do anything but mind my own business. I know my rights."

Niki stepped closer. "I saw you attacking a police officer. I know a few things, too. For instance, you aren't allowed within a hundred feet of your victim."

"She's right," Nelson said. "Go right ahead and report me, and then explain why you were here. I'd like to hear that myself. Were you planning to finish what you started?"

"No, wait. You got it all wrong." The steam blew out of Shamberg's face, and his arms went slack. "Take your hands off me, I won't fight."

Nelson held him for another fifteen seconds. "Talk." He let him go and stepped back.

Shamberg rubbed his shoulder. "Like I told you earlier, I didn't realize he was a kid. I came home and found him in the process of robbing me. He ran. I told him to stop, but he just kept going."

Nelson's jaw tightened. "What did he take?"

Shamberg looked away, and didn't answer at first. "I didn't find anything on him."

Niki and Nelson exchanged glances.

"You do an inventory to see what was missing?" Niki asked.

"Look, I'm not pressing charges against him, and my lawyer says I probably won't be charged either. It's over, all right?"

Of course he'd have a high-priced lawyer to buy him off, she thought bitterly. Probably had his number on speed dial.

"It's not over yet," Nelson said. "You haven't explained why you're here."

Shamberg exhibited the trapped look of a jackrabbit stalled between two cars on a country Texas road. "I wanted to see if the girl showed up."

Niki stared at him. Had she heard him right?

"What girl?" Nelson said.

"The one with the boy. Your guys didn't see her?" Shamberg shook his head. "Unfuckingbelievable. What kind of kids think they can get away with robbing someone in River Oaks? Did you know they had the alarm passcode to get in? How did they get that?"

"Maybe you gave it to him," Nelson suggested.

Shamberg scoffed.

"You have no idea who they are?" Nelson said.

"No, I told you."

"Besides the alarm system, how many webcams are set up in the house?"

"Just what your forensics people found. Didn't your guys see the girl on the video? I assume they looked at the one in my office."

Nelson's jaw tightened. "The webcams were turned off. You would know that, wouldn't you?"

Shamberg looked surprised. He stared at Nelson and then shook his head. "They shouldn't have been. Those kids must have turned them off."

"Whatever," Nelson said. "In any case, you didn't mention the girl in your statement."

Shamberg ran a hand through his hair, tangling the strands even more. "Look, I was distraught, okay? I shot a kid. I'll have nightmares the rest of my life."

Nelson's jaw tightened again. "Maybe you just wanted to find her yourself, see if she has whatever was stolen."

"Yeah, I mean, no. You got it all wrong. I want to talk to her, that's all. Like I told you, I'm not missing anything."

Niki said, "What made you think you'd find her here?"

He turned to her with a sigh of impatience. "She might be hurt. I thought I saw her fall. Anything else? If not, I'm going home."

"So you were worried about her?" Incredulous, Niki thought, after what he'd done to the boy.

"I didn't want to be responsible for another hurt child."

Shamberg turned to go, but Nelson stopped him. "You're going to give me a description of this girl right now." He pulled out his notebook and a pencil.

Sweat beaded on Shamberg's forehead. "I didn't get a good look at her. Like I said, she ran away."

"About how old was she?"

"I don't know."

"Guess."

"About the same age as the boy, I think."

"What color hair?"

"I don't know. Blonde, maybe? I only got a brief look."

"So she wasn't African American?"

"No."

Nelson continued to write. "Her hair, short or long?"

"Short, I think."

"What was she wearing?"

Shamberg shrugged, his face pinched. "Jeans? Yeah, Jeans, and a T-shirt."

"Call your lawyer. Tell him to meet us at the police station. I'll have a police artist there."

Shamberg's face reddened. "I have a business meeting in an hour."

"Cancel it." Nelson poked his head inches from Shamberg's. "Or don't you care about the girl after all?"

Shamberg wiped his face with his hand. "I'll talk to my lawyer."

"Damn right," Nelson said. "You can leave now."

Niki moved next to Nelson and watched the homeowner stride away.

"You believe that guy?" Nelson said, staring after him.

"No." Niki took a moment to organize her thoughts. "I think he knows exactly what they were after. That's what scares me. He can't get to the boy, so he goes for the girl. I hope we find her before he does."

"Keep a lookout on the street," Nelson said, and pointed to his notebook. "Not a very thorough description, but if Shamberg can do better with the police artist, I'll email it to you."

Niki looked at him curiously. "Shamberg's webcams were really shut off during the B and E?"

"Yup. Amazing, isn't it? I doubt the kids even knew the webcams existed. Not a chance they would know how to turn them off. They got lucky is all."

She nodded. "Yes, that is amazing. Well, I've got work to do. I have to find Sharena's kid."

CHAPTER 4

Niki pulled up in front of a shotgun house with peeling white paint and a cracked front window. The street had no sidewalks and looked deserted except for a girl riding a bike. Sparse grass poked through hard earth and the morning rain had formed mud puddles in many parts of the front yard.

Her attention was drawn to the shiny, black stripped-down Harley parked in the gravel driveway in front of an old Ford pickup with one back tire replaced by a cinder block. The Harley seemed out of place in the shabby surroundings.

She eased out of her car and hit the lock before advancing along the narrow dirt walkway. A dog yipped a warning from inside the house. The floorboards creaked as she mounted the steps to the wooden porch and knocked on the door.

A large black dog galloped around the side of the house and bounded up on the porch. Niki stepped back against the house before he could jump on her with his muddy feet. He looked like a puppy despite his size and didn't seem menacing. She put out her hand. "Good dog." The dog sniffed, wagged his tail and licked her fingers. "That a boy. Good dog."

"Rocky," shouted a woman as she rounded the corner of the house and stalked to the front. She wore a light blue plaid smock and gardening gloves and held a trowel. "Rocky, come here." The dog leaped off the porch, ran a circle around the woman before sitting next to her. "Some watchdog you are. Don't know the meaning of mean. Guess you might lick a person to death." The woman chuckled then squinted at Niki. "Do I know you? I think I seen you before."

During her cop years on patrol in the Montrose area, Niki had picked up a teenage Sharena on suspicion of shoplifting. Instead of arresting her, she drove the thirty miles to Sharena's home in Brookshire and talked to her mom. Rhonda Rockland made a lasting impression. She recalled the image of a beer bottle in Rhonda's hand, her pores oozing the odor of alcohol. Today she looked sober. Rhonda had a lean but sturdy build and the same faded blue eyes as her daughter's. Prematurely gray hair hung loose to her waist, and weathered skin spoke of time spent outdoors.

Niki came off the porch. "Mrs. Rockland?"

The woman let out a guttural laugh. "Shit, ain't been called that in a blue moon. Been married twice again since I had that name. It's Taymore now, but folks 'round here just call me Rhonda. And you are?"

Niki gave her name, and was met with a blank stare. "I visited your daughter yesterday."

Now Rhonda put it together. Any hint of friendliness left her face, and a scowl matched her tone when she spoke. "I remember you. You're the cop who brought my girl home after one of her runaways."

Niki kept her smile. "Good memory. I'm a counselor now. I work with kids at Open Palms. It's a shelter—"

Rhonda waved her hand dismissively. "Yeah, I know what it is."

"Can we talk for a minute?"

"I can guess what this is about." Rhonda pulled off the gloves and stuck them in the pocket of her smock. "I got nothin' to say and no time to gossip."

"I'm not here to cause you any trouble. Your daughter's

concerned about Jayme and asked me to check on her."

A sheen of sweat glistened on Rhonda's forehead. "That little girl's just like her mother. Smart-mouthed, got to have her way, always running off. Don't need no social worker comin' 'round tellin' me my business."

Rhonda brushed past her and went up the stairs. She stomped the dirt off her work boots with each step, and dropped the trowel next to the door. Rocky had galloped ahead of her and sat with tail wagging. Rhonda turned with a glare. "You still here?"

Niki didn't want to fight with the woman. She needed to establish some kind of connection with her, to get her to open up. She pointed to the Harley. "Nice ride. Must be good on gas?"

The question threw Rhonda off balance. "Good 'nuf. Better'n that old truck." After a moment, she added, "My ex left it here before he went away."

"My husband rode one like it on his off hours. He was a motorcycle cop."

"Yeah? He still rides?"

She shook her head. "Died in a car wreck a few years ago. Never had an accident on his Harley."

"Yeah, that's like my first ol' man, Sharena's pop. No cop, but he never had an accident neither. Car or bike. Bastard's still kicking." Rhonda stood poised with her hand on the knob, but didn't open the door.

Niki rested one foot on the bottom stair with a hand on her knee. "I'm here because your daughter asked me to come. She's worried sick. Jayme's only eleven. You remember how it was for you when Sharena would run off at that age."

Rhonda's face flushed with anger. "You bet I remember. You think I want to go through that crap again? Sharena was difficult. She never listened. Look where it landed her. You have no idea what I had to deal with."

On the contrary, Niki was all too aware of Sharena's youth, particularly her teenage years. She remembered the calls Rhonda had made to the station when Sharena disappeared. Each time she reported her daughter missing, the calls became more desperate, and her voice almost incoherent. Sharena once told her how she hated being around her mother's alcoholic binges, but found the street just as treacherous. On one occasion, Sharena was kidnapped and almost sold before she got away. Another time, Rhonda planned to ship her off to her dad's to "straighten her out." Her biker dad and his Bandito friends would "welcome" his little girl. Sharena ran off again. When she became too hungry and ran out of friends, she'd finally trudge back home, only to run off again.

To hear her mother tell it, Rhonda was the injured party, not Sharena.

Niki tried to sound sympathetic, but also wanted to convey a sense of urgency. "I see kids like Sharena and Jayme every day. I hear their stories. The street's too dangerous for any kid, but especially someone Jayme's age."

Rhonda crossed her arms. "I know how old Jayme is. Eleven going on thirty. Top of that, she's too street smart for her own good. She'll be back. She always comes back. Just like Sharena. Mark my words."

"Please, can I come inside? We really need to talk."

"There's nothing more to talk about." Rhonda turned away. "You've done your duty, now go back to Houston."

Niki sighed. She had hoped the years had mellowed Rhonda. "I'm sorry you feel that way. You do realize I'll have to report Jayme's disappearance to CPS and have the police come out. You'll have to answer their questions."

She turned and walked toward her car.

Five steps later, Rhonda's voice stopped her. "Oh, for christsake. Wait up a sec."

Niki hesitated before turning back.

"I don't need no cops coming around. Might as well come in. Too hot out here anyway." Rhonda looked at her as if she was to blame for the heat.

Relieved, Niki followed Rhonda. Informing CPS and the

police had not been an idle threat. If Jayme didn't show up right away, Niki would follow through, no matter what Rhonda told her.

The door opened into a small living room. A floor fan between the living room and kitchen circulated warm air. A small terrier met them, yipping when it saw Niki. Rocky remained outside.

"Shut up, Frosty." Rhonda shooed the little dog. Frosty jumped on a worn sofa and growled.

The house smelled musty. The garage-sale furniture was sparse: sofa, two chairs, and a small TV on a wooden stand. Rhonda brushed past a round table and four chairs pressed into a corner between the kitchen door and the side window. Niki followed and watched Rhonda take a pitcher from the refrigerator.

"I got water or lemonade. But I wouldn't trust the water. Lemonade's fresh."

The offer, made grudgingly, surprised her after the woman's hostility. Niki almost declined, but decided her refusal wouldn't help the tension between them. Besides, the heat left her throat dry, and the lemonade looked ice cold and refreshing. "Whatever you're having is fine."

"Gardening gets a body mighty thirsty." Rhonda poured two glasses, handed one to Niki, and sat, back to the window.

Niki took the seat opposite Rhonda and drank several gulps of the tangy liquid before wondering, belatedly, if it had been made with untrustworthy water. She put the thought and the glass aside. "When Jayme came home after one of her disappearances, did she ever tell you where she went?"

"Hah, that's a good'un. Lips tighter than my zipper, her's was."

"Did you call the police and report her missing?"

A pink flush blossomed on the other woman's cheeks. "'Course I called them the first time she run off, and the second, and the third. Cops finally told me what I knew already. Jayme's just like her mama, always running off, thinkin' something's better around the corner. Only better ain't where she's lookin'. Just a matter of time and she'll be back. She been that way since her mama got put away. So don't go blamin' me. It's her mama's fault she's the way she is. Plain and simple."

The cops knew? Was Rhonda telling the truth? Niki would check with the locals before she headed back to Houston. "When's the last time you saw her?"

"Like I told Sharena, she took off on a Friday, I guess about four weeks ago. I figured she was goin' to see her friend down the street. Only she never got there. Ain't seen her since. Just like her to worry me sick. Then I figured she lied. She never meant to go to Kaley's."

Rhonda acted like the girl ran off just to worry her poor grandmother. If Jayme lied about where she was going, Rhonda felt justified in not following through.

"So you didn't call the police this time?"

"Yeah, I called them," Rhonda said. "Same as before. They didn't do shit."

"But she's only eleven."

"Yeah, I know. Kids grow up fast these days. That one? Out on the street, you wouldn't even know her real age."

"If you can't handle her, if she's too much for you, CPS can take custody."

Rhonda's eyes went hard and she leaned toward her. "What do you mean? She's my kin. I don't hold still for no threats, young lady."

"It's no threat." Niki took a breath and started over. "I know it must be hard after raising one child and thinking you're through, then having to raise another." She crossed her fingers. "Nobody's blaming you. I'm sure you're doing your best."

Rhonda gulped her lemonade. "That's what I been saying. Ain't my fault."

Niki scraped the chair back and stood. "If you don't mind, I'd like to see her room."

Rhonda frowned and eyed her with suspicion. "What for?"

Bedrooms told her much about a person, but Niki doubted Rhonda would understand, even if she explained. "She might have left an address or some other clue as to where she's gone," Niki said.

"I done looked, didn't find nothin', but suit yourself."

"Which one's hers?"

Rhonda led Niki to the back room that faced the yard. She thought the woman might stand in the doorway and watch her, but after a moment of indecision, Rhonda left her alone.

Jayme's bedroom looked as if it belonged to a much younger girl. Barbie sheets and a pink blanket were scrunched up on the bed. A framed picture of Jayme and her mom in happier days stood on the dresser overlooking the room. An old poster of a Twisted Sister album hung on the wall.

Niki moved to the closet. Toward the back hung two dresses and a coat that might have belonged to Sharena. Dolls and stuffed toys were piled on the closet floor. Most looked well cared for before they'd been abandoned.

Except for one.

An oversized baby doll had been stripped of clothes, her head severed, stuffing sticking out of its cloth body. The doll's bottom and chest were crisscrossed with a red marker. The acts of violence seemed at odds with the care shown the other dolls.

Niki saw Rhonda, once again in the doorway, watching.

"Well? Find a clue?"

Jayme's room had revealed more than the girl's grandmother had told Niki. Jayme had put aside her childhood toys, had seemingly moved on, a normal transition most kids went through, but something had changed.

Niki held up the mutilated doll. "Did Jayme do this?"

Rhonda frowned then drew in her breath with a ragged sound. "I think her mama gave that to her. No, wait a minute, it was her mom's boyfriend. Ex-boyfriend, now."

"Sharena's ex-boyfriend gave the doll to Jayme?"

"That's what I said. The one whose house burned down. Bruce somebody. I forget his last name. Don't matter anyway. Punk's in jail, too."

Niki had followed Sharena's trial, just as she had kept in touch with the girl over the years. Sharena's statement never revealed a reason for torching her boyfriend's house. But Niki thought the answer lay in front of her. The connection between the markings on the doll and the torched house proved there was motivation for both Sharena's actions and Jayme's subsequent rebellion. Niki replaced the doll and stood, meeting Rhonda's eyes. The woman's lips thinned into a straight line and her eyes held no emotion. Without a word, Rhonda turned and left the bedroom.

Niki's gaze swept the room with a final glance before following Rhonda to the kitchen. "What was Jayme like before her mother's arrest?"

"What do you mean? Like, did she run away a lot?" Rhonda reached for a cigarette pack and lighter on the kitchen counter. "Hell, I don't know. She didn't live with me then. Guess she was a regular kid. Played with friends, went to school, never done nothin' crazy."

"What were Jayme's living arrangements with her mom? Did they live with the boyfriend?"

Rhonda lit her cigarette with a trembling hand. "I know what you're gettin' at and it makes me sick."

"I'm sorry to bring this up," Niki said. "I don't know the facts, but clearly something must have happened to change Jayme's behavior."

Rhonda puffed and blew out smoke. "Well, Sharena didn't say nothin' to me."

Not surprising, Niki thought. Communication between mother and daughter had always been strained.

"Sharena mentioned that Jayme had a close friend, a girl named Kaley Blunt. Do you have her address? I'd like to talk to her."

"Kaley?" Rhonda took her empty glass to the sink. "She don't know where Jayme is. I already asked."

Niki silently counted to ten. "What about other friends?"

"Nobody else her own age. Older boys live in the neighborhood, but they're mostly druggies."

Niki made a mental note to follow up later. "How long has she been friends with Kaley?"

Rhonda stared out the window toward the cluttered backyard. Niki saw a trampoline and a child's pool. "They been close since first grade," Rhonda finally said.

"Can you give me the address?" Niki repeated.

Rhonda turned to her, looking annoyed. "Why? I tol' you, it's a waste of time."

"I can find her without your help, but your cooperation or lack of it will be noted if I have to ask the police."

Rhonda's expression soured as if she'd bitten into a lemon. "Shit, you don't need to do that. I'll walk you over. Just a few doors down."

Niki wanted to talk to the girl alone. "I can find it. Give me the number."

Rhonda took off the smock that covered ratty jeans and a Harley T-shirt. "No trouble at all."

Niki followed Rhonda out the front door to the street. The neighborhood hadn't changed much since the last time she'd been there. How long had it been? A year or two? Before Sharena went to jail, she thought. Low incomes brought lower expectations. The statistics showed that drugs were readily available in small towns, perhaps because of the poor economy and nothing else around to stimulate the mind. Even an eleven-year-old going on thirty, who'd experienced too much life on the downside and had been forced to grow up too soon, might be tempted to try sweeter fruit. Niki only hoped that the fruit wasn't poisonous.

The Blunt house looked in better shape than Rhonda's. Grass grew in front, and the house had a fresh coat of peach paint. Rhonda marched to the door and summoned Mrs. Blunt, who appeared at the door looking harried and explained she was getting ready to leave for work. Kaley wasn't home, but a call to the girl's cell phone yielded quick results. Kaley appeared minutes later, riding a worn boy's bike, the same one Niki had seen when she drove up. A hand-me-down from an older brother, she guessed, or bought at a second-hand store. She found it noteworthy that no matter what the economic circumstances, children had cell phones.

Kaley pedaled to the front of the house, jumped off, and dropped the bike on its side. She had a gymnast's build, slender with muscular shoulders, large dark eyes in a pale face, and a quick open smile. Her light brown hair curved in at her shoulders, and she kept fingering the ends. She wore skinny jeans, a halter top and sneakers that looked new.

Rhonda accosted Kaley before Niki could fire her first question.

"Kaley," Rhonda said with authority in her voice, "this here woman wants to talk to you about Jayme. Since your mom has to leave, I said I would handle this. You don't have to say anything. Understand?"

Kaley looked perplexed, but said, "Sure, Mrs. Taymore. Is Jayme back yet?"

"Not yet, sweetie. Mind what I say."

Niki tried not to show her irritation. She pasted on a pleasant smile. "You can leave now, Rhonda. Kaley and I will be fine."

"I tol' you she don't know nothin', and I ain't gonna let you say anything to upset this child."

"That's not my intention," Niki said, wondering what Kaley could tell her that made Rhonda act so defensive.

She turned to Kaley and introduced herself. "Mrs. Taymore says you and Kaley are best friends."

Kaley rolled her eyes, put one hand on her hip, and pursed her lips. "That girl," she said with an exaggerated sigh. "One day she's my best friend. Next day..." She shrugged. "Off somewhere."

"That must have hurt your feelings," Niki said. "Did she explain why she left?"

"She didn't tell me anything. She's so full of herself." Another roll of the eyes. "Like she's got some big secret and can't even tell her best friend."

Rhonda crowded in closer.

Niki walked Kaley a few steps away. "That must hurt. Best friends usually confide in each other."

Kaley clicked her tongue. "I know, right? We used to tell each other everything."

"Maybe she didn't get the chance before she left. When was the last time you saw her?"

Kaley glanced at Rhonda. "A few weeks?"

"Did she seem afraid, Kaley?"

"Don't be wasting your time," Rhonda said. "Kaley, your mama wants you."

Niki made an effort to keep her voice calm. "Rhonda, please. Let me talk to the girl. Go back home."

"Excuse me? You're talkin' about my grandbaby."

Niki gave the woman the look that sent most teenagers at the shelter back to their rooms.

Kaley covered her mouth and giggled, giving Niki the impression she didn't care much for her friend's grand-mother.

"It's all right, Mrs. Taymore, really," Kaley said. "I don't mind talking to this lady."

"Well, I do mind," Rhonda said, folding her arms across her chest.

It took all Niki's will power not to physically remove her. "I'm worried about your friend," she said to Kaley. "If you can tell me anything that would help me, you'd be helping Jayme, too. I know you still care about her, and you wouldn't want to see her hurt."

Kaley flashed a nervous look at Rhonda. "She didn't tell me anything. Honest."

"What about a cell phone? If Jayme had one, wouldn't she call you, since you're her best friend?"

Kaley's large dark eyes blinked. "She doesn't have one anymore."

Rhonda grabbed Kaley's hand and pulled her away. "That's enough. You're scarin' the poor girl. Kaley, get your butt home now. Your mama's waitin' on you."

Kaley wrestled her hand free, and this time defiance and anger flashed in her eyes as she glared at Rhonda. "I'm going. Okay?"

"Wait," Niki called after the girl. She was sure the mention of the cell phone had hit a nerve.

Too late. Kaley was already pedaling her bike up the driveway to the peach house where her mother watched from the door.

Niki spun to face Rhonda. "You're not helping your granddaughter this way. If something bad happens to her, I'll come back."

"And do what?" Rhonda's voice rose until the whole neighborhood could hear her. "Don't you threaten me. You think I want harm coming to my Jayme? Government always causes the trouble. You and the system put my baby in prison. Don't come 'round here again. You hear me? I got a gun and I'll use it. All you cops and do-gooders can go to hell."

Niki's ears burned as Rhonda's threats followed her to the car.

Kaley's words came back to her. The girl had visibly reacted when Niki asked about cell phones. Was it possible the girls each had one and still kept in touch without anyone knowing? And what did Kaley know that made Rhonda so anxious?

She had to find another way to talk to the girl.

Alone.

CHAPTER 5

Niki pulled into a truck stop and maneuvered around the commercial transport trucks that crowded the lot until she found a parking spot next to the diner. There were fewer customers than she expected, judging by the cars in the lot. She ordered coffee to go at the counter.

She sat in her car, cup in one hand, drumming the steering wheel with the other. She couldn't let go of Kaley's reaction to the mention of Jayme's cell phone. Jayme trusted her. Niki pictured Kaley opening her cell phone the minute no one could see her, believing she was helping her friend by telling her of Niki's visit.

She set her half-empty coffee cup into the cup holder and started the car. She circled back toward Kaley's house and parked at the corner. Storm-darkened clouds pushed across the sky and the humidity rose with the summer heat. She turned on the air conditioner and let the car idle. The street remained quiet. She glanced at her watch. Two-thirty. If it didn't rain, Kaley might venture out on her bike again.

A half hour passed. Niki finished her coffee and thought about returning to the truck stop. Nothing happening here. She could be wasting valuable hours. Except she had no other leads.

A blue and white police car drove alongside her and stopped. She rolled down her window and smiled at the officer, hoping she looked like an innocent bystander.

The officer didn't return the smile as he lowered the passenger side window. "Can I help you, ma'am?"

Ma'am? Jeez, did that make her feel old. "No, officer, I'm fine. I'm waiting for someone." The cop looked familiar somehow.

"Waiting for whom?" the officer said.

She realized her position didn't look good. From a cop's point of view, only a stalker or predator parks in a neighborhood for hours. No matter how she explained her purpose, it wouldn't wash. If she said she was waiting for a child, he might arrest her on the spot.

"I can explain," she said.

The officer frowned then got out of his car. As he walked toward her, the feeling that she knew him grew stronger, and she felt a growing unease. He wasn't wearing a hat and his wiry black hair weaved tight against his skull. His skin was the color of fine whiskey. She couldn't see his eyes behind his dark glasses, but got the impression he was about her age.

She put her hands on the steering wheel in the ten and two position and waited for him to come to the window. She wasn't guilty of anything, but nevertheless felt stupid and embarrassed. She couldn't place where they might have met, and it was bugging her.

"Driver's license, please."

She put one hand down and reached for her purse. "I'm getting my wallet out," she said. She slowly extracted her driver's license as well as her business card and handed both to him. She watched for any sign that he recognized her name, but he remained stoic. Not even a flicker.

"My name is Niki Alexander. I'm ex-police with HPD and work as a counselor for Open Palms." Even this information didn't produce the reaction she sought. On the other hand, he had to acknowledge her credentials.

"I know of Open Palms," the officer said. "What's your business here?"

"Visiting Rhonda Taymore down the street regarding her

granddaughter, Jayme Rockland. I think you might know the name? Her grandmother said she's reported her missing a number of times in the past."

The officer gave her back the ID. "Why are you looking for her now?"

"Missing again. I saw Jayme's mother at Gatesville Prison yesterday. You're probably aware of the situation. Her name's Sharena Rockland. She used to live here." The officer's expression neither confirmed nor denied he recognized the name. "Sharena had talked to her mother, who had been given temporary custody of Jayme, and was told the girl had been missing for four weeks. Sharena was understandably upset and asked me to look for her." She tried to see his name plate over his badge, but his body was turned just enough to hide it.

The officer took off his sunglasses and stared down at her. "I still don't understand. What is your connection with Sharena Rockland? It seems strange to me that an inmate would be calling a counselor based in Houston."

"I know how it sounds, Officer…" He turned toward her and she was able to see his name. *Officer Russell Baker*. She almost choked on the name. Without thinking, she clamped both hands over her mouth and sputtered, "Oh, God. That's it. That's why I know you."

Baker's eyes widened in alarm. "Beg your pardon?" He gave her ID a second look. "Niki Alexander." He shook his head. "I'm sorry. What am I missing here? We know each other?"

Her heart rate jacked up, and she had difficulty swallowing. "No, I mean, yes. You knew my husband, Mike Alexander. From the academy? The three of us graduated at the same time. You probably wouldn't remember me. We only met once through Mike."

Baker's eyes softened. "Mike Alexander. Of course, I remember him. A nice guy. A bit of a show-off, liked to pull off stunts, as I recall. A real daredevil on the road." He winked. "But I'm sure you know that. I heard he chose motorcycles. No surprise there."

She didn't speak right away. She couldn't.

Baker frowned in concern. "Are you all right? You've turned pale."

She swiped her cheeks, embarrassed that the mention of Mike's name brought tears to her eyes after all these years. "I'm sorry. I didn't think hearing his name could still get to me. You see, Mike died several years ago."

Her car door opened and Baker leaned in. "Niki, may I call you Niki? Don't apologize. Why don't you sit in the squad car with me for a few minutes?"

She was too surprised at his offer to resist his outstretched hand. "I'm all right, really."

Despite her mumbled protest, she let Baker lead her to his squad car and settled into the passenger's seat. Baker climbed in next to her and handed her a box of tissues he'd pulled from his glove box. The motor was still running and so was the air conditioner. The squad car brought more memories, both good and bad.

Baker spoke first after an awkward silence. "What happened, if I may ask? Was it in the line of duty?"

"No, that's the stupid part. After years on the job, it was an off duty auto accident that killed him. Hit and run. They never found the other driver." Telling the story didn't make her feel any better. Her cheeks felt wet.

"Would you like some coffee?" Baker's voice was warm and sympathetic. "There's a café a block away. Their brew is better than the truck stop's."

Baker must have seen the empty cup in her car. "Sure. Why not?" She managed a smile to hide her discomfort. Why couldn't the past stay in the past? Mike's death had hit her hard. But that happened almost ten years ago. Her life had changed. Why did meeting Baker seem like it happened yesterday?

She clicked her remote to lock her car and let Baker drive her to Ruth's Café. A few minutes later they were sitting in a booth toward the back of the café. Baker waved to the waitress who brought two brimming cups of coffee to the table and smiled at the officer with casual familiarity.

"How long have you been a widow?" Baker asked when the waitress left.

"Over ten years. I can't believe I can still cry over him."

"Certain traumatic events in our lives we never get over, like losing a child or a spouse. I'm assuming you never re-married since you still have his last name." Baker stopped and shook his head. "Sorry, I shouldn't pry. None of my business."

"It's okay. The truth is I've been too busy to think of marriage. Being a counselor at Open Palms fills my life."

"I can imagine," Baker said.

Before he could pry further into her life and, in particular, her reasons for quitting HPD, a subject she wanted to avoid, she leaned toward him. "You asked why I was the one Sharena called. I first met her when I patrolled Mont-rose as a rookie. She was a runaway back then, on drugs, doing anything and everything to stay hooked. I found her on the street after she'd fought off some very bad men and took her back home to her mother."

Baker drank his coffee and watched her over the rim of his cup.

"Rhonda Rockland, I guess the name's Taymore now, looked like a hard-riding, hard-drinking biker mom. I admit she even scared me a little. But like a tiger protecting her cub, she welcomed Sharena home. A few months later Sharena was back on the street. I'd find her or she'd find me. We'd talk, sometimes for hours. When I became a counselor, she still kept in touch even as an adult. She never got along with her mother, and her father was no better."

"That doesn't explain why you took time off from Open Palms today to look for Jayme."

"A prison matron called me last night. Sharena attempted an escape and, when that didn't work, she slashed her wrists. Luckily, the cuts weren't deep enough to do real damage, but until her daughter is found, she's going to try anything to get someone to listen."

"So you didn't feel you had a choice," Baker said.

"That's right, I didn't."

Baker gazed down the street and chewed his lower lip. "I assume you already talked to Mrs. Taymore?"

Recalling her interview with Rhonda, Niki had to either laugh or get angry.

"Well, you could call it that, I suppose. I thought she'd changed since Sharena was a child, but she hasn't. Still the same rough-edged biker broad. She did let me see Jayme's bedroom, though." She thought of the mutilated doll in Jayme's closet, considered mentioning it, but decided this wasn't the time. "Rhonda claims that she reported the girl missing each time she ran away. Is that true?"

"I don't know about each time," Baker said, frowning. "Jayme's in the system as a chronic runaway. We got the judge to issue an Amber alert the first two times. Both times she returned home on her own. We called CPS. They came out, investigated, but found no evidence of abuse."

"What's been done now to find her?"

"We've investigated. We believe she may be in Houston. We've notified HPD to be on the lookout for her." Baker pushed his empty cup aside and rested his elbows on the table. "Seems to me you've done everything you could."

"Almost everything. There's one loose end I want to tie up. Jayme's friend, Kaley. I talked to her earlier today, or tried to. For some reason, Rhonda kept butting in and wouldn't let her answer my questions. Any idea why?"

Baker looked surprised. "Can't think of a reason. Except, Rhonda Taymore can be difficult."

"That's putting it mildly. She doesn't act at all concerned about Jayme, and she wasn't much help. If anything, she seemed hostile. It's like she either knows where Jayme is or she doesn't want to be bothered anymore and hopes she doesn't return." She shook her head. "I shouldn't have said that."

Baker leaned back. "As many times as Jayme's run off, Mrs. Taymore's probably angry and frustrated. She can come off as crude and uncaring, but I believe she loves her granddaughter."

"That's no reason for keeping me from talking to Jayme's best friend," Niki said. "I'd like another chance to talk to Kaley. Without Rhonda around."

"I don't see a problem with that if you get her mother's permission. Were you waiting for her at the corner?"

She stared at the coffee swirling in her cup. "I was deciding on a strategy."

"Uh-huh. I suggest the path of least resistance is going through the mother." He put cash on the table and stood. "Ready?"

As they walked out the door, Niki remembered what Rhonda had said about the teenage boys in the neighborhood. "Do you have a big problem with drugs in this town? Rhonda mentioned the teenage boys in the neighborhood were mostly druggies."

"What town doesn't have that problem? We're no different here from the big cities. You deal with drug addiction at Open Palms. You know the score."

"Yes, I do." She climbed in the passenger's side and waited until Baker slid behind the wheel to ask, "From your observations, does Jayme have a drug problem?"

"I haven't seen signs of her using." Baker started the engine. "There's one drug that's more prevalent here than in Houston, for the time being anyway. Not that Jayme's experimented with it. The street name is *wet*, among others. The main ingredient is embalming fluid. The smell alone would make you gag."

She recoiled. "Ugh. That'll kill you."

"Eventually, yes."

"How do people use it?"

"It comes in liquid form. They dunk their cigarettes in it and smoke it. Gives the user a euphoric high. Kids can hardly walk or talk afterward."

"You really don't think Jayme's smoked that stuff?"

"No, I don't. Why do you ask?"

"I'm looking for reasons she's on the street."

"Good luck finding her," Baker said as they reached her car. "Let me know, will you? Again, I'm sorry to hear about Mike. He was an excellent cop and a good man."

"Thanks." *Mike would be your age*, she thought, as she watched Baker drive away. *No. Don't go there.*

The sound of a honk startled her and interrupted her thoughts. She turned to see a truck driver pointed to the driveway she blocked. She pulled away from the curb.

Rain splattered the windshield but lasted only a few minutes. The air remained damp and humid. The darkened sky promised more showers. Kaley would probably be back home by now. Niki parked in front of Kaley's house and checked the street. Before she reached Kaley's front door, it opened and Kaley stood there, holding a plate of cookies. "Mrs. Alexander? Gosh, I thought you left."

"I was going to, but then I saw your bike." She glanced over the girl's shoulder through the open door to a small living room.

Kaley lifted the plate. "Want one? Chocolate chip."

"They look yummy. Did you make them?"

"Uh-huh. They're still warm."

"That's hard to resist." Niki took the one Kaley offered. It tasted as good as it looked. She licked a smear of chocolate off her finger.

Kaley tilted her head. "You look like a girl I know at school. I thought she was Mexican but she told me she was Hawaiian."

Niki hid her surprise, and then smiled. "You have a good eye. I'm half Hawaiian on my father's side. He was Hawaiian and Chinese. I got his eyes and his skin color."

"What about your mom?"

"Norwegian. I guess that makes me pretty much of an American."

Kaley laughed. "I like that."

"Now I'd like to ask you a few questions, since I answered yours."

"Okay." Kaley's smile faded. "Want to come in? Mrs. Dempsey won't mind."

The name startled her. "Who's Mrs. Dempsey?"

"She's my aunt. She watches me while Mom's at work."

They entered a comfortably furnished room. The smell of spices and baked desserts greeted them. A scattering of multicolored rugs covered varnished plywood floors. A well-worn sofa, cushioned chairs, and lamps on Formica tables created a homey atmosphere. From the kitchen behind the living room came an elderly blue-haired woman, her face, hands, and arms dusted with flour. "Goodness, Kaley dear, you scared me. I thought you left." Mrs. Dempsey stopped when she saw Niki and her mouth turned down. "Who's that with you, dear?"

"I'm sorry to intrude," Niki said quickly. "I talked to Kaley earlier."

"What's your business with the girl?"

"She's looking for Jayme." Kaley said.

Niki smiled at her. "That's right." She handed Mrs. Dempsey her business card. "I'm a counselor at Open Palms in Houston. Jayme's mother's a friend of mine and she asked me to help look for her daughter. I used to be a cop. I'm not here to harm anyone, just looking for information."

Mrs. Dempsey glanced at the card. "How do you think Kaley can help?"

"Best friends talk to each other. Don't they, Kaley?"

"Sometimes," Kaley said, looking at her shoes. "But I already told you everything I know."

"See there? I don't think she wants to talk to you." Mrs. Dempsey didn't sound as sure as she did before.

"Kaley?" Niki waited until Kaley looked up and met her eyes. "You want me to find your friend, don't you? What if she's in trouble? If you know something, anything that can help me locate her, Jayme's mother would be very grateful and so would I. We just want her safe."

Mrs. Dempsey turned to Kaley. "Sweetie, do you know something? If you do, maybe you should tell this lady."

When Kaley didn't answer, Mrs. Dempsey frowned. "We haven't seen Jayme in weeks."

"I understand, Mrs. Dempsey."

The woman nodded. "I have to check on my pies. Kaley, I'll be right in the kitchen if you need me."

After Mrs. Dempsey left the room, Niki turned back to Kaley. "There are ways to keep in contact if two people have cell phones. Right, Kaley?"

Kaley glanced at the kitchen before lowering her voice. "She used to have a cell phone but her grandma took it away. Now we can't talk anymore."

"Do you know why her grandma took it?"

"I think it's on account of a boy we both know. Her grandma don't like him 'cause he's black and got sent to a camp."

Niki couldn't help but think of the unknown boy in the hospital. There had been a girl with him, according to Shamberg. The description he gave sounded like Jayme. Was there a connection? "Kaley, how old is this boy?"

"Twelve. He likes to tell people he's thirteen, but he's not. I know because we went to the same elementary school, and he was a year ahead. He's not bad or anything."

"Do you think Jayme might be with this boy?"

"Maybe. He don't like that camp, I know that. He was always running away."

"Where are his parents?"

"They died. That's why they put him in that camp."

A dozen more questions immediately came to mind, but they needed to be directed to someone else. "What's his name?"

"Curtis Ray. I don't remember his last name. He can be really nice." Kaley fingered her hair. "I don't want to get Jayme in trouble."

Niki lifted Kaley's chin so they were face to face. "You're not getting her in trouble by talking to me. I'm not a cop. I help kids who are on the street. I can help Jayme and Curtis Ray. Kaley, please listen to me. Her mom's worried, like your mom would be if you disappeared. She called me and begged me to find her daughter. What is it you know that you haven't told me? Is she with Curtis Ray? Tell me the truth."

Kaley's brown eyes pooled. "I don't know," she said, her tone defensive. "Last time I saw her she was with him. I told her I'd go with her, but she wouldn't listen."

"She probably didn't want you to get into trouble. That's what best friends do for one another. Help me out, Kaley. Where did they go? Think. Did they go to the camp?"

Kaley blinked. "No, they'd never go there. Curtis Ray hates the camp." She hesitated. "I think they got a ride to Houston."

Niki took Kaley's hands in hers, trying not to squeeze them. "With who?"

Kaley pulled away. "I don't know. I'm just guessing. Maybe they took the bus. I don't know where they are. I swear. That's the truth."

Niki went to the front door. "I'm going to find your friend, Kaley. When I do, I'll let her know you're worried about her. Okay?"

For several minutes Niki sat in her car, pondering what she'd learned. Did Officer Baker know about Curtis Ray? She thought about calling the station and asking for him. Instead, she dialed a Houston number.

Rube Hernandez's voice growled in her ear.

"Did I wake you?" she said.

The young black man, who liked to call himself the "King of the Street" and who appeared whenever she needed an ear to the ground, laughed. "Niki, it's afternoon. What's up?"

"I have a missing girl, Jayme Rockland, age eleven. Might have been seen with a black kid a year or so older. Name's Curtis Ray. There's a good chance they're in Houston. Probably in your area of crazy."

"Eyes on the street," Rube said. "Get back with you soon. I think I know where to look."

CHAPTER 6

Jayme desperately wished she and Curtis Ray hadn't gone to that ugly house. After two days and nights hiding in a corner of the Freed-Montrose library, she could still see her friend on the ground, that horrid man standing over him holding the gun.

Back on the street, desperate for something to eat and drink, she panhandled enough from a man who looked like he wanted to buy *her*, but ended up giving her enough for a hamburger at Captain Jack's. The thin soles of her shoes made a sucking sound across the sticky floor. She slumped in a chair, sweaty, weak, and aching all over. The heat had stolen all the moisture from her mouth. If she didn't get a Coke soon, she wouldn't be able to talk again. Her stomach growled and visions of Granny's kitchen table, the cornbread and homemade soup, made her feel hollow.

A wave of nausea came over her when she saw catsup smears on the table, a terrible reminder of blood on Curtis Ray. Feeling sick, she hobbled to the restroom. After relieving herself and spitting up sour green liquid, she stared into the mirror. Anyone seeing her like this might call the cops. Her face was streaked with dirt and sweat, her hair a tangled mess. She splashed cool water over her exposed skin, rubbed her face shiny and finger-combed her hair. She felt a little better.

At the counter, she ordered a dollar hamburger and a cup

of water from a bored clerk. She sat down in a booth and gulped half the water, wishing it was Coke instead. After staring at the hamburger while her stomach did flip-flops, she forced herself to eat and hoped the meal would stay down.

She kept an eye on the door. Her street friends hung out here sometimes. One of them might tell her if Curtis Ray was alive. She had swallowed the last bite when the door swung open. She recognized at once the shaved head, the multiple piercings through eyebrows, lips, tongue and nose. But it was the signature full-sleeve tats that gave the older teen his name. She groaned. *No, anyone but Snake.*

Snake nodded when he saw her. She shivered all the way down to her toes. "Don't let him smell fear," Curtis Ray always told her. She turned away from Snake's cruel smile.

"I been looking for you." Snake knocked the edge of her table with his knee, splashing her water onto the table. "Thought you might be here. Old habits and all that shit."

She stared at the rattlesnake's open jaw, the poisonous teeth bared menacingly on Snake's bicep. She tried to swallow the bulge in her throat. "So? Ain't no law against it."

Snake squeezed in next to her and spoke in her ear. "You broke into my boss's house. He ain't happy."

Snake worked for the man? Her knees clicked together and she tried to make herself shrink into the wall. Water dripped on her cut-off jeans. "Don't know what you're talking about."

Snake licked his lips. "You stole something from him. You and Curtis Ray. Don't worry, he didn't blab your names to the cops. Not yet. He just wants his shit back. He figures since your boyfriend's in the hospital and nothing was found on him, you must have it. Time to give it up. Now."

Curtis Ray was alive. She felt the insane urge to giggle from relief. Instead, she gritted her teeth. "Told you—" she began, but his hand clamped over her mouth. An arm curled around her neck.

Snake's mouth covered her ear. "Tell me where it is or I'll break your neck right here."

Her face felt as if on fire. She raked the hand covering her mouth with her nails, aimed her elbows at his ribs, but he moved out of reach. She kicked his shin and felt her big toe crunch inside her thin tennis shoe. The pain brought tears to her eyes, but she blinked them away.

Snake laughed and the sound landed on her ears like an insult. She screamed and thrashed. He let go of her and his arms flew up. He jerked away so suddenly she lost her footing and started to slide down the chair. Her fingers caught the table's edge and she held on. She looked up and saw a black man lift Snake by the collar and power-walk him out the door.

Her muscular savior returned, brushing his hands together, as if he'd handled rotten meat and needed to get rid of the stench. His dark skin gleamed under the bright lights, his neatly matted dreadlocks swinging against his back. His mean expression softened as he approached her.

"Don't be scared." Her savior's voice was low and husky. "You be safe."

Now that she was free and unhindered, she recognized him. A lot of kids she knew were scared of him. He had a nickname. They called him the King of the Street.

"You—you're Rube," she stammered. "I've seen you before."

"That right. You ready to get outta here?"

"I'm not going with you. You crazy? Why did you—"

"Don't like bullies. You want Snake back? He's waiting for you. Right out that door. Or take your chances with me." Rube extended his hand toward her.

She felt glued to the chair. "Where to?"

"Safety. You worried about me?" He looked offended.

"How do I know you won't hurt me?"

He sighed and folded his hands. "You have nothing I want, little girl. Now come on. Ain't got all day. You choose, King of the Street or Snake?"

A scream of fury and a crash from outside made her jump in terror. Rube grabbed her hand, pulled her between tables and chairs, and out the back door. A black Harley Davidson waited, partially obscured by Snake. A broken chain dangled from both wrists. Snake leaned against the Harley. Rube pushed her behind him and stood with feet apart and hands fisted.

"Got no fight with you, Rube," Snake said and pointed at her. "She's the one I want."

"Get the hell away from my bike."

Snake ignored him. "Hey, Jayme, where's the shit you and your boyfriend took? Give it to me now, and I let you walk away with this guy."

The rage that had been building since she left Curtis Ray behind made her skin burn. "Go to hell, asshole. Tell that to your pervert boss."

Snake's eyes widened. "Hey, bitch, watch your language. I'll take your skinny ass and make sausage with it."

Rube stepped closer to Snake. "Shut your fool mouth before I shove my boot in it. What the fuck's wrong with you? Fight someone your own size, you coward."

"No problem." Snake shoved Rube's bike over, and a long knife appeared in his hand. He made slashing motions as he danced toward Rube. The blade sliced through the air, easily missing its target.

Rube bent forward and came back up under Snake's arm. Both his hands closed over Snake's wrist and twisted until the knife clattered to the ground. Rube's leg pumped between Snake's thighs. His fists pummeled Snake's face and throat.

Jayme watched Snake slither to the ground, moaning and holding his crotch. Rube righted his bike and tossed a helmet to her. She shoved it on, jumped on behind him, and wrapped her arms around his waist. The roar of the engine drowned out Snake's moans. The wind blew in her face and she held on. She closed her eyes, the smell of Rube's leather jacket transporting her to another time and place, riding on the back of her grandpa's Harley as they raced the back roads of small town Texas.

The ride came to an end all too soon when Rube stopped in front of a small house. He opened the garage door and drove into the dark. She got off, letting her eyes adjust and noticed the fraction of light coming through another door. Rube had his back to her as he secured the bike.

She had heard the stories about Rube from others on the street. He once helped a girl abandoned by her father solve a murder. He helped a Mexican child brought to the states by a drug mule. She also heard he worked closely with an old friend of her mom's. Niki Alexander was her name. Her mom talked about Niki like she was some kind of saint.

Rube opened the side door and the light poured in.

They entered a small kitchen. There was just room enough for the essentials. Rube pointed to a chair at a small table. She sat and ran her fingers over the tabletop. The finish was polished wood with a dragon design carved in the middle.

"You make this?" she asked.

Rube's brows curled. "How did you know?"

She shrugged. "Heard you fixed furniture."

"Sometimes."

"Is that how you make money?"

"More of a hobby." Rube paused and studied her. "Working with my hands takes me to another place."

"I wish I had a hobby that would take me places," she said wistfully.

Rube rubbed his hand over his chin. "What d'you like doing?"

She shrugged. "Don't know. I like to take pictures." She spared him a glance. The camera phone felt heavy in her pocket but she wasn't ready to trust Rube with its contents.

Rube opened the refrigerator and brought out a carton of eggs, a roll of sausage, mushrooms, red onion, and green and red peppers. "Anything here you don't like, you tell me, okay?"

She watched him cook, saliva filling her mouth. Her stomach answered with a growl, the hamburger a brief memory.

Rube didn't speak again while he cooked omelets. After the meal was served and eaten, her eyes drooped. She looked longingly at the sofa in the next room.

"Not yet," Rube said, observing her. "First we talk."

Her throat tightened. "About what?"

"Everyone looking for you, Jayme."

She rose at the sound of her name, but Rube put out his hand and gently pushed her back onto the chair.

"Your ma is worried about you. You ain't been home in a month. She called Niki Alexander to find you. You know Niki?"

My mom called? Jayme rubbed her neck. "I met her once. She's a cop. Mom used to talk about her all the time like she's some big deal."

"She's not a cop anymore. She be a counselor at Open Palms."

Her heart raced. She couldn't get past the idea of her mom calling someone besides Granny to check up on her. "Why would my mom call her?"

"Niki helped your mom when she's young like you. That's the kind of person she be. She helps street kids. She drives all the way to Gatesville to see your ma. Then she call me 'cause she know what I do. My eyes on the street, girl."

A mix of emotions fought within her. "I can take care of myself."

"Yeah, that right. Until Snake, he come along." Rube's eyes narrowed. "Why Snake after you?"

She studied her hands. "Don't know." She felt Rube's eyes on her. They made her squirm. "He's just mean, I guess."

"I think it be more than that. He works for some big shot. Who this boyfriend of yours he talk about?"

"Don't know who you're talking about. Can I lay down now? I'm really tired."

Rube folded his arms and stared at her. "Niki plenty worried about you. I like Niki. She been good to me. I want to tell her you okay but 'less you tell me what trouble you be in, I can't do that."

She stood, wanting to run, to be anywhere but here. "I said I can take care of myself."

Rube unfolded his hands and placed them on the table. "Yeah, I saw how you take care of your little self. You see the door where we came in? It goes both ways. You ain't no prisoner."

She took a step toward the door, but her body was sore and weak. Every muscle felt like ice cubes.

"Know anything about that boy in the hospital?" Rube asked, drawing out his words. "The one Snake's boss shot in front of his house? Pretty bad off, nobody knowing who he is and all. Guess they'll have to put him in a cell somewhere since he has no one to help him. Word's out he had a girl with him. Guess you wouldn't know anything about that. Too bad she don't care enough to help him."

The ice cubes started to melt. She stumbled back to the table, tears squeezed from her eyes.

"I care," she said with a whimper. "Will he live?"

"Oh, yes. Be good as new in a few weeks. What's his name, Jayme? And what you be hiding in your pocket? Best tell me, girl."

CHAPTER 7

Niki got Rube's call while parked across the street from police headquarters at Travis Center. Relief flooded her, followed by anger.

"I'm glad she's safe, Rube. That poor, dumb kid. Doesn't she realize she could have been shot, too?"

"She knows. She secure in my crib. For now."

"What am I going to tell Nelson? He wants me to listen to the nine-one-one tape, hoping I can identify the speaker. I suppose that will be Jayme's voice."

"You be right. You gonna tell him?"

"I need to talk to her first, after I let Sharena know she's okay. She'd kill me if I got her little girl arrested for a B and E."

"I think Jayme more scared of Snake," Rube said. "He say she's holding something they stole from Shamberg's, and he wants it back."

Niki groaned. "Is she?"

"Didn't say either way. Showed me the phone she used. It got a camera feature. There're pictures you should see. I got me a bad feeling about them."

A patrol car came out of the underground parking garage. The driver glanced her way as he slowly drove past. She watched him turned the next corner. "Explain."

"Shows a bedroom with a twin bed and a movie camera with a spot light next to it."

Niki knew at once where this was heading and she didn't like it. "Anyone in the pictures?"

"No."

Her phone beeped. Nelson. "I have to go. Can you keep Jayme until I can get over there and talk to her?" She opened the car door.

"She not going anywhere. She wants to see her friend. Got something for him."

She had one foot on the ground. "Don't tell me. Was it taken from Shamberg's house?" His silence was answer enough. "Shit. She say what it was?"

"A DVD. Says it rightfully belongs to her friend."

"Yeah, sure it does. So what, a music video? Some cute boy band?"

"Didn't say."

"You haven't watched it?"

"She hid it before I found her. Won't say where."

"You're just full of good news, aren't you?" She was out of the car and slammed the door. "I'll try to get over there tonight."

"Be square." He ended the call.

Inside Travis Center, she had to go through security and get a visitor's pass before boarding the elevator to the sixth floor. Nelson met her inside the door marked Homicide.

"It's a girl's voice," Nelson said, walking her to his office, one of several cubicles that lined the sides of the room. Portable partitions provided privacy. "Maybe you'll recognize it. It's a long shot, but nobody knows those kids like you."

"Hello to you, too," she said, pushing him inside, away from prying eyes. "I know you're busy, but don't I get a kiss?"

For a fraction of a second, Nelson looked annoyed. She knew he hated being distracted when his mind was focused. His expression changed when she moved in close. His mouth curved up in a smile and he touched her lips with his. Not good enough, she thought, and wrapped her arms around him and deepened the kiss, leaning into him. When she released him, she whispered, "Much better."

"Hmmm," Nelson murmured, and his olive skin turned a deeper tint. "Better stop that or I'll have to close the blinds."

She laughed. "What blinds?"

His white shirt was wrinkled and unbuttoned at the collar, his tie askew. His blue-black hair curled along the back of his neck. A well-worn leather jacket hung on the back of his chair, which he returned to as if he'd never left. It was back to business. One of the traits she loved about him was his dedication and single-mindedness to his job. Next to his partner, Luis Perez, Nelson was the best detective in the squad.

He spoke in a monotone as if reading from the computer in front of him. "The voice on the nine-one-one call definitely belongs to a young female. We traced the cell number to a Davey Tanner, with an address for a townhouse rental in Montrose. When we checked with management, they said Davey Tanner hasn't been seen for several months. They were told he was working out of town. The rent's been paid regularly by a corporation." He turned on the recording. "See what you can make of this."

She hadn't heard Jayme speak since she was five. This agitated, shrill tone came from a terrified girl who had just seen her best friend gunned down.

"I may be mistaken, but it sounds like Jayme," she said carefully. "Sharena's daughter."

Nelson looked surprised. "You could tell that fast? If that's the case, we have to find her, and not just because of her mother. She could ID the boy in the hospital. I'd like to know how she got this phone."

"Just a guess, but maybe Davey Tanner gave it to her."

His eyes flashed at her. "You're being sarcastic? I can never tell. My guess is, the boy in the hospital gave it to her."

"And he got it from Davey. There's your connection."

He shrugged. "In any case, we better find her before

Shamberg does." He turned back to the computer and tapped keys.

She watched him. "What've you learned about Shamberg?"

"Asshole's squeaky clean on the outside. CEO of a real estate corporation that buys up commercial land all over Texas, Utah, and Wyoming. He's also on the board of several other corporations, including one or two in the oil and gas industry. Then there are the political connections, the police chief included, and the current DA. Of course, he gives generously to several causes, including a boys' camps."

"Probably gives to the Humane Society, too. I wish you'd kicked his ass at the hospital. I know you wanted to." She caught his grin before it disappeared into a frown of concentration. She hesitated before continuing. "Maybe there was more to the shooting than we're aware of."

Nelson peered at her over the top of the computer. "Like what?"

"Maybe they discovered a secret about Shamberg that could ruin him. It could explain why he went after them with a gun."

Nelson pushed his chair back and gave her his full attention. "You know something?"

"No, of course not." Her mouth felt dry. "I'm just speculating, throwing suggestions out there."

"Well, don't." He turned back to the computer.

"What about Davey Tanner? You said a corporation paid for his townhome. Which one?"

Nelson looked up, seemed to consider the question. "I'll look into it."

His phone rang and he picked up. A frown deepened as he listened. "He showed up at the hospital? Hold him there. I'm on my way." He hung up and looked at her. A slow grin spread.

Niki said, "Well? Who showed up? Where?"

"That was Luis. He said a man showed up claiming to be

our young suspect's uncle. Says he recognized him from the television's account. The media is bringing out the nut cases."

"What if he's really a relative?"

"The way Luis was laughing, I kind of doubt it. In any case, that boy is going nowhere."

"Did Luis let him into the room?"

"Not a chance. No unauthorized visitors allowed." He stood and grabbed his jacket. "I got to get over there. Want to come along?"

Surprised by the invitation, she reached the door before him. "You bet I do."

"We'll take the cruiser. That way you won't have to worry about hospital parking."

When they arrived, Sergeant Luis Perez met them in the lobby. She hadn't seen her ex-partner in months and his familiar face lifted her spirits. She had first met Nelson when he replaced her as Perez's partner. That had been five years ago. Luis hadn't changed his dress habits over the years. His blue suit was a shade too lavender, and his space age tie came out of Star Wars. He could have taken retirement last year, but he refused to admit or accept age restrictions. Only the lines in his face and the gray at his temples betrayed his cop years.

She gave him a quick hug. They dispensed with the greetings and walked to the elevators.

"Where is this so-called relative?" Nelson said.

"I put him in the visitors' room. Oh, forgot to mention that he's a preacher. Preacher Webster Capp of the Follow Jesus Camp for Boys."

"Seriously?" Niki tried unsuccessfully to suppress a laugh.

"That's what the man said." Luis chuckled.

The elevators doors groaned open and they got in. Luis pushed the button for the ward where injured jail inmates and those in custody were kept.

"How is the patient?" Niki asked Luis.

"Awake and alert enough to give his name. He's Curtis Ray. So I guess we don't need the preacher man to ID him." Luis winked at her and put an arm around her shoulder. "The nurse reported the prisoner ate a light breakfast this morning. The doctors are encouraged. His kidney survived the surgery."

The elevator ground to a stop and the doors creaked open. The three got out and walked down the hall. A uniformed officer sat in the hall between two doors.

"Tell me about this preacher," Nelson said. "Where was he all this time? Has he filed a missing person's report?"

Amusement colored Luis's tone. "Preacher Webster Capp runs a boys' camp in Hercules, Texas. His story is that Curtis Ray's parents died while Curtis Ray was at the camp. Somehow, Capp got custody, or so he claims, and continued to provide a home for the boy at the camp. About a month ago, Curtis Ray ran off. Capp sent one of the counselors to look for him. Said he didn't hear anything from him until he heard the news on TV. Said he knew right away it was Curtis Ray."

Niki couldn't wait to hear what Jayme would tell her about her friend. "Has Child Protective Services been called?"

"We notified them, but haven't heard anything since," Luis said. "They don't have to get involved in one of our cases. Usually they're too busy and understaffed. I'd be surprised if anyone shows up."

"We need to talk to Curtis Ray, with or without CPS or a guardian giving permission," Nelson said. "If this Preacher Capp shows us some proof he has custody, we can get his okay."

"He couldn't provide any paperwork," Luis said.

"I'm a counselor, certified with the state," Niki said. "Let me sit in."

At Open Palms, it was her job to comfort, console, treat, and protect each and every runaway, or throwaway, who found their way to the shelter. As far as she was concerned, the job extended to any street kid who needed her help.

Luis conferred with Nelson briefly before he nodded to her. "Okay, you can come in. We're not taking a formal statement at this time."

Niki followed the two detectives inside the room. Since he was a minor, Curtis Ray didn't have a roommate. His surroundings were bleak, plain, devoid of flowers or framed pictures on the walls. The antiseptic smell permeated the room.

Curtis Ray's eyes fluttered groggily at his visitors. His chocolate brown skin showed an unhealthy gray tint.

Luis approached him first. "You remember me? I was in here earlier."

"Yeah, you're that detective." Curtis Ray looked from him to Niki.

"I brought in my partner, Detective Spalonetti. We have some questions for you. The woman with us is Niki Alexander. She's a counselor at a shelter for teens."

A blanket covered him to his chin. Only his arms stuck out on either side. His right wrist was cuffed to the bed rail. She stepped close to him. "Hello, Curtis Ray. I'm glad to finally meet you."

"We're here to get your side of what happened in that house," Luis said.

"You gonna arrest me?" Curtis Ray's said in a thick voice. "I'm the one who got shot."

"We're not arresting anyone until we get all the facts," Nelson said.

Niki took the boy's hand. She turned to Luis. "Can I have a moment alone with him? His stress level is elevated. His pulse is racing. I can calm him down."

Nelson looked about to argue, but Luis nodded an assent. She waited until they stepped out of the room, then pulled a chair close to Curtis Ray and sat.

"I'm glad you're feeling better. The doctor says you'll be getting out soon." She leaned toward him. "I know of one girl who'll be relieved at the news."

His eyes widened. With an effort, he raised his head. "Is she—is she okay?"

"She's with a friend. Safe." She tilted her head toward the door. "I haven't told them yet. I'm seeing her tonight after I leave here. Is there any message you'd like me to pass on?"

"Tell her—" Curtis Ray squeezed his eyes shut as if in pain, then opened them again. His voice grew stronger. "Tell her to give the DVD to the cop. Tell her, be careful of Snake." His eyes closed.

"What cop?" When he didn't respond, she said, "Okay, I'll tell her."

Luis knocked, and he and Nelson came back into the room. "Is he all right?"

"Better, I think," she said.

Luis took her place next to the bed. He waited until Curtis Ray opened his eyes. "Son, we need to know what happened before you were shot. But before we take your statement, we have good news for you. Your Uncle Webster is here. He's eager to take you back home with him when you're recovered enough."

Curtis Ray's eyes bulged and his shoulders bucked. "Oh, fuck! Hell no! Fuck!" he screamed, and kept screaming obscenities as he struggled to sit up.

None of them had anticipated his reaction. Or maybe Luis had. Niki took a second look at him, not liking what she was thinking at that moment.

Luis lunged forward to hold Curtis Ray down. Nelson reached the other side of the bed. Neither could stop Curtis Ray from yanking out the needle that connected him to the bag overhead. He twisted wildly to his side. Only the handcuff held him by cutting into his wrist.

"He's going to tear the stitches," she cried.

A nurse rushed in, instantly appraising the situation and acted quickly.

"Clear the room. Everyone out," she ordered.

With a backward glance at the hysterical boy, all three

left the room. When they reached the nurse's station, Nelson said, "Let's talk to this Webster Capp. I want to get his story before he sets foot in that room."

"I don't want him in that room at all." Niki whirled on Luis. "Did you know what he would do?"

Before Luis could confirm or deny, the elevator doors opened and a tall, imposing black woman swept into the hall like Mother Hell.

"Oh shit," Niki muttered, forgetting about Luis. "Not Lavinia Roselle." Past experience with the woman rushed back. She would rather have the plague than have to deal with Lavinia Roselle again.

The head supervisor from Children's Protective Services plowed through them. When she reached the door to Curtis Ray's room, Lavinia Roselle turned with the fire of a dragon in her eyes and zeroed in on Niki. "What are you doing here?"

CHAPTER 8

Lavinia Roselle was a force of nature in Children's Protective Services. Niki respected the regional supervisor who had earned the title by working a zillion hours without the comparative pay scale. Lavinia handled cases other workers couldn't. That's not to say, however, that dealing with the woman was always easy.

"Niki is here in her capacity as a counselor," Nelson explained to Lavinia. "She's been looking for a friend of the patient."

"Is that so?" Lavinia's gaze fixed on her. "Did this friend happen to be with Curtis Ray when they decided to break into the house?"

How much did this woman already know?

To Niki's relief, Luis answered for her. "If Niki knew where the girl was, she would have told me or Nelson. Can we get back to Curtis Ray?"

Niki felt a stab of guilt and hoped Lavinia didn't see through her.

Lavinia didn't waver from her questions. "Why did you come here today, Niki?"

"I was with Nelson when he got the news that Curtis Ray had a visitor. He invited me along."

Lavinia turned to the detectives. "Why was he screaming a minute ago?"

Again, Luis took charge. "We have a situation, Lavinia,

as you might have guessed. A man arrived claiming to be Curtis Ray's uncle."

"So I heard. Have you talked to him yet?"

Luis's mouth twitched. "I met with him briefly. I personally look forward to hearing his story."

Lavinia's eyes narrowed. "You don't believe he's the boy's uncle?"

"Nope. Furthermore, Curtis Ray became hysterical at hearing the man's name. Since the boy's in our custody, we don't have to let anyone into the ward."

"Where is this visitor? Webster Capp is his name?" Lavinia's tone was crisp and no-nonsense.

"Pastor Webster Capp is in the visitor's waiting room down the hall the last I saw him," Luis said.

Lavinia pressed her burgundy lips together.

Nelson intervened. "The nurse had to give Curtis Ray a sedative after he ripped out his IV."

Lavinia frowned and addressed Luis. "Capp can wait. I need to talk to the boy if he's calmed down enough. I'd like you and Nelson to come with me." She turned to Niki. "Your job is finished. You may go."

The frank dismissal rankled, but there was no reason to stay. She watched the two investigators disappear into Curtis Ray's room with Lavinia. Instead of taking the elevator, Niki looked down the hall. It only took her a minute to make up her mind.

Her flat-heeled shoes made snapping noises against the soft linoleum floor. She reached the waiting room, which looked like someone's idea of a living room with chairs and end tables. She didn't see anyone who looked enough like Curtis Ray to be his uncle. A man dressed in jeans, snakeskin boots, and a felt cowboy hat eased out of a chair. He reminded her of an old poster of John Wayne, but a shorter, thinner, more bow-legged version. She looked past him.

"I'm looking for Webster Capp," she announced.

The cowboy took a step toward her. "I'm Webster Capp, ma'am. Most call me Preacher Capp."

She stared at him. Now she understood why Luis kept laughing. This white man couldn't be a blood relative unless Curtis Ray was half white.

She found her voice. "Mr. Capp, what is the name of the patient you're here to see?"

"That's my business, ma'am. Should I know you?"

"Niki Alexander. I'm a children's counselor. I'm here about a patient."

"You're talking about my Curtis Ray?"

"Yes, sir," she said. "We should step out in the hall and talk privately."

He looked annoyed, but walked out with her. "There was a cop here earlier. He was supposed to come get me to identify Curtis Ray. I been waiting all day, and I come a long way. I aim to take him home with me where he belongs."

"How are you related to Curtis Ray? You must forgive my confusion. You don't look like a relative."

He chuckled. "I see. I run into this all the time."

She waited for him to continue.

"Listen, miss, no offense, but I don't know you. I want to talk to his doctor. That cop said he'd take care of it. Where'd he go?" He looked both ways down the corridor.

Once again she was being dismissed. This time brought anger. His casual attitude about Curtis Ray's injuries didn't help him either. "I can only talk to a relative about a patient."

He turned slowly and pierced her with a look meant to back her down the road and out of his way. "I don't mean to be rude, little lady, but I am the boy's legal guardian, and that gives me the right."

"And I am the first one of many you will have to go through before you will be allowed in his room," she said.

That wasn't entirely true. Only the police or maybe the doctor had any say, but if Capp thought he could bully his way in by shoving his nonexistent rights down her throat, he was dead wrong. She gritted her teeth. If she had her way, this man wouldn't get within a mile of Curtis Ray. There was a reason for the boy's reaction, and if she had to pry out the dirt by the spoonful and examine each noxious granular to find the answer, so be it.

His look of outrage gave her some satisfaction. "I repeat. I am his guardian," he sputtered. "No one can keep me from seeing him."

"Show me proof. You do have legal documents to back up your claim, don't you?" she said. "We don't let just anyone walk into the children's ward and leave with a patient, no matter who he claims to be. Not without documents signed by a judge. Curtis Ray is in police custody. He's handcuffed to the bed. CPS and the arresting cops are all with him right now. So if you have proof of legal custody, better dig it out."

The bluster on Capp's face faded, but red patches on his cheeks flowered. Niki wondered how much alcohol he'd consumed before he came. His breath stank of whiskey. He took off his hat and ran his fingers through gray stringy hair before fitting it back on his head.

He took a step closer to her. "Maybe no one explained this to you, miss, but I run a boot camp for troubled boys. Judges and other authorities see fit to send these children to me. I try to instill in them good morals and behavior so that someday they might fit into a society of good, decent folk. Now I come a long way from Hercules, Texas, to find this boy, and I aim to stay here as long as it takes."

Not if she could help it. Niki said, "What is his full legal name?"

He sighed, as if his patience were running thin. "Curtis Ray Johnson. You can ask the cop who brought Curtis Ray to my camp and put him in my care."

"What cop? What's his name?"

"I don't rightly remember at the moment. Paperwork's back at the camp."

"Did a judge sign an order giving you legal custody?"

"As I stated before, in case you weren't listening, I got full legal custody."

"So you say. You must at least have brought his birth certificate."

"No, not with me. I didn't think I'd have to prove anything. Have to go back to the camp to get it. You can take my word, the word of a God-fearing man and preacher. Now take me to my boy."

"Not possible," she said. "Like I said before, he's in police custody. No visitors allowed."

"My lawyer will take care of those charges. The boy was shot, for God's sake. He's a minor. Why haven't they arrested the gall-dang shooter instead?"

She smiled and stepped closer, invading his personal space. "Now there's something we can both agree upon. Mr. Capp, do you know what Curtis Ray was looking for in that man's house?"

His demeanor abruptly changed to defensive. His cheeks turned a brighter scarlet and he backed away. "Of course not. Anyway, you have no proof he was in there."

"Do you know a Davey Tanner?"

He frowned. "Davey? He's a counselor at the camp. What does he have to do with anything?"

"That's what I'd like to know. Were they friends?" she asked.

Capp frowned. "I'd be dang surprised if they were. Davey's older and helps me run the place. Why the interest in Davey?"

She ignored the question. "Do you know if Davey is missing his cell phone?"

"For that you got to ask him. He ain't reported no loss to me."

She wasn't sure she believed him. But the matter of the cell phone and how it got into Jayme's hands were not important at the moment. "Let's get back to Curtis Ray. Why do you suppose he ran away? He must have given you some grief."

A change came over Capp. A caginess crept into his voice. "You understand, miss, being a counselor and all.

This ain't the first time he left camp," he confided, as if she were now on his side. "This time he's been gone a few weeks. He's got an attitude. Don't get along with the other boys. Fights all the time. Don't think he's got any friends. I been doing my best for the boy. When I read about the shooting, I dropped everything, hopped in my truck, and got here as soon as I could. All I want is to take him home where he belongs. He don't deserve what he got."

At that moment, Lavinia Roselle burst into the room, flanked by Nelson and Luis. She bypassed Niki, ignoring her.

"Are you Webster Capp?"

Capp looked straight at her name badge. To Niki's amazement, he transformed once again. He stretched out his hand to Lavinia with a beatific expression of fatherly concern.

"I'm Pastor Capp," he said softly. "And you must be the angel protecting my boy."

Niki wanted to gag. "I'm out of here, boys. Good luck, Lavinia. If you need any help, and I doubt you will, but just in case, look for someone else."

Nelson followed her into the corridor. "Luis and I are finished here for now. You saw the officer at Curtis Ray's door. He won't let anyone in who isn't authorized."

"Good," she said, relieved for the first time since her visit. "Thanks."

"I don't know about you," Nelson said in a Texas drawl, "but I'm starved. You in for dinner?"

Food. Images of a hamburger and French fries flashed. When was the last time she ate, or even thought about eating? Then she remembered Jayme. She was supposed to stop by Rube's. "I have to make a phone call first."

Luis joined them. "Don't see how that cowboy preacher thought he could get away with his story." He chuckled.

"You could have warned me," she said.

Luis grinned. "Where're we eating? There's a cafeteria downstairs."

"No cafeteria food for me," Nelson said adamantly. "There's a coffee shop in the next block. I say we go there."

"If they serve hamburgers, I'm in," she said. "Meet you outside?"

While Nelson and Luis made their getaway, she visited the hospital ladies room and made a quick call to Rube to check on Jayme.

"She asleep," Rube informed her. "Maybe you should come in the morning instead."

"I hate to wait that long, but you're right. Call me when she wakes up, and thanks again."

She met up with Nelson and Luis and they walked down the street together.

The diner wasn't crowded and they found a booth toward the back. She filled them in on her conversation with Capp. "Even if the judge doesn't send Curtis Ray to Juvie, I wouldn't let him go back to that camp. Not after the way Curtis Ray reacted."

"Someone should look into that place," Nelson said. "I'll do some research on the computer."

"Ah, the computer," Luis said. "Know all, be all. Won't ever take the place of pounding the streets and talking face to face with real people."

In many ways, Niki agreed with him. "But it does lay the ground work. Have you ever seen a crime scene with Google Earth?"

"Nope, and I don't want to," Luis said. "If you can find hard evidence that way, then I'll take a look."

The waitress arrived carrying tall glasses of water and took their orders.

Niki waited until the waitress had left. "This is just a thought, a crazy idea, but what if Capp knew about the robbery ahead of time?"

Nelson shook out his napkin. "What gave you that idea?"

"I asked him about Davey Tanner, the owner of the cell phone used to call nine-one-one. Turns out Davey's a counselor at the camp."

"You're saying Davey gave the phone to Curtis Ray, or Curtis Ray stole the phone from Davey?" Luis said.

"Or, maybe they're all in on the robbery together. Maybe Capp or Davey was the mastermind," Niki said.

"Sounds like you been watching too many thrillers," Luis said.

Their food arrived. She doctored her hamburger and took a bite, savoring the juices before swallowing. "I've been thinking." The men groaned. She flipped them off, and continued. "Look at the big picture for a moment. Curtis Ray and a girl break into Shamberg's house, but they don't take anything of value that a common burglar would be after. So ask yourself, what were they after? Whatever it is, poor Curtis Ray gets shot before he can carry the stuff out and get away. Nothing is found on him."

Nelson chewed on a fry. "What's your point?"

"Motive. What was Curtis Ray looking for?"

"Maybe," Nelson said, drawing the word out, "that's something the girl could tell you when she's found."

"Good idea." She sat back. "And maybe someone should go to the camp and talk to Davey."

Nelson looked at her and nodded his head slowly. "Thank you for that suggestion. I'm sure we never would have considered it on our own."

She ignored the sarcasm and finished her hamburger in silence.

After they left the restaurant, Nelson drove her to Travis Center where she had parked her car. He promised to call later, but warned he probably would be working late.

The first thing she did when she arrived home was to run upstairs and change into her sweats. Rube still hadn't called. There wasn't much she could do about Jayme until she heard from him.

She went downstairs and into the spare back bedroom she had converted into office space, and switched on her computer. Nelson wasn't the only one who could do research in cyberspace. Later she could relax with the new Kay Finch cozy until she fell asleep.

She found Texas camps and Hercules on Google and read the various articles that popped up. She barely acknowledged her doorbell until it rang several times. She looked at her watch. After eleven. How had the time passed so fast? The bell sounded again. She looked at the screen before she reluctantly closed her laptop. She stretched her arms toward the ceiling and rolled her neck. The bell rang again. Whoever it was could damn well wait a few minutes. She wasn't expecting anyone, and she doubted Nelson would stop by. Anyway, he would use his key. She went to the door and peered through the peephole, but couldn't see anything but darkness.

"Who is it?" she demanded.

The strong female voice that answered sounded uneasily familiar. She flashed on a face from the past, and her chest tightened. No, it couldn't be. She had to be mistaken. Why now? Why after all this time? For a second, she was tempted to turn and hike upstairs. Easier than letting the past back in, she thought. Then she heard her father's voice as clear as if he were beside her, chiding her as he did back then, and a longing overcame her resistance. She unlatched the locks and swung open the door.

She stared at the well-dressed woman for several seconds before she spoke.

"Lilith? Is that really you?"

CHAPTER 9

Niki couldn't take her eyes off the woman standing on her porch. No word from her in fourteen years except for a couple of sightings. Once, when she graduated from the police academy, she spotted Lilith in the audience. A bittersweet moment came on her wedding day when she saw her stepmother leave before the ceremony ended. Later she found a wedding gift from her. No physical contact either time.

Last she heard, Lilith had remarried and became a widow twice, and spent long vacations touring Europe. There had been no calls, no emails. Niki didn't miss her. She had resented Lilith from day one. She wasn't over her mother's death when her father deserted her, too, only to come home three years later with her "new mother." The fights she witnessed between her father and Lilith only cemented her resolution never to accept that woman in their lives. They divorced when Niki turned eighteen and had already left home.

"Niki dear? Aren't you going to ask me in? I'd forgotten how muggy Houston summers could be."

Niki didn't know how long she'd stood there staring at the woman. She moved aside, feeling numb. "Sorry, how rude of me."

Lilith arched an eyebrow. "I hope I'm not interrupting anything. I've been driving most of the night. My eyes are absolutely bleary from the road."

"No, you're not interrupting. You'll have to excuse my shock. It's been a few years since I've heard from you."

"Fourteen, exactly. Look how much we've both changed. It's a wonder we even recognized each other. That's a mistake I hope to correct." Lilith laughed self-consciously. "Silly me, I seemed to have misplaced your phone number, if you ever gave it to me."

Niki turned away without responding to the not too subtle barb, and showed her to the living room. What *had* she come here for? Niki almost wished she hadn't opened the door. Couldn't the woman have waited until morning?

Lilith strolled around the room, glanced at the paintings on the wall, and stopped at a writing desk. She glanced at Niki. "I know it's late, but I didn't want to wait until morning and miss a chance to see you."

Already she was reading her thoughts like when she was a teenager. "Its fine, Lilith, really. Don't worry about it." She couldn't quite keep the irritation out of her tone.

"I can tell you're not overjoyed to see me. I don't blame you. We haven't been good at communication. But life is too short, Niki dear. We can't let the past go unresolved. We have a lot of catching up to do."

Is she serious? She wants to make up for past mistakes now? Like I don't have a life or my own problems to handle? Damn her.

"You'll have to excuse me, Lilith," she said. "You're the last person in the world I expected to see. Where are you staying? Maybe we can get together for lunch sometime."

Lilith put a hand on her shoulder, eyes searching hers. "I know we haven't been close and the years apart haven't helped, but this is a new day. I really want this, Niki. When you've thought about it, I hope you'll want it, too."

"This is a bad time," Niki said, refusing to let this woman get to her. "My life is complicated right now."

Lilith frowned. "I'm sorry. I didn't think to ask. Do you have someone here with you?"

"What? No, I'm alone. I am expecting a call, though, and

might have to leave." *The nerve of the woman. What if Nelson was here? What business is it of hers?*

Lilith swayed, catching the arm of a chair. "Forgive me. The ride to Houston was long. I didn't realize how tired I was."

For the first time since Lilith had come in, Niki took a closer look at her. Lilith had always dressed impeccably. That hadn't changed. Her dark hair had the finished look that only a salon could give. Lilith's posture and poise were always perfection. But now Niki could see the puffy flesh under her eyes, the lines of fatigue showing under her makeup.

The manners and good taste Lilith had drummed into Niki's teenage years came back to her. She relented. "Let me get us a cup of tea, unless you'd prefer coffee? I have both."

"Tea is fine, dear." Lilith gave her a grateful smile and followed her into the kitchen.

Niki glanced at the woman as she filled the teapot. In the brighter light of the kitchen, Lilith appeared almost fragile. Maybe she'd come to Houston for the Medical Center, God forbid. "Have a seat, Lilith. You look tired. Where are you staying? I don't believe you said."

Lilith smoothed her skirt. "I just arrived. I hadn't booked a room in advance, and all the hotels seem to be filled up. But don't worry about me. I'm sure I'll find a motel somewhere."

Didn't sound like Lilith, who used to plan everything in advance. What was going on with her?

"I don't want to burden you," Lilith said, examining her polished red fingernails. "I've just come from burying my husband in his family's hometown in Kentucky."

That's why she was here? "Oh. Sorry, I didn't know." What else could Niki say? She never met the husbands who followed her father. She only knew about them from the formal wedding or death notices Lilith sent her. Niki had never responded to any of them, except to toss the cards in the trash. "So what brings you back to Houston?"

Lilith touched her hair, in a self-conscious manner.

Jeez, the woman doesn't have a single strand of gray. At her age? Good genes or good chemicals?

"My late husbands, since your father, were very generous," Lilith said. "When they passed, they left me enough so I could revive my career. I need to take all the CLE classes again, but that won't be a problem. I can help you out, too, if you let me. I know we didn't get along while I was married to your father, and I understand how you felt at the time. I wasn't your real mother and never could fill that particular emptiness. I think it's time we got to know each other as adults."

No, this is wrong, Niki thought. *This woman comes back into my life after fourteen years and expects to be instant friends? No way. What is my stepmother's real reason for upsetting my life?*

Her hands were shaking as she poured water over teabags in the cups. She put the kettle down and gripped the counter with her back to Lilith, not wanting the woman to see how visibly upset she was. *Relax. Count to ten. Tell her to leave.* She didn't have time to deal with this now. She picked up the cups and carried them to the table, managing the effort without spilling a drop.

Lilith reached out her hand and touched hers. "I should have called first. But, honestly, I didn't have your number. You probably would've hung up on me anyway. Give us a chance, Niki. Let me help you."

Nike jerked her hand away as if burned. "Help me how?"

Lilith picked up her cup and blew on the steaming liquid. "You know I used to work for the DA. I still have connections."

Now Niki was really confused. "So what? I work at a teen shelter. If you've kept up with my life, as you alluded to, you know that already. I have my own connections with the police, with lawyers, and the different agencies. Do you have a specific reason for bringing up your connections?"

"What got you so suspicious all of a sudden? I'm planning ahead, eager to start a new life here in Houston. Is that so wrong?" Lilith finished the rest of her tea and put down the cup. "I suppose I should be off. I need to find a motel somewhere. Any suggestions?"

Niki sighed. Before she could respond, her cell phone rang. She checked the screen and saw Rube's name. "Sorry, I need to take this. I'll be just a moment." She stepped into the living room and answered.

"Niki, you better come now," Rube said. "She's upset. I don't know how long I can keep her here."

"Don't let her out of your sight. I'll be there in five minutes." She rushed back into the kitchen. "Sorry, but I have to go. Make yourself comfortable. I don't know when I'll be back." She paused. "You can stay here tonight. Take the guest room downstairs."

She grabbed her purse and flew out the door. She came to an abrupt stop at her car and looked back at the house. *Shit. What did I just say?*

CHAPTER 10

Niki heard the sobs before Rube opened the door.

"I didn't touch her." Rube raised his hands, palms out. "She goin' on 'bout Curtis Ray."

Niki dove past him to where Jayme sat huddled in the kitchen. She pulled up a chair and sat next to her. "Jayme? Look at me. Do you know who I am?"

Jayme lifted a tear-streaked face and focused cornflower blue eyes on her. "Rube said you're Mama's friend. I remember you. Once, when she stopped to visit you, I was there, in her truck."

Niki smiled. "I remember that day, too. You've grown some."

"Mama used to talk about how you helped her get out of trouble."

"That's right. This time I'm here for you."

"It's Curtis Ray who needs help," Jayme blurted. "Don't let that preacher take him."

She looked questioningly at Rube. "How—"

"Curtis Ray called her."

They let him use the hospital phone? Curtis Ray must have been persuasive with the nurses or the cop on duty.

She took Jayme's hand. "What did he tell you?"

"He was scared. He swears the preacher is lying. That guy isn't his uncle. He just wants to take him back to the camp. You got to stop him."

"Don't worry," she said. "The police have Curtis Ray in custody. He isn't allowed visitors, especially not the preacher."

"Like he's in jail?" Jayme wailed. "He didn't do anything wrong."

"It's for his own protection, and so the doctors can fix him up and make him all better. This way the preacher can't get to him. He's going to be fine, Jayme."

"He—he said if he's sent back to the camp, he'll be killed. Just like the others."

Had she heard her right? "What others? Jayme, what are you saying?"

Jayme looked miserable. "I don't know. I'm just telling you what he told me. He's been looking for his friend, Markey. Said they took him to Houston, but he never came back. Markey's got no family. Curtis Ray says they probably killed him."

"That's a very strong accusation."

Jayme expression hardened as she faced her. "Curtis Ray believes it. He says the guy who shot him takes pictures of boys. Dirty pictures and videos to sell. He says they took Markey there."

"Who's *they*? And who's Markey? Why haven't I heard about him before?" What kind of story was Curtis Ray telling Jayme? Niki expected to hear a confession about a burlary gone badly, not something this sick. Rube had told her about the pictures on the cell phone. They must be connected.

Jayme stared at her for a moment and then turned away. "I knew you wouldn't believe me. Curtis Ray said you wouldn't. No one will."

Niki collected her thoughts before she spoke again. "Jayme, did Curtis Ray ever tell you how he knows this?"

Jayme hesitated then understood. "You mean, did that guy take pictures of Curtis Ray?"

Niki nodded.

"He wouldn't tell me." Jayme hesitated. "But I think so."

Niki didn't say anything for several moments. Jayme's story of possible perversion and murder, as sick and warped as it sounded, was by far not out of the realm of reality. Niki dealt with street kids every day. Vulnerable and initially trusting, they were fresh meat to the predators and sexual deviants who sought them out. Jayme's own mother had been grabbed off the street when she was fifteen by a sex trafficking ring. Fortunately, she had been able to escape. Now Jayme was being exposed. Second hand, thank goodness, but still too close.

"Jayme, look at me," she said, and waited until Jayme turned back to her. "I know what can happen to runaways and throwaways who come across a pervert or a pimp. I don't often see kids fight back. What were the two of you looking for when you went into that house?"

"You—you believe me?" Jayme sounded incredulous.

"Yes, I do. Were you looking for the room that was pictured on the cell phone?" At Jayme's look of surprise, she added, "Rube told me you showed it to him."

Jayme nodded. "Curtis Ray wanted proof."

"The police tracked your nine-one-one call, which showed the number belongs to a Davey Tanner. Did Davey take those pictures?"

"Curtis Ray's friend, Markey, took them. I don't know how Markey got the phone. Want to take a look at the pictures? Show her, Rube."

Rube had downloaded the photos from the phone and already had his laptop powered up. Niki looked carefully at each of them, noting the placement of the twin bed and video camera. The room was an improvised studio.

Shamberg. The sonofabitch was into child pornography. A rich man who thought he was protected by his connections.

There were other pictures as well, Niki discovered, showing the pool and tennis courts in back of the house. More showing interior shots of the kitchen, dining room, and living room.

Jayme looked sheepish. "I took those," she admitted.

Niki surmised this. "Did you find the room?"

Jayme shook her head. "We looked everywhere, even had to open some of the doors."

Niki forced down her anger. She had to remain calm for Jayme. "Rube mentioned you had a DVD."

Jayme looked miserable. "We found a bunch of them. He probably kept them to watch all by himself. Pretty sick, huh?"

"Yes," she agreed. "Very sick. What did you do with them?"

"Curtis Ray dropped them by accident when I bumped into him. All except one. He put that one in my pocket."

A bright spot, a ray of hope, something tangible to use. She crossed her fingers. "Where's the DVD now?"

Jayme leaned back, retreating in more ways than one. "Curtis Ray made me promise to keep it safe. So I hid it. Good thing, too, 'cause Snake would have grabbed it when he found me. If it wasn't for Rube—" She looked down at her hands knitted tightly together.

"I know," Niki said, and stole a glance at Rube, who sat impassively. She put her hand over Jayme's. "Curtis Ray gave me a message to give to you."

Jayme looked up, eyes widening. "What message?"

"He said to give the DVD to the cop. Do you know what he meant?"

Confusion clouded Jayme's eyes. "What cop?"

Disappointed, Niki said, "I thought you might know."

Jayme shook her head, looking unhappy. "Won't do any good. The rich always get away."

How did this kid get so cynical? Oh, wait. Biker dad? Mom in jail? Grandma who couldn't wait to get rid of her? Yeah, that could do the trick. "Curtis Ray told you this?"

"Mom told me." Jayme struck a pose with one hand on her hip and mimicked Sharena's salty attitude. "Money buys everything." She glared angrily at Niki. "Are you still a cop?"

Niki was having trouble keeping up with Jayme's swiftly changing moods. "Not anymore. But I'm close to the cops who are investigating your friend. I get involved when there are kids in trouble. If we can prove what Shamberg has been doing to boys like Markey and Curtis Ray, they'll go after him, not you and Curtis Ray. Sometimes you have to trust a cop."

"Hmmm. I don't know," Jayme sniffed, sounding exactly like Sharena.

"One of the cops is my ex-partner. His new partner is a good guy, too. Both are worried about you. I'd like to tell them I've found you, and you're safe."

Jayme stiffened. "Won't they arrest me like they did Curtis Ray?"

"They'll want to find out what you know. You're a witness, Jayme. You can tell them what Shamberg did to Curtis Ray. He had no right to shoot him. But first, we need that DVD so we can show evidence of child pornography to a judge and convict the bad guys."

Jayme chewed on her lower lip. "Rube said you talked to my mom."

"Yes, she called me to ask for my help in finding you. I went to see her in Gatesville. She's very worried about you."

"If she trusts you," Jayme said slowly, "then okay. I guess I should call her and Gran, but I don't want to go back home yet."

"I've already called your mom and your grandmother. They know you're safe and with me. That's all that matters."

A mischievous grin spread across Jayme's face. "I bet Gran was mad."

Niki winced, remembering the stream of obscenities coming across the line. "She's relieved, knowing you're okay."

"Yeah, that's good, I guess," Jayme said.

"I'm curious about something else. Where did you go that night after what happened?"

"Hid in someone's back yard, hoofed it back to Montrose in the morning, and hid for a while in the library." Jayme looked up at her. "That's where I hid the DVD."

Jayme walked all the way from River Oaks to the library? Had to be more than three miles. Niki glanced at Jayme's callused feet and the worn tennis shoes in the corner of the room. Probably used to walking everywhere like most street kids.

She drew a long breath. "Will you show me?"

Jayme nodded.

"First thing in the morning," Niki said, "when the library opens. Meanwhile, young lady, you should get some sleep."

She stood, but before she took a step, Jayme jumped up and hugged her. Niki held the girl close, feeling a beating heart next to her own. That feeling stayed with her all the way home. It wasn't until she pulled into her own driveway and saw the rental car still parked there, that she remembered what waited for her inside the house.

CHAPTER 11

Niki opened her front door and crept in like a thief in case Lilith might be asleep or, better yet, gone. A second later she berated herself for acting like an intruder in her own home. She started to slam the door but stopped herself in time. No sense in acting like a teenager.

Lilith slept, not in the offered guest room, but on the sofa in the living room. Her stepmother didn't stir even when she stood a foot away and looked down at her. In repose Lilith lost the gloss of sophistication and, instead, looked tired and pale.

She had to admit she was more than a bit curious about her stepmother's real intentions. At this hour, though, she had no inclination to wake her and went upstairs to her own room and undressed for bed. Under the covers, staring at the ceiling, she refused to dwell on Lilith's motivations. Her real concern was Jayme. But after a while, she drifted off. Evidently, the night had taken more of a toll on her than she thought.

The next morning the sofa was empty, but the door to the downstairs guest room was closed. She figured Lilith had chosen the more comfortable bed and decided not to wake her. She didn't have time for a protracted confrontation. After making a pot of coffee, she ate a bowl of fruit with her cereal, filled her travel mug, and quietly left the house. The longer she could put off dealing with Lilith the better. She needed to concentrate her efforts on helping Jayme and Curtis Ray.

She picked up Jayme from Rube's house and twenty minutes later parked in a covered garage behind the Freed-Montrose neighborhood library. The historical ivy-covered building graced the south side of a brick courtyard that fronted three restaurants. The Black Lab, Cezanne Jazz, and the Eatsie Boys Café were all favored by students and professors from the nearby University of St. Thomas.

Niki took Jayme through two double doors and stopped in front of a circular desk occupied by two busy librarians. Jayme turned left and examined a red wire stand that held a row of nondescript DVD cases.

"I was so tired when I got here," Jayme said. "I remember thinking why not hide a DVD in a case with another DVD?" A look of concentration deepened the tiny lines between her eyes as she flipped open cases. As she got closer to the middle of the row, Jayme's frustration showed. "I don't remember which one."

"Take your time and relax," Niki advised.

Jayme continued until she threw the last case down in despair.

Niki went to the desk and asked one of the librarians if they had changed the DVDs recently. The woman looked puzzled. "Not unless new ones came in and needed to be added. I can't tell you if any of them have been checked out."

"Why?" Jayme asked, looking more desperate.

"It's the privacy act," Niki explained. "They can't give out any information."

"There are more DVDs behind you," the librarian said, helpfully. "Is there one in particular you're looking for? I can check the computer."

"Thanks, but she's forgotten the title, so that won't help," Niki said.

With fresh energy, Jayme went through row after row.

"What made you think of the library to hide the DVD?"

Niki asked, to take the edge off Jayme's frantic search.

Jayme paused. "We used to go here when we wanted to get out of the heat or just rest and read. This is Curtis Ray's favorite place. He loves to read. Now I do, too."

So the street orphan who grew up in a boy's camp was both smart and resourceful. She made a note to tell Nelson.

Jayme finished with the shelves and sank to the floor with a choking sob. "It's not there."

Niki knelt and put an arm around her. "How did you manage to stay the night? Where did you sleep?"

Jayme turned toward the staircase. Next to the bottom step was a sign printed with the words, Adult Section. "I hid upstairs."

Halfway up Niki heard Jayme say, "I wish he'd never given it to me. I wish we never went to that house."

"If wishes were diamonds, we'd be rich," Niki intoned.

On the second floor, a uniformed cop stood at a tall podium several feet away from the stairs. The head librarian's office, an open file room, and the elevator were to his right. Niki guessed the file room would have been locked at night.

The other side of the room held tables with computers and more rows of bookshelves filled with books and magazines. She noted a separate fiction section, and several rows holding foreign books. The non-fiction took up the rest of the space.

She roamed the room with Jayme and finally came to a row of reference books opposite the guard's post. In the far corner was an alcove next to a high window that overlooked the street. A rolling stand with books to be shelved occupied the space.

Jayme pointed. "I slept there. Nobody saw me. I hid in the ladies room until closing. Not even the guard found me." She slumped against the wall, looking defeated.

"There's nothing more we can do here," Niki said, glancing at the guard who had been watching them.

Jayme wiped tears from her eyes and got to her feet.

Outside they passed the patio outside Eatsie Boys Café.

Jayme stiffened and slipped behind her. She whispered, "Snake. Do you see him?"

Niki almost missed him. The moment before he disappeared, she caught a glimpse of a bald head, a yellow and black T-shirt, and one arm covered with tattoos.

Did Snake follow them to the library? Or had he already searched?

By the time they reached her car, Jayme's tear-streaked face didn't attempt to hide her anger and frustration. "What are we going to do?"

"Only one other thing we can do," Niki said calmly. "You're going to talk to the police."

"They'll arrest me," Jayme shrieked, reaching for the door handle.

Niki clamped onto Jayme's arm to steady her. "Hold on. Remember what I told you? They need to get your statement to back up Curtis Ray's story. You want to help him? This is the way to do it."

CHAPTER 12

Niki braced for Nelson's reaction when he returned to his office after recording Jayme's statement.

He strode around his desk, plopped into his chair, and swiveled to face her. "Why did you wait this long to tell me you found Jayme?"

"You saw her. She was scared. I had to find a way of getting her story without having her run away again. If the police grabbed her first and asked questions later, she would have clammed up."

Nelson folded his arms. "You believe we're that insensitive when we pick up a minor? You don't trust us after all this time?" Every word sounded like an accusation.

"It's not that I don't trust you, but Jayme doesn't. I needed to talk to her first. Sharena gave me that responsibility. My job was to find Jayme, so I decided to do it my way, even if that meant you'd get mad at me later." She allowed the hint of a smile to soften her face. "Don't get on my case. It all worked out, didn't it? I gave her to you. You got her story. You haven't arrested her. Happy ending."

"I didn't arrest her. Yet." Nelson gave no sign of thawing. "I have to interview Shamberg."

"Good idea. We should."

Nelson frowned. "*We?* What do you mean?"

"I mean, you should take me with you," she said.

"Why you, a civilian, instead of Luis, who's my partner? In case you've forgotten."

"Shamberg knows who I am. He must suspect we found Jayme. What he doesn't know is if Jayme and Curtis Ray found something that can be used against him. That's why he'll let us in if I'm with you. End of discussion."

"You're giving me orders now? Just because you used to be Luis's partner doesn't give you special privileges."

She leaned back and put her feet on the edge of his desk, letting the bottom of her shoes scrape the wood. "I thought we were equals and could discuss a case rationally. If you object, I want to hear why."

Nelson didn't answer. The silence extended uncomfortably. Any other cop would have arrested Jayme as soon as they spotted her. They would never take the word of a street kid caught breaking and entering over the word of a River Oaks homeowner and businessman. She gave Nelson credit for listening to the girl.

She broke the silence. "Not talking to us will make him look like he's hiding something. When we confronted him at the hospital, he said he wanted to cooperate. Good, let's give him that opportunity. He also wants to find Jayme, because she might have whatever he thinks Curtis Ray stole. He may see a way of getting to her through me." She let her feet drop to the floor and leaned toward Nelson. "Let's try it my way, please? If it doesn't work, you haven't lost any ground. What if Curtis Ray is right and Shamberg is a pedophile and pornographer? You'd go to any lengths to send him straight to hell. I know you."

She saw a blue vein pulse at his temple. For a moment she was afraid she'd lost the battle. The stoic Cherokee stubbornness showed in his face. He also had his father's Italian temper. She had to think fast to keep up with him.

To her relief, he sucked in a breath and nodded. "You're right about one thing. If this guy is abusing and exploiting minors in any way, I'll go after him with everything I got. But so far there's no evidence that indicates he's guilty."

"That's why you need fresh eyes. We have one advantage. Shamberg doesn't know pictures were taken.
You've seen the photos of that room. We need to find his
studio."

Nelson stood and grabbed his keys. "Maybe a surprise
visit will catch him off guard."

She jumped to her feet. "I'm ready. Let's go."

Twenty minutes later, they arrived at Shamberg's River
Oaks house. As they passed the ground where Curtis Ray
was shot, grass still rusty with old blood, Nelson paused.
His eyes narrowed, and his jaw tightened.

Niki hadn't the advantage of being there previously like
Nelson. This was the closest she had been to the crime scene and was repelled by the sight. She thought of Curtis Ray
and wondered if two children could bring down Shamberg's
shadow world.

Nelson touched her elbow, indicating it was time to
move forward.

Shamberg opened his front door, dressed casually in a
white Polo shirt and brown slacks. In the daylight, his dark
hair formed a vee on his forehead showing more scalp than
had appeared at night in front of Ben Taub Hospital. He
frowned, shifting his gold-rimmed glasses halfway down his
nose. "The investigator and the counselor. What brings you
here? More questions?"

"Only some follow up," Nelson said. "May we come
in?"

Shamberg stepped aside. "I told you both, I got nothing
to hide. By the way, have you found the girl yet?"

"Still worried about her?" Niki asked.

He didn't respond like she'd hoped. He ignored her.

"The description you gave the police artist was helpful,"
Nelson said.

Shamberg didn't say anything for a moment, then he
laughed. "Nicely done, detective. That's the best non-
answer I've heard in a long time." He led them into a lavishly furnished living room that Niki recognized from the

pictures Jayme had taken. "May I get you something to drink?"

"No, thank you, Mr. Shamberg," Nelson said.

"Call me Clay."

"Tell me again, Mr. Shamberg," Nelson continued. "What happened when you came home and saw the two kids in your house?"

"I went over this twice." Shamberg held up his hand before Nelson could protest. "When I arrived home that evening, I heard voices. I spotted a boy and a girl, inside. They both ran out. It was dark early. The boy looked to be in his teens and black. We've had a lot of robberies in the neighborhood, and I thought he fit the description other victims reported to the police. I didn't want him to get away with anything valuable."

"Were you carrying a gun or did you have to go inside to get it?" Nelson asked.

"I have a license and my gun is registered. In my business I sometimes carry a large amount of cash. It's better to be prepared than sorry later. As it turned out, I was sorry I shot the kid."

"Have you determined what *is* missing?"

"Nothing. That's the part that hurts. As a matter of fact, I'm going downtown later to have the charges against the kids dropped."

That's a switch, Niki thought. Why the sudden change of heart? She drifted around the room, noting the pictures on the mantle. There were several with Shamberg and a beautiful blonde in different settings. Expensive looking paintings and black and white framed photographs lined the wall. Glass figurines were encased in locked cabinets.

She paused at a sketch of a building plan laid out on a long table tucked in the corner of the living room. She recognized the location of the condominium that had stirred up a recent outrage in the Rice University neighborhood. Another strike she had against the man. She had friends who were protesting at the construction site.

She caught Shamberg looking at her.

"The kids didn't break anything," he said. "If they did, I'm fully insured."

As if that meant anything, she thought.

"The charges against the children are up to the district attorney, not you." Nelson said. "On the other hand, you can still be arrested for shooting a minor. That's called attempted murder."

Shamberg's face reddened. "I know the law, detective. I'm a homeowner protecting his property. In Texas, I'm within my rights. No judge or jury would convict me."

"The boy was unarmed," Nelson said evenly.

"How would I have known that? Do I wait until he produces a weapon? By that time, I'd be dead. I shot him in self-defense. Pure and simple."

"You shot him in the back," Nelson said with gritted teeth.

Niki cut in before blood was shed. "Mr. Shamberg, is that your wife in those pictures with you?"

Shamberg turned to her. "My fiancé."

"She's beautiful. Have you set a date for the wedding?"

"Nice of you to notice. No, the wedding's been postponed until after this unpleasantness is resolved."

"I also noticed you had several framed photographs. Is photography a hobby of yours?"

Shamberg hesitated. "I used to play around with the camera. Not much time for it anymore, I'm afraid."

"What about video?" she pressed, hoping to see some kind of reaction.

He had none. Not even a twitch. "Don't have time," he answered. "Why do you ask?"

She shrugged. "No special reason. Just that photography and video seem to go together."

"Wish I could squeeze that in my schedule. Maybe when I'm retired."

She noticed he wasn't looking at her, but watching Nelson retreat to the den adjacent to the living room.

"Is that a pool house out back?" Nelson called out.

She followed Shamberg into the den, curious to see what had caught Nelson's attention. From the French doors, she could see the pool and tennis court. Jayme had captured most of the grounds with the camera.

"Why, yes," Shamberg said. "Next to the pool, as anyone might expect to find a pool house." His tone conveyed impatience with an edge of sarcasm.

"I'd like to take a look inside," Nelson said.

Shamberg frowned. "Why?"

"Are you hiding something in there you don't want me to see?"

"Of course not. I don't know what you expect to find in there besides dressing rooms and a bar. I've got the best whiskey in the world for my guests. Would you care for a taste? I can see that you do not. Maybe another time."

"I could come back with a warrant."

"Ridiculous," Shamberg said, shaking his head. "I told you I have nothing to hide. What possible reason—Wait. You think the kids were in there? I didn't think about that. I don't keep drugs around if that's what they were looking for."

Shamberg led them outside, across a large patio, and down a brick path. Lounge chairs and tables were placed around the pool. He opened the door to the pool house. They entered a spacious room with pale pink walls and filled with comfortable sofas and chairs. An indoor wet bar displayed the expensive whiskey of which he boasted. A pool table filled more space. Shamberg opened a door closest to the entrance and indicated the showers and changing areas.

Niki shook her head at Nelson.

"Satisfied?" Shamberg asked. "By the way, I've been meaning to ask, how is the boy doing in the hospital? Hope he's on the way to recovery."

The bastard's enjoying himself, Niki fumed.

"I can't discuss the boy's condition," Nelson said, his

tone sharp. He beckoned to Niki. "Let's take a walk." They left Shamberg to lock up the pool house, and headed toward the trees that lined the back fence.

Shamberg lit a cigarette and called after them. "Let me know if you find any varmints digging holes under the fence."

Nelson's look of frustration mirrored what she was feeling. "Jayme said they couldn't find the studio," she whispered.

She hadn't told him about the photos of this house that Jayme took. In fact, Rube had deleted them from the camera once he put them on his laptop. They both knew the DA could use those pictures as physical evidence she was in the house with Curtis Ray. Not that Niki believed either child would be prosecuted, but she wouldn't give them any ammunition either.

Nelson fingered the cigarette pack in his shirt pocket. "This is a dead end. Forensics went through his house and did a thorough search. Those photos of that room could have been taken anywhere. They could have nothing to do with Shamberg."

"You don't really believe that," she said.

He shrugged. "You got any other suggestions? No? I didn't think so. Let's say our goodbyes and get the hell out of here."

"You find anything?" Shamberg asked when they returned to the pool area.

"We've seen enough for now, Mr. Shamberg. But don't leave town. We'll be talking to you."

"You'd better have another talk with that boy. Tell him burglarizing a home is dangerous business. That kind of behavior won't get him what he wants in life. Take it from me. I didn't have the greatest childhood either, but I succeeded in making something of myself."

"Good for you," Niki said under her breath.

"Thank you for your time and patience, Mr. Shamberg," Nelson said.

"Anytime, detective, anytime."

Once they were back in Nelson's car, she leaned her head back. "We need that DVD."

"Ah, yes, the missing DVD," Nelson echoed. "If it doesn't show Shamberg breaking the law, we'll still have nothing. I'll talk to Curtis Ray again."

"Can I come with you?"

"You're asking now?" He gave her a sideways glance. "Sure, why not? You'll just argue until you get your way. Anyway, you seem to be a calming influence on him."

"Thanks," she said, not trusting her easy win. "Where's Webster Capp? I hope he's not hanging around the hospital all day."

"Got a motel room last I heard," Nelson said.

"What happens after Curtis Ray recovers from his injuries?"

"The state pays his bills as long as he's in custody and too injured to leave. After the doctor releases him, the state stops paying. The court will appoint an attorney ad litem to protect his interest."

"What happens to him between his release and his court date?"

"His attorney ad litem can suggest a shelter or group home."

"Group home? What about Open Palms?"

Nelson paused while he considered. "The judge may decide Open Palms is too open. Curtis Ray could leave too easily."

Niki disagreed. "We have an armed guard and a weapons detector. I don't know how we can be more secure. Will he be released from the hospital soon?"

"A week or less."

"We've got to find that DVD and hope whatever is on it proves Shamberg is the lowest form of the human race."

Without looking at her, Nelson said. "You know that Snake may have it by now. If so, the DVD's as good as destroyed."

"We still have the photos. Maybe we missed something in the background."

Nelson didn't seem impressed. "Let's go to your house. I need a decent cup of coffee. We'll retrieve your car later."

She barely listened to him as she brooded silently on the way. He parked in front and took her hand in his, and with his other hand touched her cheek. She faced him and he kissed her gently. She pulled him closer and deepened the kiss.

"Been a long time," he murmured, his hand covering her right breast. She buried her head into his neck.

Seconds later she felt him stiffen and he let go of her. He was staring up at her house. With a quick, fluid movement, he reached for his gun. "Stay here. There's someone in your house."

"What?" She turned to follow his gaze, and almost choked. "Oh, shit, I'm an idiot. Lilith. I forgot all about her."

He drew back, his confusion evident. "Who?"

"She arrived last night. My subconscious must have blocked her temporarily."

Nelson's hand brushed against his holster. "You make her sound dangerous."

She couldn't help a short laugh. "You've no idea."

"Are we going in?" Nelson prodded.

She opened the car door. "Sure. Come on, meet my stepmother."

CHAPTER 13

Niki was not surprised to find Lilith impeccably dressed in a sapphire suit, the tired lines she had last seen on her creamy complexion smoothed to an elastic tightness. She made herself promise to act like an adult and let past resentments slide. For now, at least, and in front of Nelson.

"So this is the new man in my daughter's life," Lilith said, after the introductions were made in the living room. She circled Nelson as if he were up for auction. "Nice specimen."

"Lilith, stop it, you're embarrassing him," she said, feeling her face go warm. "And me."

As if she hadn't spoken, Nelson grinned at Lilith. "Thank you for the compliment, Mrs. Winegold. It's nice that someone notices."

Was he flirting back? She felt her good intentions slip sideways.

"Niki never mentioned her mother," Nelson continued. "I knew she didn't come fully formed out of the police academy's womb, but she's never told me anything about her family."

"I can say the same about you," Niki retorted. "All I know is you have a wildly antagonistic gene pool, Cherokee and Sicilian. It's all I can do to deal with that combination."

"Honey, you know you love it." "Honey" was not a word

he usually used on her. As if that wasn't enough, Nelson chucked her chin with his forefinger. She grabbed the finger and twisted, harder than she intended. He didn't flinch, but blew her an air kiss. She let go with a warning look. *Don't mess with me.*

Lilith covered her mouth and coughed politely. "Didn't mean to start an argument. To clarify, I'm Niki's stepmother. The wicked witch, as she likes to think of me."

"Liked to think of you, as in the past. I actually haven't thought about you in fourteen years. Maybe because that's how long it's been since I've heard from you." She turned to Nelson. "She's another Italian. You two should get along great."

Nelson grinned and offered Lilith his hand. "A pleasure to meet you."

"Likewise." Lilith clasped his hand with both hers, and held it. "I understand you work in the Homicide Division. Did you two meet on the force?"

"No, she had already quit by the time we met. We have my current partner in common. Even though she's not a cop anymore, she has this bad habit of inserting herself into our cases."

"Only when it involves a street teen," she objected.

Nelson continued as if she hadn't spoken. "Niki likes to think she's still a cop when it suits her."

"She's always been like that," Lilith said. "She knows what she wants and she goes for it."

"Yes, I've noticed that, too. What part of Italy are you from?"

"Oh, I was born here. My grandfather came from Tuscany. And you? That's quite a combination you were born into."

"That's what Niki keeps telling me. My mother was Cherokee. My father was Sicilian. They met when he was stationed in Oklahoma."

"You're an army brat then?"

"For a few years, yes. Got to see the world before age ten."

Niki cleared her voice. She had never heard any of this before. She should be delighted Lilith and Nelson were getting along so well, but in the process they seemed to have forgotten her. "I'll go make a pot of coffee."

"Oh, you needn't bother," Lilith said. "I just made a fresh pot."

"You must have been expecting us." Nelson looked pleased.

"I'd just made it back to the house after running a few errands and needed a jolt of caffeine while I contemplated where to go for dinner. Then you two bounced in the door."

"Coffee sounds wonderful," Nelson said.

"Perfect." Lilith beamed at both of them and hooked an arm through theirs and practically danced them into the kitchen. "Niki has such a homey atmosphere, especially in the kitchen. I'd never have expected it of her."

"What did you expect? White and shades of beige?" She was getting tired of feeling left out, and after the curved nail imbedded in the last remark, she'd about had it with both of them.

Lilith looked surprised "Of course not, dear. I was paying you a compliment. I think you've shown exceptional decorating taste."

Nelson stepped beside Niki and put his arm around her shoulders. "Niki is actually an amazing woman," he said. "Once the two of you get acquainted again, you'll realize how talented she is in so many areas."

His words surprised her and gave her the boost of confidence she needed. It was almost like he had read her state of mind. She squeezed his hand gently. "You didn't need to go to any trouble," she told Lilith. "This is my home and you're a guest."

"Oh honey, relax," Lilith said. "I'm not here to disrupt your life." She dug through the cabinets until she found three mugs and poured the coffee. After putting them on the table, she brought a container of milk from the fridge and sat down. "I couldn't find any sugar."

"Don't keep any," Niki replied.

"That's all right," Lilith said with a wave of her hand. "I don't use any either."

Nelson took a long swallow and held the cup with both hands with elbows on the table. "Why *are* you here, Lilith?"

This time Niki spoke up before her stepmother could answer.

"The new widow inherited some money from her latest catch, so she decided to come to Houston and open a law office. She used to work for the DA here years ago. I assume she returned because of some misdirected urge to make up for old times. Am I right so far, Lilith?"

"Almost right." Lilith met her eyes, and then smiled as if acknowledging Niki's right to speak for her. She turned to Nelson. "Her quick mind has a tendency to jump over a few details at times. We did get off on the wrong foot when I married her father three years after her mother's unfortunate death from cancer. I met and married her father in San Francisco while Niki stayed with her grandparents in Los Angeles. We never had a chance to meet before I was thrust into her life. Not the best way to form a mother and daughter relationship. She was hell bent not to accept me no matter what. Under the circumstances, we didn't have much of a chance."

"Not just that," Niki said. "You were always fighting with dad. You never got along with him either."

Lilith sighed before answering. "The truth is he knew from the start I had lost my mother when I was your age and had to deal with a stepmother. I think he picked me just for that reason. Your father decided I would be the perfect replacement because I would understand how you felt. He was wrong. My experience didn't help."

Niki scoffed. "Are you saying that's the only reason he married you?"

Lilith smiled sadly. "He never loved me like he loved

your mother. I stuck it out because of you. I did try to be a good replacement."

Niki glanced at Nelson, suddenly embarrassed for him. "Let's change the subject."

"I agree," Nelson said, watching both of them carefully.

"Okay," Niki said. "Start by telling me why you chose this time to come back into my life."

"I'm curious, too," Nelson said. "Has it really been fourteen years?"

Lilith answered flatly, "Yes."

"That's a long time," he said. "Long enough that your differences can't and won't be resolved in five minutes."

Niki remembered her earlier promise to herself. "We're both adults. We can deal with this."

"Very good. See? You're not a teenager anymore," Lilith said, her green eyes shiny.

The remark felt condescending and brushed her the wrong way. Niki was reminded of why they used to fight. She glared at Lilith.

Lilith reacted at once. "Oh, my goodness, do I have to watch every word I say? Are you still the overly sensitive Daddy's girl?"

Nelson broke in before Niki could form a retort. "Why don't we all take a breath and relax."

The silence lasted for several seconds. Lilith spoke first. "Nelson's right. I have a suggestion. Let me take you both out to dinner. Tomorrow I'll look for other digs."

It seemed too easy. How could she trust this woman's motives after all these years? Her cop instincts made her question everything. Those instincts had served her well in the past and especially when she dealt with troubled teens. She hoped she was wrong about her stepmother.

"Come on, babe," Nelson said, taking her hand. "I'm hungry. Aren't you?"

"Dinner sounds great." She forced a smile. Maybe over a meal she could pry more information out of Lilith. "Where?"

"How about Carrabba's?" Nelson suggested.

Of course, it would be Italian, she thought wryly.

"Excellent," Lilith said.

They rode in Nelson's car, since hers was still parked at Travis Center. The restaurant was crowded and noisy, but the food surpassed her expectations. Conversation was minimal and noncontroversial. She decided not to push for information and enjoy the meal instead. Lilith and Nelson shared a bottle of wine. Niki, as usual, abstained and ordered iced tea. Her stepmother didn't appear to notice, and she didn't feel the need to explain that she still attended AA meetings on occasion. She kept in the background while Nelson and Lilith compared notes about countries they'd visited. When their plates were cleared, Lilith picked up the tab.

It was still early when they arrived back at Niki's. Lilith suggested a dessert of Italian sherbet she had bought earlier, and they retreated to the kitchen.

"Unless you had other plans." Lilith winked at them. "Don't mind me."

"Not tonight," Nelson said, with a glance at Niki. "My shift starts at seven, and I don't want to disturb you that early. I'll stop by on my way to work and take Niki to her car."

Niki didn't like the idea of not having wheels even for one night. "I'd rather we get my car now."

Nelson nodded. "You're right. You might get a call in the middle of the night."

"Then we must have dessert before you go." Lilith took down tulip-shaped dishes from the cupboard and scooped sherbet in each. Nelson settled in a chair while Niki washed her hands.

Once they were seated, Lilith savored a spoonful before speaking. "Since you're both leaving, there's a matter of importance I've wanted to bring up. I didn't want to spoil dinner. I hoped this could wait until tomorrow, but I realize that wouldn't be right."

Here it comes. Niki's gut twisted. No time to prepare for whatever was coming.

"You're working the case of the boy who got shot," Lilith said. "I read about it in the paper."

Niki exchanged a look with Nelson, who put his spoon down.

"I'm wondering why homicide has the case since the boy is obviously alive," Lilith continued, as if unaware of the renewed tension in the room.

"When someone discharges a gun that hits a person, homicide division gets the case," Nelson explained. "Even if nobody dies."

"How is the boy's condition?"

"I can't really discuss the case," Nelson said. "You should know that."

"Of course, I do. Did Niki mention I used to work for the DA's office?"

Nelson looked puzzled. "She might have mentioned it."

"Is the boy represented?"

"Not yet."

"He was on the street for at least a month, wasn't he? After he ran away from the wilderness camp?"

"How do you know that?" Niki interrupted. "That wasn't in any paper."

"I have my sources," Lilith said.

Nelson leaned toward her. "What's your interest in this case?"

"What's always been my interest," Lilith said curtly. "Cases involving children were my specialty in the DA's office. I prosecuted mostly sex crimes."

Nelson kept his expression blank. "Do you plan on going back to the DA's office?"

Lilith gave a short laugh. "Oh my, no. A lot has changed. New DA in place. I was thinking of going into criminal defense."

"You want to defend Shamberg?" Niki said, feeling an acid flush in her stomach.

"No." Lilith's expression hardened. "I want to defend Curtis Ray."

Finally, the truth was out. Even though Niki expected an answer other than reuniting with her, the words still delivered a sock to the gut. "That's why you're here. I knew there had to be a reason." *Other than me.*

"What's your plan?" Nelson's knee bumped into Niki's under the table. "Are you counting on a family member to hire you?"

"It's my understanding no one has come forward except the preacher who runs the camp. I know Lavinia Roselle. We discussed all this earlier today. Between the two of us, we can get the judge to appoint me attorney ad litem for Curtis Ray. I'm willing to take the case pro bono."

Niki digested Lilith's words. Met with Lavinia earlier? How much did she know about the case already?

"Curtis Ray has to agree," Nelson finally said.

"He will," Lilith said with confidence.

Niki shook her head, trying to silence a buzz like a swarm of bees around a hive. "I knew you had an ulterior motive for coming. It wasn't a sudden need to connect with your stepdaughter after all these years. You came here for the sole purpose of defending Curtis Ray. The only question I have left is why."

Lilith lifted her chin. "I haven't lied to you about wanting to see you again. I've wanted this for years, but the timing was off. But, yes, I did come for the case. I want to see Clayton Shamberg buried in jail, far away from young boys. He's not going to get away from me this time."

CHAPTER 14

Lilith's stunning admission left Niki speechless. Clayton Shamberg had been Lilith's target all along?

Nelson held a spoonful of sherbet in the air. A drop of icy orange hit the table. His eyes narrowed. "How do you know Shamberg?"

Lilith's calm demeanor belied the anger behind her words. "His name came up when I worked for the DA's office. Even back then he was suspected of picking up runaway boys off the street and dealing in pornography. His real estate corporation, his friends in high places, his influence in politics all formed a wall around him. The boys wouldn't testify against him, and the cases went away. Since then he's been more careful about his perverted activities. He has more to lose. His corporation has grown and expanded. He owns real estate all over Texas, including the camp where Curtis Ray was staying."

The enormity of her stepmother's accusations against Shamberg didn't surprise Niki as much as the length of time Lilith had spent monitoring his life. "He's been under suspicion for that long?"

"In my opinion, and I'm no psychologist, he's probably been hiding his perversity since college. A pedophile doesn't change. They become expert at hiding their nature and choose professions that let them work with children, such as sports coaches or gym teachers. Many are married and have children. Most are heterosexual. To his friends and business affiliations he appears normal. The pedophile, if caught, might claim he's only expressing his love for the boys, and not guilty of a crime. I could never prove any of my suspicions, but I know what Clayton Shamberg is hiding underneath the mask he presents to the world."

"Any witnesses or victims come forward to testify?" Nelson asked.

"One boy almost did." Lilith dropped her gaze to her hands.

When she didn't elaborate, Nelson said, "I looked into the ownership of the land where the camp is located. That's a hundred acres. His name isn't listed in any of the corporate documents filed as owning the property."

"Of course not," Lilith said. "The corporate documents don't have to show his name. All he has to do is put the land in the name of one of his other corporations that's held by another corporation. He knows how to hide behind paperwork. Believe me, I've done the research. He owns that land."

Niki listened to their exchange with a growing concern. "You think by representing Curtis Ray against the B and E charge, you can achieve, what?"

Lilith faced her. "Would you want a pedophile loose with your shelter kids? Would you want to see any of your kids perform sex acts on the Internet? Let's work together. You've been protecting the girl who was with Curtis Ray when they broke into Shamberg's house. We know they were after something they could use against him. Curtis Ray took the risk of breaking into his house for only one possible reason. He's one of Shamberg's victims and wants revenge."

"I can see why you want to use him," Niki said. "Yes, he's been abused, but I don't want to see him hurt more in the process, whether it's emotionally or legally."

"I don't either. Don't you see? He doesn't have to become more of a victim. We need to find whatever proof he was after. He showed a lot of spunk by going after Shamberg. I want to help him."

"First of all, he hasn't told us anything," Nelson said, interrupting.

Lilith acknowledged him with frustration written all over her face. "What do you expect when he's already under arrest?"

"He told Jayme he was looking for his friend, Markey, who disappeared after a visit to Houston," Niki said.

"That doesn't mean Shamberg had any contact with Markey." Nelson dropped his spoon. "You're assuming more than you may be able to prove."

Lilith snorted. "I've been after that sonofabitch for sixteen years. He finally lost his cool when he shot Curtis Ray. He's exposed now. He's afraid. This is the time to strike."

Sixteen years? Niki reeled with the realization that Lilith was after Shamberg while still married to her father. As a teenager Niki once ran away after a fight with Lilith and she'd stayed on the street for days. Back then she'd thought her stepmother overreacted when she listed the dangers and what could have happened to her. As an adult, Niki admitted how lucky she had been to survive.

"Shamberg didn't act guilty when we paid him a visit," Nelson said.

Lilith glanced up sharply. "You didn't tell me about that."

"We went earlier today," Niki said and filled Lilith in. "We didn't find anything suspicious."

Lilith scraped her chair away from the table. "He owns property everywhere. He wouldn't do anything in his home."

Nelson took out his notebook and wrote something down. "I'll look into his other holdings." His cell phone rang. He checked the caller ID and rose from the table. "I have to take this. Save any more ideas until I get back."

Niki stared at her dish as she stirred the sugary remains of her dessert.

Lilith watched her. "I like to think my return to Houston serves two purposes. One, it gave me an excuse to see you again. Maybe recover the lost years when we didn't communicate."

"That's not what brought you here." Once the words were out, Niki realized the anger she expected to feel was gone. "You came because of the newspaper article about Shamberg. The fact that I was here made it possible for you to get your foot in the door. My door, specifically. My primary role is not going after Shamberg. It's protecting Jayme. I promised her mother."

"We can do this together, Niki. Save Jayme and Curtis Ray. Put away a monster."

"You don't have doubts that he is that monster?"

"No doubt whatsoever," Lilith said firmly. "I'll do anything to see that he pays for what he's done."

Niki gathered the dishes and put them into the sink. "Were you close to the child he molested years ago?"

Lilith nodded. Her eyes glistened with moisture. "The mother came to me. Single parent. She worked in one of Shamberg's offices. She thought his attention to her fatherless child was special. How nice of him to take an interest in her and her eight-year-old son. A short time later, the boy hid when Shamberg came to her house and refused to come out. One day she came home and found her son trying to hang himself. That's when she discovered the truth. Her boss, Clayton Shamberg, had been molesting him during their outings together. She came to me, wanting to prosecute. I said I would, but the child might have to testify against him. Instead, the mother chose to quit her job and leave town with the boy. Shamberg laughed it off. Said the boy was lying. I couldn't prove otherwise."

Niki looked at her stepmother with new understanding. "Something terrible happened back then. You tried to fix it, that's what counts." She knew her words were a salve that would never heal Lilith's pain. She knew that kind of pain and the residue guilt. She put a hand over Lilith's. The other woman looked up in surprise. "What matters is Curtis Ray. He needs us to fight for him."

Lilith's eyes searched hers and finally nodded with the barest of smiles. "We agree then."

Nelson appeared in the doorway. "We better get over to the hospital if you want to talk to Curtis Ray. He'll be released tomorrow morning baring any complications. My partner is there now."

"Your partner?" Lilith said. "I look forward to meeting him."

Niki gave a short laugh. "I believe you already have, if you remember my early career with HPD. He used to be my partner."

"Luis? Luis Perez?" Lilith's smile widened as she turned to Nelson. "It's been years. He's your partner now?"

"What a coincidence, huh? That's how I met your daughter."

"So that's what you meant earlier when you said you had a partner in common."

"Right." Nelson grinned. "We ended up working a case together."

"I had to fight him for that," Niki said. "He didn't think I was qualified because I no longer wore a badge."

"Bet he knows better now." Lilith's smile warmed. "Luis is an old friend. It'll be a treat to see him again."

"What do you mean *old friend*?" Niki felt caught off balance. Again.

Lilith laughed. "How do you think I kept up with you all these years? Not lately, of course, but during the years you were with HPD?"

"I'm not sure how many more surprises I can handle. Remind me to thank Luis for going behind my back." She didn't wait for a response but went to the door.

Behind her, she heard Lilith asking, "Who's the sitting Juvenile Court Judge?"

"Judge Woods," Nelson said. "Why?"

"We're in luck. I know him from way back. I'm going to convince him to appoint me as Curtis Ray's attorney ad litem."

CHAPTER 15

The hospital at night was as bright as daylight, but the change in the atmosphere struck Niki as noticeably different from her last visit. The air didn't crackle with the same electricity. Even the attitude of the night nurses seemed relaxed and their pace slower. Maybe that explained why she could watch the reunion between Lilith and Luis with the detachment of a casual observer.

The revelation that Luis had kept in touch with her stepmother as long as he did disconcerted her. She knew he could keep secrets, but why this one? Watching their warm embrace made her wonder what else he had kept from her.

While Nelson left to check with the doctor, the three retired to the waiting room down the hall where a half dozen people sat in chairs against the wall. Luis guided Niki and Lilith to an empty corner. They lowered their voices so as not to be overheard. Lilith explained to Luis her mission to convict Shamberg of pedophilia and pornography. When she finished, Luis glanced at Niki. She read the concern in his eyes. The protective side of his nature was revealed with that one look. She hoped to convey her reassurance with a smile. He nodded, and the furrows on his forehead smoothed out.

Nelson came in and announced to Lilith that she could meet with Curtis Ray. He turned to Luis. "The nurse let me know there was a young man waiting to see him. She told him visitors weren't allowed. He said he'd wait and talk to the officer in charge."

Luis chuckled. "Oh yes, almost forgot. I talked to him earlier and told him the same thing. Guess he's not taking no for an answer. We might as well interview him now and save us the time later. He's from the same camp as Curtis Ray. Does the name Davey Tanner mean anything to you?"

Niki tapped Nelson's arm. "The nine-one-one call. His phone."

He nodded. "Tell the guard to send him up."

"I'd like to meet him before I see Curtis Ray," Lilith said.

While they waited, the others in the room got up. One man glanced furtively at Luis before leaving with the others. When they were gone, a guard brought in the new visitor.

Davey Tanner was approximately five-eleven with muscular shoulders, bulging biceps and almost no fat on him. When he smiled, he exhibited teeth so white they almost didn't look natural. Blond, tanned and good looking as a magazine model, Davey appeared clean-cut, with soft features—full lips, blue eyes with long dark lashes, and smooth skin except for his hands, which were callused. His fingernails were clean and shone with a coat of clear polish.

Niki glimpsed his driver's license, which he handed to Nelson. Date of birth showed he was twenty. "You're older than the other boys," she said.

He had an easy laugh. "Yes, ma'am. I'm one of the counselors."

"Been with the camp long?" she asked.

"Since I turned seventeen when Preacher Capp took me on." He took notice of Lilith and stared at her as if seeing royalty.

Lilith acknowledged him with a smile. "Hello, Davey. I'm Lilith Winegold. I'm here to see your friend. How long have you known Curtis Ray?"

"Gee, guess it's been a couple of years, ma'am. We lived at the camp together. Can I see him now?"

Nelson answered. "He's not allowed visitors, I'm sorry."

Davey jerked a thumb toward Luis but kept his gaze on Nelson. "He said I had to ask you. So what's the prob, Captain?"

"Thanks for the promotion, but Sergeant Perez and Officer Spalonetti will do for now," Nelson said. "The problem is, he's under arrest."

"But it was Clay who shot him. Right? I'd think that's worse than attempted burglary. Why don't you arrest ol' Clay?"

Nelson frowned. "Clay?"

Davey gave a high-pitched laugh. "That's what the big man's name is."

"The big man?" Nelson repeated. "Clayton Shamberg, you're talking about?"

"Yeah, the one who shot CR. Never thought he'd do that to one of his boys."

"You know him well?" Nelson asked.

"Yeah, pretty much." Davey shrugged.

Lilith's reaction was visceral. "What did you mean by *one of his boys*?"

"Nothing, ma'am. I just thought since Clay owns all that hundred acres of land I should call him the big boss. He looks after us, in his way. He's the one talked Preach into hiring me."

Lilith's mouth trembled, and she pressed her lips together. She breathed deeply through her nose. "You're tight with Shamberg then?"

"Not so much since I've been working at the camp. Lately, he's been too busy with that condo he's building. Got lots of people pissed at him over that business, I hear." He looked at the faces around him as if judging their reaction.

Lilith kept her voice even. "Why do you think he shot Curtis Ray?"

Instead of answering, Davey turned to Niki. He winked at her, as if sharing some secret joke.

Before she could respond, he turned back to Lilith. "Haven't a clue, lady. You a cop, too?"

Her mouth twitched. "I'm a lawyer."

"Clay hired you, huh?"

"No. I'm here to defend Curtis Ray."

Davey looked surprised. "Really? Really and truly? Wow. Why you doing that?"

Nelson moved in front of Davey, blocking his view of Lilith. "Enough. I'll ask the questions from here on. Save us a trip to the camp to look for you."

"Me?" Davey said, bouncing another glance off the others. "Sure, why not?"

"We can go somewhere private, if you'd like."

"Hey, I got nothing to hide. Go ahead, Pop, shoot." He erupted into a laugh. "Not literally, of course."

"Why did you give Curtis Ray your cell phone?"

"My cell phone?" Davey looked up at the ceiling as if he might find the answer there. "I didn't. Kid must have grabbed it before he ran away." He lowered his head and met Nelson's eyes.

"Are you accusing him of stealing your cell phone?" Nelson asked.

"Well, never gave it to him, so guess you can call it that. Could be either him or his little buddy, Markey. Both been little pests. Been wondering what happened to it. You have it? I'd really like it back. Got some personal numbers I'd rather not share. If you know what I mean."

"Unfortunately, we'll have to keep it awhile. It's evidence in a crime."

"You mean, like a gun?" He turned to the others, laughing like he thought it was a joke.

"This is funny to you?" Nelson said.

Davey worked his mouth until he looked sober. "Hey, I feel bad for CR. He had a hard time adjusting. Some kids do." He looked around as if seeking agreement. "What did he do with my cell phone? It's got a camera. He take some pictures? I'd like to see that."

"That's what we're trying to find out. You want to press charges against him for stealing?"

"What? Hell, no. After what he's been through? I feel sorry for the kid."

"We need the truth, Davey," Nelson persisted. "Maybe you loaned your phone to Curtis Ray or to Markey so he could take pictures of Shamberg's house."

A look of unease crept into Davey's expression. "Why would I do that?"

"Maybe you were in on the plot to expose Shamberg and his studio."

Davey's eyes narrowed. The smile disappeared. "What studio?"

"You said you and Shamberg were buddies, so I assume you've been to his house."

"Not buddies. More like he's my boss. Don't know shit about a studio."

Nelson changed the subject. "Have you been in touch with Curtis Ray since he ran away?"

"No," Davey said, looking warily at Nelson. "You'll let me know when I can pick up my phone?"

"Sure," Nelson said. "Won't be until the trial is over."

"A trial? That sucks. When can I see the kid?"

"We're not letting him see visitors yet."

"This ain't right," Davey said. "You know he don't have family. That's why he was at the camp. Does Preach get to see him? He's the closest person to family the kid's got."

"No visitors," Nelson said.

Davey stared at him for a long moment and then burst into nervous laughter. "Boy, ya'll got it covered, don't you? What a racket. Sewed the boy up tight." He leaned toward Nelson and stuck his forefinger in his face. "I'm his friend, see? Fuck the cell phone. If he needed it, so be it. Just want him to know I'm here. You tell him that."

"I'll tell him." Nelson brushed Davey's finger away from his face. "By the way, how did you and Shamberg meet?"

For a moment, Niki didn't think Davey would answer.

He seemed to withdraw and lose the animation. "He picked me off the street when I was messed up. I got no family. He was the only one who cared. That enough for you?"

"One more thing," Nelson said. "Where are you staying? I might have more questions for you."

"Why?" Davey's tone became more belligerent. "I came to you, not the other way around."

"What if Curtis Ray wants to see you and we can arrange it?" Nelson persisted.

Davey hesitated.

Lilith stepped forward. "Davey, are you staying with Shamberg?"

Davey glared at her. "Fuck you all." He whirled around and stomped out of the waiting room. He headed for the elevators. When they didn't open right away, he sprinted to the stairs.

"Well, there goes our one lead," Luis said.

"He'll be back," Lilith said, but her voice had a shaky quality. "He doesn't seem the type to be scared off that easily. He knows more than he's letting on." She turned to Nelson. "Can I see Curtis Ray now?"

"Go ahead."

Niki stopped her. "If Curtis Ray agrees to let you represent him, or if the judge appoints you as his lawyer or attorney ad litem, whichever, can you request counseling for Curtis Ray? I don't want the boy ending up at the Texas Youth Commission. He's still in bad shape mentally. I can treat him at Open Palms. It's the best private shelter in Houston and I can guarantee his safety and the safety of others."

"I'm not sure that's a good idea," Luis interrupted.

She ignored him and waited for an answer.

"I'll recommend Open Palms," Lilith said to her. "If he's still the same judge I remember, once he hears the circumstances, he'll allow it. Would you give me a tour when we're finished here?"

"Sure," Niki answered without hesitation.

When Nelson left to accompany Lilith, she cornered

Luis. "Just how well do you know my stepmother, Luis?"

He grinned. Rather sheepishly, she thought. "Whether you like it or not, Lilith kept in touch with you through me. She's always been a forceful and attractive woman. One who's very difficult to resist when she wants something."

Did his eyes glaze over when he mentioned her name? "How close *was* your relationship with her?"

He had a mischievous glint in his eye. "What're you saying? Young lady, your stepmother was married to your father at the time we met. Never was any hanky-panky between us. Mrs. Winegold always has been a high-class lady with impeccable morals."

"Don't give me that shit. I know you better." She gave him a soft punch in the shoulder. "Better than I know Lilith."

"You two will hammer it out somehow," he said. "It's a new day for both of you."

"Oh, stow it," she said. But she smiled in spite of herself.

Lilith returned, looking upset. "He's one angry kid. I don't think he knows or cares who I am, at this point. But I got his okay to go to court with him. Niki, we got to win this thing, whatever it takes. I'll see Shamberg gets punished, and I promised Curtis Ray he'll get the help he needs."

CHAPTER 16

The miracle Lilith achieved took place the following morning and had Niki scrambling. Open Palm's supervisor, Alice Voss, as well as the volunteers and Vince, the guard, were prepped in advance to protect and restrict the movement of an underage boy living there under what constituted house arrest. Niki expected some resistance, and even anger, when she sat Curtis Ray down in the game room and tried to explain to him the lack of evidence found in Shamberg's house.

His reaction hit her worse than she expected. His face crumpled, but he didn't cry. For a long moment, he said nothing. Finally, he look up at her. "Did you find the videos?" The anger and accusation behind the words betrayed what didn't show on his face.

"He denied making any videos."

His lips trembled. "Did you ask him about Markey?"

"That's your friend you've been looking for?"

"I bet he killed him." His voice cracked, and tears filled his eyes. He rubbed them angrily. "He'll get away with it, too."

"No, he won't, Curtis Ray. He won't get away with any child he's harmed, including you. But there is no evidence your friend is dead. There's no reason to give up hope." She could see he didn't believe her. "What about Davey Tanner?"

He looked startled at hearing the name. "How did you know about him?"

"We traced the cell phone Jayme had to him. Did Davey take the pictures we saw on the phone?"

Curtis Ray shook his head. "No, Davey gave it to Markey. He took the pictures."

"We couldn't find that room in Shamberg's house."

"Markey didn't say where he took the pictures. I just wanted the videos."

"What made you think you would find them at his house?"

He looked away from her. "Markey and me, we talked about it. He said Clay would keep them in his house so he could look at them whenever he wanted to."

The feelings of disgust and loathing filled Niki. This child had been through enough. She wanted to hold him close and comfort him, but she knew he wouldn't accept any touch from her. "Davey Tanner came to the hospital to see you."

His eyes widened. "He did? I don't remember."

"You couldn't have visitors."

He bit his lip and looked down at the floor. "What did he want?"

"He said he was concerned about you. He also wants his cell phone back." She watched Curtis Ray carefully for his reaction, but he seemed distracted. "The police told him it was evidence."

He jerked with agitation. "He used to live with Clay. Did he tell you that? He knows about that room. Ask him where it is."

"We did ask him. He said he didn't know anything about a room used to shoot videos or the existence of a separate studio."

Curtis Ray's face flushed with anger. "He's lying. Why is he lying like that?" He pounded the wall so hard it shook. Bits of plaster fell to the floor.

Jayme, who Niki surmised must have been listening in

the hallway, ran in. "Why don't you believe us? The pictures are real."

"Calm down, both of you. I don't doubt they are real." She gave Jayme a stern look for interrupting, but it did no good. "Curtis Ray, are you sure Davey used to live with Shamberg?" When he nodded, she took out her cell phone and punched a button. Nelson answered after the second ring. "I'm with the kids. Do you know where to find Davey Tanner?"

"He left the hospital with the preacher," Nelson said. "I'll check the motel where Capp was staying. They may still be together. I'll get back to you if it's important."

"It is. Davey lied to us at the hospital and I need to talk to him. " She ended the call and turned back to Curtis Ray.

Curtis Ray had stopped listening. His hands curled into fists, then pressed them against his temples, squeezing his eyes shut.

"Are you hurting?" she said gently.

"My head. On fire," Curtis Ray moaned. He crawled on the long, worn sofa and curled into a fetal position.

Jayme sat next to him and rubbed his back, making soft murmured sounds of comfort. He didn't flinch from her.

Niki brought him the medication the hospital had prescribed for his headaches. After she gave him the pain pill, she left him with Jayme and retreated to her office.

She opened a new file and had started preparing her report when her phone rang.

"I caught Capp as he was checking out," Nelson said. "He said he's going back to the camp. He'll pray for Curtis Ray's soul."

"Swell. What about Davey?"

"Wasn't with him, and he couldn't or wouldn't say where the young man went. Davey was supposed to leave with him, but hasn't shown up."

"Is Capp going to wait for him?"

"Don't think so. He sounded anxious to get out of Houston. Says the kids need him."

"He didn't make a stink about not taking Curtis Ray back?"

"What could he say? The boy's under arrest and can't travel."

"Does he think he's locked up?"

"I didn't tell him different."

"Good."

"What about Jayme?" he asked.

"She's staying at Open Palms to be near Curtis Ray. She's his only friend, and I thought it would be good for both of them. They need each other right now. I made another trip to Brookshire before Curtis Ray was released. Jayme's grandmother gave me some grief but, in the end, gave Open Palms her written permission to let Jayme stay. I got the impression she was glad not to have to put up with Jayme for a while. In fact, I think she would've signed temporary custody over to me if she could."

"Not the storybook granny, I take it," Nelson said.

"Not hardly. I also stopped at the Brookshire police station and told Officer Baker that Jayme wasn't missing anymore and where she would be staying."

"Did you ask him what he knew about the camp?" Nelson said.

"He knew of the place. He even transported some boys there that the local court ordered. Didn't say anything negative about the preacher or the camp. "

"Why would he, unless he actually witnessed abuse?"

She paused. "Did I tell you he went through the academy the same time Mike and I did? He didn't remember me, but was friendly with Mike."

"No, you didn't mention that."

"Well, it was a long time ago."

"I bet he did remember you, just didn't want to admit it."

She grinned and wished he could see her expression. "That's nonsense. He would've told me."

"Maybe. Where's your stepmom?"

"Lilith? Who knows? She said she wanted to tour Open Palms but I haven't seen her yet."

"When you do, wish her the best for me."

Niki heard something in his voice. "You like her."

"Yeah, I do. She's very proud of you."

"How do you know that? She tell you?"

"In so many words. See you tonight?"

"Call me. I'm not sure when I'll make it in. If you see Lilith before I do, tell her—"

"Tell me what?" said a familiar voice.

She turned to see Lilith standing in the doorway. "Never mind. She's here."

"So I am," Lilith said, with a smile. "Is that Nelson? Tell him I said hi. If you're not too busy, I'd like that tour now."

"I'm not busy, but Curtis Ray is here already. So is Jayme."

"Are they all right?" Lilith asked.

"Not really. I wouldn't expect them to be. Curtis Ray is angry, and so is Jayme."

"Curtis Ray needs her, and she can help him. We can do the tour later. I want to see them first."

Curtis Ray and Jayme were sitting on the linoleum floor in the game room playing a card game. The medication must have worked. The boy no longer appeared to be in pain. Jayme looked up when Niki came in with Lilith. Curtis Ray kept his head down.

Niki settled on the couch, ready to observe. It would be interesting to see how Lilith handled the boy.

Her stepmother sat on the floor between Curtis Ray and Jayme.

"What are you playing?" she said conversationally.

"Poker," Jayme answered.

"My favorite," Lilith said. "Who's winning?"

Jayme pointed to Curtis Ray. "He always wins."

"No I don't," Curtis Ray said, still not looking up. "What do you want?"

"To get to know you better," Lilith said. "So I can help you."

"Won't do any good," Curtis Ray whispered, barely loud enough to be heard.

"You know, lawyers can work miracles sometimes. I got you here, didn't I?"

Jayme spoke up. "He can't pay. Lawyers cost a lot."

"Sometimes lawyers work pro bono. That means—"

"Free. I know what it means." Curtis Ray raised his head and peered at Lilith over his cards. "No one works for free that's any good."

Lilith met his eyes with a solemn air. "I prosecuted and put away creeps like Shamberg many times when I was paid as an assistant district attorney. Now I can pick and choose my battles. I'm doing this for free because I want to see him punished as much as you do."

He tilted his head slightly as if weighing her words. "Why?"

Lilith's gaze didn't waver. "Because many years ago he hurt another boy, but the mother took her son out of town so he wouldn't have to testify. So he didn't get put away. Now I have another chance."

Curtis Ray looked away and studied his cards for a long moment before he spoke. "You sure you gonna do it this time?"

"That's right."

"I wish he were dead."

Lilith nodded. "That's too good for him. Too easy. I want him to pay in ways that will hurt him more."

Curtis Ray threw down his cards. "He got money. Money wins."

"Evidence wins," Lilith answered with equal certainty. "We're going to find that evidence and use it to put him away in a dark cell where he won't ever see light again."

Curtis Ray stared back at her with hardened, weary eyes. "If you say so."

Lilith extended her hand, but Curtis Ray moved out of

reach. She kept her hand on the floor between them. "You were looking for evidence in his house. What exactly were you hoping to find?"

Curtis Ray shifted slightly.

"You can tell me," Lilith said. "You know better than anyone what's needed. I know how to use that information."

He took his time answering. "He made movies of us. Made us do nasty things to him and others. He liked to watch. Put the videos on the web. Some he kept on DVDs." He turned to Jayme. "You got the one I gave you? Show her."

Jayme looked miserable. "I can't find it."

Before Curtis Ray reacted, Niki spoke up. "She hid it in the library. We'll go back and look again."

Instead of showing anger, Curtis Ray looked resigned.

Lilith moved closer to him. "Curtis Ray, I need to ask you something. If you don't feel comfortable answering, just say so." Lilith waited until the boy raised his head. "Were you in some of those movies?"

Dark anger burned in his dry eyes. He nodded.

"What about your friend, Markey?"

His head shot up. "They took him away from the camp, and he never came back. They did something to him. That's when I ran away, too."

"Who took him?" Lilith asked.

He shook his head.

"If Markey's in Houston, someone will know where he is," Niki said. "We'll find him, Curtis Ray."

He shook his head slowly. "He's gone."

"You don't know that," Niki said. "What's his last name?"

"Lockner," he said finally and spelled it for her.

She exchanged a look with Lilith, who gave a short nod.

"That's enough questions for today," Niki said. "Finish your game, and I'll bring up some dessert later."

There was no answer from either child.

Outside in the hallway, Lilith said, "Kid's a hard case. No wonder. We need to find his missing friend."

"Do you really think he's alive?" Niki said.

"What makes you think he isn't? His body hasn't shown up. Any idea where to look?"

Niki didn't have to think long. "The street church is happening tonight. Let's ask Pastor Jim Haynes. He knows most of the kids in the area."

CHAPTER 17

After a stop at Niki's house to eat and change, she and Lilith headed back to Open Palms. They arrived early enough to find an empty parking space next to the shelter. Lilith eased out of the car, staring across the street as if the noise and chaos of teenagers streaming in from all directions was a sight she hadn't expected.

"Where'd they all come from?" Lilith stared open-mouthed as a girl in short shorts and a bra top ran past her.

Niki watched her with amusement. "Didn't know there were so many homeless kids? Wait till you see Hermann Park at night. Come on, I'll introduce you to a few I know by name."

They crossed the street. There were no cars in the paved parking lot because this was Wednesday night, and the lot was reserved for the street church. Niki recognized a few older men and women, mostly homeless from other shelters, who regularly attended. The rest, however, were young, mostly in their teens to early twenties. A majority were white mingled with a lesser number of Hispanics and African Americans. Most wore shorts and T-shirts to deal with the unpredictable weather.

The late October heat hadn't dissipated and Niki's skin felt wet and clammy from the humidity. She twisted her long hair into a tight knot at the top of her head.

Lilith's short black curls frizzed, and her face turned a

shiny shade of pink. "Does fall ever come to this city?" she mused.

"Yes, but some people call it winter," Niki replied. "Are you all right?"

For a moment, Lilith looked insulted. She huffed in response. "What do you mean? Do I look like I'm about to stroke out?"

"No, but you wouldn't be the first if you did. I'm trying to look out for you. The sun will go down soon, and we'll only have the humidity to contend with." She glanced at Lilith. "I didn't mean to insult you."

"Honey, I'm almost a native. I remember Houston's seasons. You needn't worry about me. Do you see Jim Haynes?"

They were halfway through the crowd, jostling elbows as they made their way to the front where Pastor Haynes usually stood. "Not yet."

Lilith looked around. "I hope you didn't tell Curtis Ray and Jayme our plans. Five minutes in this crowd and he'd wander off looking for his friend. It's a shame they have to be treated like prisoners."

Puzzled by the remark, she turned to Lilith. "Curtis Ray *is* a prisoner, just not in a jail. Jayme stays with him out of loyalty and friendship. If he's lucky, Curtis Ray may get probation."

Lilith was silent for a long moment. "Maybe," she finally said.

The noncommittal answer bothered Niki. "Tell me you don't plan to put him through a full-blown trial just to get to Clayton Shamberg."

Lilith stopped. Her eyes hardened. "You give me too much credit. I don't have any say in what the judge decides. I'll talk to the DA and tell him the whole story. There's a good chance Curtis Ray will not go to trial at all. It's Shamberg I want to see face a jury for his crimes against children."

"What if the DA doesn't see it your way? What happens

to Curtis Ray if he goes to trial and his story gets out? How scarred will he be for life?"

"You don't think he's already scarred for life?" Lilith's tone softened. "There are ways to protect him during a trial. He won't have to give live testimony in a courtroom." She paused to let a group of older boys cut in front of them. "Curtis Ray took a chance and broke the law to expose that monster. I will do everything I can to protect him, but he wants the same result I do."

"No argument there," Niki said.

They followed the sound of rap and a rumbling bass coming from a boom box ahead. A line began to form in front of two long tables. She watched Lilith who despite her height had to strain her neck to see the attraction.

Niki knew what lay ahead. She smelled the food before they pushed through to the front. A variety of entrees, salads, and desserts filled the picnic tables. She pointed to a slim figure off to the right of the tables. Pastor Jim Haynes, dressed in white, was surrounded by teenagers. The preacher seemed to feel their presence and turned their way. To Niki his tanned, freckled face looked forever youthful. His sun-streaked hair ruffled as a warm breeze swept through the parking lot, sending a stack of napkins flying off the food table. No one bothered to pick them up.

A familiar voice, loud and raspy, came from behind them. Niki turned and recognized Tara Barlow's tangled orange hair. The once homeless woman knew almost everyone who attended street church.

She seemed thinner each time Niki saw her.

Tara's toothless smile widened. "Hey, girlfriend, what you doing here?"

Her cigarette rasp was more pronounced than Niki remembered.

"You lookin' for me?" Tara asked. "I think I owe you a house cleaning."

Niki laughed. "Hadn't occurred to me, Tara."

"Well, it should." Tara looked with undisguised curiosity

at Lilith. "Who you got there? Anyone I should know?"

Niki glanced at Lilith and tried not to laugh. Lilith's expression couldn't hide her quick assessment of Tara. A street person. Probably a drug addict. Tara had been both at one time. Niki guessed Tara had probably lapsed more than she would admit. Nevertheless, over time Tara had proven to be a loyal friend and now had a home with Ric, a paraplegic as the result of a gunshot, and an alleged drug dealer. Ric brushed elbows with as many prominent community leaders as he did with ex-gang members. Tara stayed with him, despite other women and young girls who came and went. He had picked her off the street a long time ago, and she repaid him by nursing him, cleaning, and cooking his meals. He in turn gave her an apartment in back of his house in the mostly Latino neighborhood of South Houston.

"Tara, meet my stepmother, Lilith Winegold. She's a lawyer."

Tara's eyes widened. "My gawd, is that right? Well, what do you know? I always suspected my best girl had a blessed upbringing." She let loose a raucous laugh. "Wait 'til I tell Ric. A lawyer. We can sure use one of them around here. Someone's always getting into trouble. You looking for a criminal, don't come here. We're all God-fearing in this place." Another laugh erupted from her.

Lilith recovered and gave Tara a warm smile. "I'm glad to meet all of my daughter's friends."

Tara gave Lilith a hearty embrace, which Lilith accepted after a moment's shock.

"That's how we welcome Niki's friends around here," Tara said. She peered closer. "You really her stepmother?"

Lilith's cheeks flushed, but she laughed with good humor. "Yes, but I treat her as if she were my own daughter."

"Why didn't I meet you before?" Tara said.

"We both have had busy lives," Niki answered for Lilith.

"I guess you know everyone here," Lilith said.

"That's right." There was pride in the way Tara said the words. "No one's a stranger to Tara Barlow. Tell her, Niki."

"She's right," she agreed.

"So who you looking for this time?" Tara said. "I know you don't come here to get blessed by Brother Jim."

"You got us pegged, girl," Niki said. "We're looking for Markey Lockner. Ring any bells?'

"Markey Lockner?" Tara rolled the name around her tongue. "Nope. Got nothing. But for you, I'll check all my sources."

"Do that." Niki turned to Lilith. "Tara's got more connections than Justin Bieber has on Facebook."

Tara wiggled her nose. "Who?"

Lilith cracked a laugh. "I'm with you, gal." Then her tone turned serious. "We think Markey might be around eleven or twelve. What we know so far is that he came from a religious boy's camp near Hercules, and hasn't been seen since."

Someone shouted Tara's name. She turned toward the sound and waved. "See?" she said to Lilith. "Told you. They all know me."

Lilith said, "We really need to find Markey."

Tara gave them a shrewd stare before she said, "This got to do with Curtis Ray?"

"You know him?" Lilith looked surprised.

Tara glanced first at Niki. "Seen him around the street some. I know what I heard about him robbing Shamberg and getting shot. Rotten deal you ask me. Clay's a prick."

"How do you know Clay Shamberg?" Niki asked.

Tara shrugged. "Sometimes he brings food down here to the church. Probably to get close to the boys. Have you asked Brother Jim about Markey?"

"That's why we're here," Niki said.

A tall, skinny red-haired boy with a splattering of freckles riding a skateboard bumped into Tara. She grabbed his arm before he could run off. "Barry? Better slow down, boy."

"Aw, Tara, I'm just hanging," Barry said, ducking someone's arm that almost hit him.

"Well, hold on a sec. These people are looking for Markey Lockner. Know him?"

Barry shrugged. "What's he look like?"

"That's the problem," Niki said. "We don't know."

"Curtis Ray's friend," Tara said.

Barry shook his head. "Sorry. Name don't mean nothin'. Gotta split. See ya around, Tara."

He waved and skateboarded away.

Niki watched him until he disappeared into the crowd. "Do you know anything about the Follow Jesus camp?"

Tara put her finger to her temple as if the answer would come from there. "I heard they only take boys who been in trouble and sometimes orphans."

Orphans? Niki made a note to ask Nelson to check on that. "Know anyone who graduated from there?"

"*Graduated?* Never heard it put that way. Not about the camp." Tara laughed like it was the funniest word she ever heard.

A woman holding a baby against her chest and juggling a plate of food with her free hand squeezed past them. Niki had been so intent on Tara she hadn't noticed how the atmosphere had changed. Almost all the space in the parking lot had filled up with teens, some in groups, others alone, a few with small children. Some sat on the ground, with blankets or without. The scene reminded her of when she was a teenager back in California, on a beach filled with picnickers, the hot sun beating down. Only here there was no sand and no water, except in bottles. The color of the sky turned into a rainbow of rose, orange, and mauve. Grackles squawked at them from the branches of nearby trees.

Tara asked, "Say, how's Curtis Ray? Is he out of the hospital? They gonna put him in Juvie?"

"He's recovering and safe," Niki told her, realizing Tara knew more than she had let on.

Tara nodded with a smug smile. "I got it. You don't want everyone to know he's at Open Palms. Don't worry about me. I won't say anything."

"How well do you know Shamberg?" Lilith said. "You ever been to his house?"

Tara looked taken aback. "Now why would I go to his house?"

Niki was afraid Lilith might lose her by asking the wrong questions. "Maybe you know someone who works for him." She pointed to the head of a snake inked on Tara's upper arm. "Someone who gets his tattoos the same place you do." The image was smaller than what Jayme had described to her, but the artist could be the same.

Tara sobered. "Snake be friends with Ric. Not with me."

"Why?" Lilith asked. "Is Snake dangerous?"

"Only to his enemies."

"Are you a friend or an enemy?" Lilith said, softening the question with a smile.

Tara sniggered. "Depends on his mood."

"Does Shamberg let Snake stay at his house?" Niki said.

Tara's eyes widened. "Not *in* his house, the apartment over his garage. That's where Snake lives some of the time."

The garage apartment? How had she and Nelson missed that? "Have you ever seen the apartment?"

"Why would I go to that creep's crib?" Tara scoffed.

"You said Ric's a friend of his," Lilith said. "Maybe he took you there with him."

"Ric can't go upstairs," Tara said. "Niki knows that. He's got no feeling in his legs. He's in a wheelchair. He wouldn't let me go up there alone, either. If you want, I can ask Ric what he knows."

"Do that," Niki said. "Does Snake stay at the apartment when Shamberg's not in town?"

Tara folded her arms and stared at her. "What's all this about?"

Instead of answering, Lilith said, "Have you heard that Clay is using a studio to make movies?"

Tara scowled. "What kind of movies?"

Before Lilith could respond, a male voice boomed out of

a microphone twenty feet away. Niki turned toward what sounded like an introduction. Pastor Jim Haynes stood at the edge of the parking lot, poised to greet the gathering crowd. His flowing white shirt floated behind him like angel wings.

She grabbed Lilith's arm. "Hurry, we have to catch him before he gets to the podium."

CHAPTER 18

Niki and Lilith met Pastor Jim Haynes before he reached the podium. There were still several teenage girls surrounding him, but his attention focused on the man introducing him. Niki stepped in front of him. Recognition flashed in his eyes.

"Niki?" Pastor Jim looked surprised to see her. "Good to see you here."

"Sorry to hold you up, Jim," she said, "but I need to talk to you. We can wait until you're finished with your message, but it's important that we speak today."

Jim put his arm around Niki's shoulders. "I wouldn't dream of having you wait. It must be serious. God is all patient and wise. These children have no sense of time so it won't bother them if I don't lecture right away. That young man speaking in my place will gladly speak for hours if I don't show up." He noticed Lilith and directed his smile at her. "Hello. I don't mean to be rude. I assume you're with Niki?"

"Lilith Winegold," she said, extending her hand to Jim who captured it in both of his. "Yes, we're together."

"She's a lawyer," Niki said. "Used to be with the DA's office years ago. Oh, she's also my stepmother."

She expected Jim to laugh or otherwise remark about her parentage. She was getting tired of explaining Lilith to everyone. But Pastor Jim didn't do either. Instead, he smiled at

Lilith with a question in his eyes. "I always wondered about Niki's family. Good to know she has someone. Many in this crowd have trouble connecting with family members. That's why they're here. How can I be of help?"

"We're looking for a runaway," Niki said bluntly.

This time he did laugh and the wave of his hand encompassed the whole of the parking lot. "Look no further," he said.

Niki swallowed, realizing her mistake. "Sorry, I wasn't clear. A specific runaway who escaped from the Follow Jesus camp in Hercules. Know the one I'm talking about?"

Jim's expression changed. She saw a shadow of darkness descend over his face. He pointed toward the street and led her and Lilith away from the crowd.

"What's this boy's name?" He lowered his voice even though they were out of earshot.

"Markey Lockner," she said. "You know him?"

Jim gritted his teeth. "I know Webster Capp." He turned to face the street. "I have made many mistakes in my life, but none so egregious as to send a boy to his camp once I discerned the devil ran the place. I even reported him to the authorities. They did nothing."

"I'm confused, Jim," Niki said. "It's my understanding that it's a boot camp for boys in trouble with the law. You make it sound like a version of hell."

"Good analogy. I might use that someday with your permission." He gazed out over the crowd. "What can I say about Webster Capp? I'm sure he once believed he was doing God's work, but pride and the love of money can overtake the best of us. Though I'm not certain he was ever in a class I'd consider honorable."

"What do you mean, 'love of money?'" Lilith said.

Jim grimaced. "It's my understanding, though I can't prove it, that Capp gets paid by the state, while ignoring the rules. He doubles his take by entering into a contract with the devil."

"Does that devil have the name Clayton Shamberg

stamped on him?" Lilith said, almost before he finished.

He looked surprised. "You know that name?"

"Very well." A note of bitterness came into her voice.

Several teenage followers approached, and Jim raised his hand to stop them. Their disappointment turned to hard stares before they walked away. He ignored them. "Niki mentioned you worked in the DA's office. When was that?"

"Almost two decades ago. But even back then, Shamberg was in my sights. I suspected he was luring homeless boys into his home, promising them money, food, clothes. Those boys didn't know what this would cost them until it was too late. I'm sure he turned many to prostitution. Unfortunately, I couldn't get anyone to make a complaint. I didn't suspect him of making movies back then. Today is a different story, thanks to boys like Markey Lockner and his friend. This time, I'm determined to put his ass away."

Jim glanced toward a group of kids gathered nearby. "You believe Markey was one of Shamberg's victims?"

"I have reason to believe he took pictures of a room we believe was used by Shamberg to film his movies," Lilith said.

"If you can tell us anything, we can keep your involvement out of the investigation," Niki said. "There's another reason to find him. Someone in my care needs to know his friend is alive and well."

Jim turned slowly and faced the crowd. Dusk turned the sky a darker shade of blue, though a full moon cast a pool of light over the street church. He answered in a soft voice. "There's nothing I can tell you right now."

"If not now, when?" Lilith asked.

Weariness shadowed his eyes. "I'll be at the church office later tonight. If you want to come around ten, I may be able to give you a lead."

Niki wanted to press further, but Jim turned abruptly and headed toward the podium. By the time he stood in front of the crowd, he presented a serene countenance. His arms spread out like an embrace that encompassed every boy or girl before him. Niki watched him for several moments before she turned to Lilith. "Markey's alive."

Lilith nodded her agreement. "I'm going with you tonight."

"We can't tell Curtis Ray until we have proof," Niki warned.

"I have a more serious problem," Lilith said. "I want an explanation as to why Curtis Ray or Markey Lockner isn't in the system. I checked with Lavinia earlier. She can't find a record of either boy in CPS. No school records for them either. I need to check on their birth certificates and their parents' death certificates, if any..." Her voice trailed off.

"What're you saying?"

Lilith's eyes challenged her. "I have nothing to go on, but a gut feeling. What if they were kidnapped and kept at the camp?"

At first the accusation seemed outrageous. "Kidnapped by whom? Are you suggesting that Webster Capp and the camp harbored missing boys? How is that possible?" Niki's probe into the camp hadn't taken her down this road. Once the idea was spoken, it hit a nerve. Perhaps somewhere in the back of her mind, she'd already sown the seeds of this possibility. In Curtis Ray's case, they had found no court order or paperwork to substantiate his living at the camp.

"Nelson needs to check the different cities and counties for reports of runaways, abductions, anything suspicious," Lilith said.

"I'm sure he's doing that already," Niki said. "You're suggesting Webster Capp had taken boys without the necessary paperwork? Without a court order?"

"It's just a theory right now," Lilith said. "I know what it sounds like. I don't like it either. But look at Curtis Ray. Did he just spring out of nowhere?"

Her words echoed Niki's own suspicions. Still, she found it hard to accept. "Capp said his parents were both dead and he was given custody."

"Given custody, how? Where's the legal papers? He had

to conveniently rush back to the camp before he could answer questions. Wonder how many other orphans he's claiming to have custody of?"

"That's a serious charge."

"We'll see what an investigation turns up." Lilith sounded as if she already believed Capp was a kidnapper and worse.

"Nelson works homicides," Niki said. "Right now there's no homicide to investigate. They haven't arrested Shamberg. There's only minimal investigation, if any, and most of that is in the B and E charge on Curtis Ray."

"Which won't go anywhere," Lilith said. "I'll investigate Shamberg and Capp myself if need be. Curtis Ray is my client and I'll do whatever it takes to get justice for him."

Niki raked her hands through her hair. She didn't have a rebuttal. "We've got an hour before we meet with Jim. What do you want to do?"

"Let's talk to Curtis Ray. The more information he gives us, the easier to run down answers."

They crossed the street to Open Palms. The shelter was nearly empty, with most of the inhabitants attending the street church. Both children were in the game room. Jayme had fallen asleep on the sofa. Curtis Ray was playing pinball, flicking the levers with single-minded punishing strokes.

Niki looked at the score board. "You're good at that."

He grunted and flicked the lever again. The numbers rolled up and bells rang.

"We need to talk to you," Lilith said. "This is important."

He ignored her.

"If I'm going to represent you, I need more information."

He slammed the lever and bells rang. Over the noise, he said, "Did you find Markey?"

"We're following a lead," Lilith said.

He turned slightly. "What lead?"

"If you want me to help you, then you need to cooperate," Lilith said firmly. "I need to learn more about your background. After that, whatever we find about your friend, we'll share with you. Fair enough?"

The simmering anger, barely visible in the coal blackness of his eyes and pulsing vein in his temples, didn't change. But he jerked away from the game to face her. "You'll tell me if Markey's dead?"

"I'll tell you when we find him, and we will." Lilith took out a notebook and turned it toward him. She handed him a pencil. "Write down your full name, the name on your birth certificate. Then write the full names of your parents, and your date of birth."

Niki watched his expression as he picked up the pencil. This information would satisfy two requirements. Lilith could get birth certificates, and they'd know if he could read and write. When he was done, Curtis Ray handed the paper back to Lilith. Niki read the scrawled script over her shoulder.

Curtis Ray Johnson. Mother: Lucy Vaughn Johnson. Father: How should I know?

"Where's your mother now?" Lilith asked.

"Dead. Car accident." A simple statement, no inflection in his voice.

"I'm sorry," Lilith said. "When did that happen?"

His eyes bore into hers. "I was eight. Just turned. October twelveth, my birthday." He remained impassive.

Lilith put a hand over his. He didn't jerk away.

"Want a drink of water?" Niki asked when he shot a glance at the door.

He shook his head. "I'm okay."

Lilith resumed the questioning. "Where were you living back then?"

"Home."

"You remember your address?"

"Some country road. Nearest town was Smithville, maybe."

"Where did you go to school?"

"Ma taught me at home." He scratched his nose. "You got any soda?"

"I'm sure we do." Lilith pushed her chair back ending the interview. "You did well, Curtis Ray. I'm impressed. You're a smart boy. Your ma was a good teacher."

Niki went into the kitchen and returned with an orange soda. He gulped it down and handed her the empty can.

"Can I go to bed now?"

Niki exchanged glances with Lilith, who nodded.

Curtis Ray said nothing more as Niki led him upstairs and turned left to the boys' bedrooms. The girls' rooms were on the other side of the floor, separated by bathrooms and showers specified for each gender.

When Niki came back downstairs, Lilith was in the kitchen. Jayme was sitting up, groggily rubbing her eyes. Had she overheard their conversation? Jayme's eyes were red from sleep.

"Let's get you upstairs and into bed," Niki said to the girl.

Jayme got to her feet, weaving to catch her balance. "Where's Curtis Ray?"

"In bed, like where you will be in a few minutes." Niki put her arm around Jayme and once more climbed the stairs.

When she returned she found Lilith pacing.

"I was right," Lilith said. "There's little paper trail. No schooling, except at home by his mother, and whatever Capp provided at the camp. I'll send for his birth certificate and his mother's death certificate. A start, Niki. It's only a start."

Niki nodded. "I know." She pointed to her watch. "Almost ten. Let's go talk to Jim."

CHAPTER 19

The building where Jim Haynes held Sunday morning services stood next door to the parking lot Haynes used for his street church. The pale blue structure was often mistaken for an office building.

Niki took Lilith through a lobby area with walls decorated with portraits of Jesus in such scenes as feeding the crowd by the sea with fish. One sculptured gold-plated cross hung between two doors. The open door on the left revealed folding chairs in rows of ten in front of a raised stage. A podium faced an audience of none.

They walked down a narrow hallway. Niki knocked on the first door they saw. There was a shuffling of feet and the scraping of a chair before Jim's tall form appeared and let them in. His office was larger than Niki's at Open Palms, but not by much. It did hold more file cabinets, she noticed.

"Have a seat. I was just working on Sunday's devotional." He looked troubled. His eyes clouded, and there were lines in his face not visible earlier.

"You have a major influence over these kids," Niki began, but Jim stopped her.

"I don't need your words of praise," he said. "I know what you want, but I don't think I can help you. The news media is all over the shooting of a burglar in River Oaks. I've had some time to think about your request. Even if I knew anything about this boy you're looking for, I couldn't in good conscience subject him to a spotlight that might put him in danger."

"What danger?" Lilith said. "We'd be protecting him."

"You can't guarantee that."

"What if the wrong person finds him?" Niki said.

"They won't." Jim turned his back to them and went to his desk.

"You seem sure of that." Lilith was not to be silenced. "Are you hiding him?"

When he didn't answer right away, Niki said, "We won't reveal his whereabouts to anyone. We need to assure his friend that's he's alive."

Jim shook his head wearily. "You assume too much."

Niki perched on the edge of his desk. "You asked us here tonight and then changed your mind. Why?"

He gave a sigh of resignation. "I know you are helping Curtis Ray and Jayme, but what makes you think no one is after Markey?"

"We don't know," Lilith admitted. "But we can protect him. Has he asked about Curtis Ray? Markey might be as concerned about his friend, as Curtis Ray is about him."

Jim picked up a pencil and wound it through his fingers. "If I happen to see him, I'll give him your message."

Once they were back on the street, Niki took another look at the church. "What do you think?"

Lilith grimaced. "The same as what you're thinking. Your friends are very protective of their own people. I thought they trusted you. Or is it because I'm with you? Maybe you should talk to them alone."

Niki understood her point. "In this case, it doesn't matter. They may trust me in some circumstances, but not all."

"Well, we know something we didn't before," Lilith said. "Markey Lockner is alive, and Jim knows where he is. I don't want to give Curtis Ray any false hope, but maybe some reassurance will help him sleep easier."

Ten minutes later, they climbed the stairs to the shelter's bedrooms. Niki's heart beat double time when she saw his empty bed. For a panicked moment, Niki thought he'd boogied. She peered into the girls' bedroom. Jayme lay curled up in a twin bed. Her breathing was steady.

"Let's check downstairs," Niki said.

They found him in the game room at the pinball machine.

"Couldn't sleep?" Niki said, standing behind him.

He shook his head without looking around.

"I have a question for you." She waited, but he didn't move. "Why are you so sure Markey's dead?"

He turned slowly and stared at her without answering.

"There's been no sign of a body," Niki continued. "We think there's a good chance he's alive and hiding."

Next to her Lilith nodded in agreement.

Niki couldn't come out and say what she suspected. Not without proof. She agreed with Lilith that Jim either hid Markey in the church or knew his whereabouts. If she was wrong and Markey turned out to be dead, well, she'd have to deal with that. Her sixth sense was telling her they were both right.

Curtis Ray turned hard looks on each of them. "Why you saying that?"

Niki glanced at Lilith before answering. "We met with Pastor Jim tonight. Does Markey attend his church?"

"He used to," Curtis Ray said. "Does Pastor Jim know where Markey is?"

"He didn't say. Maybe he went to Pastor Jim for help," Lilith suggested.

Curtis Ray's eyes narrowed. "He don't trust preachers."

"No? Why not?"

Instead of answering, his voice hardened. "Don't trust any church people."

Because of Webster Capp. "Why would Markey be scared to come out in the open? The police don't have a file on him."

"That ain't it. It's Clay."

Lilith sighed. "Clayton Shamberg isn't going to hurt him."

"No, he'll send Snake to do his dirty," Curtis Ray said.

"Sit down, Curtis Ray," Lilith said gently. She waited until he sank into the middle cushion of the couch. "You said Markey took the pictures of the room. Right? Okay, remember Tara? We talked to her tonight, too. She knows Snake through her boyfriend, Ric. She says Ric might help us find the studio."

"What she want?'

Lilith frowned. "She didn't say. Maybe she doesn't like Clay either."

He nodded as though considering the idea. "How's that going to help Markey?"

"We could get evidence against Shamberg to put him away."

He didn't look convinced.

Niki sat next to him. "What's the problem?"

His mouth twitched as if looking for the right words. He swung his feet back and forth. "Markey's like me. We got no home, but the camp. Clay owns the camp. I won't go back. Markey won't either."

Lilith rested one hand on her hip, the other pressed against her forehead. "Who first brought you to the camp?"

"Preacher Capp came and got me when my folks passed."

"You never saw the inside of a courtroom or talked to a counselor or a judge or anybody?" Lilith asked.

He shook his head. His mouth drooped down at the edges, and he closed his eyes. After about five seconds, a bolt of anger wiped away all signs of self-pity. "I got nobody. Markey don't either. What we supposed to do? Where we supposed to go?"

His cheeks turned red, and he blinked rapidly. With a furious movement, he twisted and pummeled the couch. Dust specks flew into the air.

Niki waited until his anger ebbed. "You never went to

school?" The enormity of what she'd heard filled her with anger.

"We had to take these stupid classes at camp," he said, shifting away from her.

"So as far as you know, no authorities were notified of your existence," Lilith said.

His chin jutted out. "Guess not."

Lilith shook her head and paced around the room. "How's this possible? These boys were basically kidnapped. I knew it." She could have been talking to herself.

Curtis Ray's gaze followed her. "Preach Capp said I had to go with him because my parents were dead and I had no one else."

Lilith stopped and faced him. "You should be wards of the state if no other family members came forward."

His tone turned defensive. "Preach said he was my uncle now. He told Markey the same thing."

Niki sat back. "But you know that isn't possible."

The red-faced anger faded. He looked down at the floor. For several moments, he said nothing. Finally he looked at Lilith with flat expressionless eyes. "You're saying they kidnapped me. That's what you said. Right? But where would I be if they didn't take me there? An orphanage?"

"Or foster care." Lilith said.

"How'd that be different from camp?" Curtis Ray said.

Lilith looked at Niki, clearly stymied how to answer him.

Niki wasn't sure either. Curtis Ray had benefited from the academics at the camp school. He was smart, had skills, read books. Webster Capp could make a strong argument for the wilderness camp. Curtis Ray had been surrounded by other boys, and he learned survival skills.

Then she caught herself. Yes, the boys had all that, but they'd been brought there illegally to be victimized, sexually used by men, photographed, videoed, and exposed. Niki shuddered. Did Webster Capp know what Shamberg was doing? He had to know, didn't he? Shamberg was paying him.

"How would foster care or an orphanage be different?" she repeated. "For one, there wouldn't be a Clayton Shamberg." As soon as she said the words, everything she knew about the world of kids kicked her back. There would always be a Shamberg lurking on the street ready to prey on the young, the homeless, and the defenseless. She started again. "But there could be others like him out there. So you have to be vigilant. Know what that means? On your guard. Watch for the signs."

Lilith gave Niki a warning look and sat beside Curtis Ray. "You won't be alone. Children's Protective Services will be involved in your case now. The same for Markey when he's found. In the meantime, you'll be staying here and Niki and her crew will watch out for you."

Curtis Ray slumped against the back cushion.

"How about a glass of milk?" Niki said.

He shrugged as if he didn't care.

Lilith stayed with him while Niki went into the kitchen. When she returned with the milk, Curtis Ray had slid down until his back curved. His eyes were shut.

"Guess he didn't want the milk after all," Niki said.

"Is there someone who could carry him upstairs?" Lilith said.

Instead of answering, Niki shook the boy's shoulder. He jerked awake. "Here's your milk," Niki said. "When you're finished, I'll take you upstairs. It's late."

He didn't argue or protest. He finished off the milk with one long gulp and gave Lilith the glass. He stumbled a few times on the way. Once he was in the bedroom where three other boys bunked, Niki wished him goodnight and gave him privacy.

"You look as tired as Curtis Ray," she said, wearily, when she found Lilith on the couch in the same position Curtis Ray had been. "Let's head home. We have another busy day ahead."

Lilith yawned noisily and heaved herself up. "I won't argue with that."

Niki gave last-minute instructions to Robert, the night volunteer before they left. The ride home was quiet. Niki heard soft snoring sounds by the time she pulled into the driveway. She shook her stepmother awake. Lilith went straight into the guest room and shut the door. Niki hiked up the stairs. She thought of Nelson as she undressed, wondering how the investigation was going. She hadn't heard from him all day. That was unusual. She checked her messages and email on her Blackberry and deleted most of them. Nothing from Nelson. Maybe he didn't want to disturb her while Lilith was staying there. No, that couldn't be it. She dialed his cell number. It went straight to voice mail.

An old fear nagged at the edge of her consciousness. She tried to push it away. This was why she shouldn't be involved with a cop. Nelson told her once that investigators don't get killed on duty. That's a lie, she'd retorted. True, detectives didn't stop cars on the road or answer domestic violence reports, both the kind of calls that put cops at risk. The crazy part, her reason for not wanting a relationship with a cop, was not because Mike was killed on the job. He wasn't. Not even while riding his motorcycle. He was off duty driving to the store when the accident happened. No, it was the fear and anticipation she faced daily that a call would come, and this time the loss would be truly unbearable.

She stared at her Blackberry, willing it to ring. She tried Nelson again. Hung up before the robotic voice ended. Finally she dialed Luis's cell. He answered on the second ring. She heard music, loud voices, the clinking of glasses and a television in the background. *They were in a bar?*

His gravelly voice sang out, "Hey, sweetheart, what's going on? You looking for Nelly?"

"I was just wondering how the investigation was going," she said, wishing she hadn't called. "I didn't think you'd be partying."

"Partying? You know us better, sweetheart. I'm nursing a club soda with lime and watching the customers. Nelson's keeping distant company with a certain preacher who didn't make it out of town."

"You're both working?" she said, surprised. "At a bar?"

"You know how I love the nightlife, sweetie." The sarcasm was thick. "You at home?"

"Yes," she said, mollified and a little ashamed she had suspected the worst.

"Get some sleep. We'll talk tomorrow."

She hung up, didn't move from the side of the bed for a long moment, smiling to herself. Finally, she roused enough to get into her night shirt and stretch out under the covers. She started to review the conversation with Curtis Ray.

The next thing she heard was the telephone. She glanced at the bedside clock. Three-fifteen. A sharp pain stabbed her stomach. *Something happened to Nelson.*

She grabbed the phone and listened.

"Is this Niki Alexander?" said a vaguely familiar voice she couldn't place.

She inhaled and slowly let out her breath. "Yes, this is Niki. Who is this?"

"Jim Haynes. From the church?" He paused. "I know Curtis Ray is staying at Open Palms. I'm assuming you told him about our conversation? Well, he showed up at the church. I think you better come down here right away."

CHAPTER 20

Niki grabbed the clothes she had tossed on the chair by her bed and put them on. She dragged her shoes from under the bed, slipped her feet in them while stumbling toward the door. In the hall she stopped and braced herself with one hand on the wall. She was forgetting something. What? Her keys. Back in her room, she dug them out of her purse along with her ID, looked around, and tried to keep the panic out of her sleep-befuddled brain.

Down the stairs, through the living room, and out the door, locking it, and getting in her car before she remembered Lilith. No sense in disturbing her. Niki glanced at the darkened window as she started the engine. A miracle she hadn't wakened her during her flight through the house.

She backed out of the driveway, tires squealing as she wrenched the wheel, cursing Curtis Ray. Had he taken Jayme? No, he couldn't have been that stupid, she hoped. She was glad Jim had called her, not the police.

Unless he had, but not told her. So many ifs. So much uncertainty.

Damn that kid!

Maybe she should call Nelson.

No. Bad idea.

Jim had called her, not wanting to get Curtis Ray in any more trouble than he was already, and Jim might be protecting another lost boy.

Five minutes later, she rolled up next to the parking lot on Lovett across from the church. A couple of cars were parked in the lot where earlier in the evening nearly a hundred teenagers gathered. She let the engine idle as she scoped out the area. From where she stood she could see Open Palms across the parking lot.

She started to drive into the parking lot, but movement among the trees along the cross street stopped her. Clouds drifting across a full moon made visibility difficult. The video store's neon sign shone over the buildings. A street lamp cast shadows below.

She focused on two forms, one near the trees and another by the buildings. She cut the engine and peered out the open car window. Nothing moved. She hesitated. Who else would be out there at three or four in the morning? Even the nightclub hangers-on would have stumbled home by now. Maybe she'd seen nothing. Maybe her imagination was playing tricks on her.

No, someone was there, moving away from the building, bent in half, loping silently toward the trees. She wanted to call out to whoever was there. Maybe Curtis Ray and Markey?

She slid out of her car, careful when shutting the door to muffle the sound. Stood still, listening, but heard only her heart rap against her chest.

A new figure appeared, coming from Montrose Boulevard a block away. A jogger at this hour? She spotted black shorts that clung to his skin and a black T-shirt. Definitely male.

Suddenly the jogger sprinted into the middle of the street, and she recognized him under the street lamp.

Snake.

She threw a panicked glance toward the trees as two shadows moved and came together. She could barely make out the two forms when a boy's cry of alarm shattered the quiet.

Snake hadn't seen her pressed against her car. His attention was focused on who she could now see were Curtis Ray and a smaller boy who had to be Markey. Niki didn't hesitate. She leaped into the street. With long strides she reached Snake before he could react. She jumped on his back. Her nails dug into his exposed flesh. He grunted in surprise, twirled around to shake her off. She wrapped an arm around his neck and squeezed with all her strength. He tried to buck her off, but she held on.

With her legs tight around his waist, she punched Snake in the head with her free hand. At the same time, she screamed to the boys who stood on the curb, not moving. "Get in the church!"

"Bitch! Get the fuck off me!" Snake hollered.

He gave up trying to buck her off. Instead, he grabbed the arm, encircling his neck, and squeezed. With his other hand, he attempted to catch her fist that tried, but failed, to damage his face.

Pain from his grip shot up her arm to her shoulder. She thought she heard a crack as he squeezed even harder, but still she refused to let up the pressure against his throat. While her legs tightened around his middle, he whirled around in circles, trying to throw her off. Finally, he squatted and fell back, pinning her to the ground underneath him. She felt the air whoosh out of her as he flattened her. His muscular back was hard and she felt gravel from the street scraping and digging into her flesh.

She gasped for air. His hand tightened over her arm and twisted cruelly. She cried out in pain.

"Let her go!" a man's voice bellowed.

Instead of rolling off her, Snake rocked his body up and back, slamming hard against her. She attacked his face again with her free hand and clawed at his eyes. He turned his head back and forth, intent on smashing her face. The back of his skull smacked against her nose and chin. The pain was excruciating.

"I said, let her go!" the voice shouted again.

Snake's scream pierced the air. His upper body rocked

up, and he flipped over and off her onto his side. With his weight gone, she scooted away. A hand reached down and helped her to her feet.

She looked into the eyes of Pastor Jim Haynes. The baseball bat was in his hand. She looked down as Snake moaned. He was using both his hands to cradle his genitals as he curled up.

"Niki! Can you hear me? Are you all right?" Jim's voice finally penetrated her shock.

"I'm okay," she said, trembling. Her arm felt numb and useless. Her head pounded and her nose felt about to burst. She looked at the preacher's face, smooth, almost babyish, not the face of a warrior. But his eyes, dark with fury, told a different story.

"I'm fine. Really," she lied. She breathed through her mouth and looked around her. "Where are the boys?" Her voice sounded funny.

"Inside." He indicated the church with a jerk of his thumb. He stood over Snake, who writhed on the ground. "What should I do with him? Should I call the police?"

She cradled her injured arm against her chest, and gave Snake a look that could turn a volcano to an iceberg. "He's got a cell phone. He can call the police. I bet he'll call his boss. If he's not too afraid."

Snake forced open his eyes. "Fuck you. This ain't over."

"Son, you are in front of a church," Jim said. "Watch your language. Don't dirty our street anymore."

She felt a warm liquid run down her upper lip, and wondered if he'd broken her nose. She couldn't move. Jim wrapped his arm around her waist, helped her stumble inside, and took her to the bathroom. He fixed a wet towel for her nose. "You need a hospital."

"Later, Jim. I'm okay. Better than I look."

"Are you sure you don't want me to call the police?"

"No, won't do any us any good," she said. "I don't want them knowing Curtis Ray left the shelter in the middle of the night. Did he find Markey?"

Jim nodded. "I couldn't tell you before. Not until I talked to him."

"Would have saved us this trouble," she said, avoiding his eyes. "This is my fault. I gave Curtis Ray just enough information for him to follow through. And he did." She pressed the towel against her nose. "Where are the boys?"

"My office," Jim said.

"Let's go talk to them." The bleeding finally stopped. She decided her nose wasn't busted after all. She handed the towel back to Jim. Didn't want the boys to see her bloodied.

The moment she entered his office, she focused on Curtis Ray and the other boy. They slouched in wooden chairs like rebellious students sent to the principal's office, unrepentant, ready to break the rules all over again. Markey looked painfully thin. His yellow hair looked dry as straw. But his clothes were of surprisingly good quality. Jim's gift?

What a pair they made. They could be poster children. One light, one dark. Together, they could make a study for a more balanced world.

Jim took his place behind his desk and opened his laptop. Niki leaned against the desk and faced the boys. She pointed to the boy next to Curtis Ray.

"You're Markey, right?"

Markey's eyes darted to Jim then back to her. "Yeah, what of it?"

"I'm not going to scold either one of you," she said. "That's not my job. Curtis Ray knew what could happen if he left Open Palms. We can discuss that later. Right now, Markey, I want to know more about you so we can figure out what's next and how best to help you."

Markey looked unsure and turned to Curtis Ray, who nodded.

"Okay," Markey said.

"When did you run away from the camp?"

Curtis Ray broke in. "He didn't run. They took him away."

"I'm asking Markey," she said patiently

"I didn't run," Markey said.

"Who took you? I need a name."

Markey glanced at Curtis Ray, eyes pleading.

"Tell her," Curtis Ray said briskly. "She's okay."

"Davey," Markey said in low voice.

She kept her gaze steady on him. "Does Davey take all the boys?"

Markey shrugged. "I only know about me."

"Where did he take you?"

Markey looked confused. "Uh, Houston?"

"I mean, after you got to Houston. Did he take you to someone's house?"

"Oh." Markey looked down at his hands which were clasped together in his lap. "Yeah."

She told herself not to let her feelings show. "Whose house, Markey?"

"Don't know." His voice quivered.

"Did you take pictures while you were there?" She saw the fear in his eyes. "You're safe now, Markey. No one's going to hurt you again. You can trust me. I protect children from monsters. I'll protect you and Curtis Ray."

Curtis Ray turned to him. "She's seen the pictures, okay? I was gonna tell you."

Markey stared at him wide-eyed. He mumbled, "He didn't tell me his name."

She let that go. "You see the address?"

Markey shook his head.

She glanced at Jim, discouraged. She tried again. "If we drove by his house, could you point it out?"

Markey didn't answer right away. He gnawed on his lower lip. Once again he checked with Curtis Ray, who shrugged and nodded.

"I think so," Markey said at last.

She took a deep breath. "That's a start, Markey. That helps."

A doorbell sounded, causing her to jump. She turned to Jim, who was frowning and staring at his laptop.

"That's enough for one night," he said at last.

"You always get people at your door at—" She looked at her watch. "—almost four in the morning?"

"Not always." He stood. "You better wait here with the boys."

He already knew who was out there, she realized. Then she remembered he had a camera set up over the church door. He had seen the visitor on his laptop. She followed him to his office door. "Who is it?"

He looked solemn. "Police. Maybe your pal Snake called them, after all.

CHAPTER 21

Niki waited by Jim's office door and wondered who could have seen what had happened outside and called the police.

"You stay with the boys," Pastor Jim said. "I'll see what he wants."

Niki ran her good hand over her injured arm. "If he's a cop, I should talk to him. I'm the one who tackled Snake. Though why he'd call the police is a mystery."

"The boys need you right now." He pointed at her arm. "You should get that taken care of. The ER shouldn't be too crowded. It's almost morning."

The thought of waiting in the ER, always crowded at night, despite Jim's optimistic statement, made her furious at Snake all over again. She swallowed. "I'll go later." She returned to Jim's office. Both boys watched her. Curtis Ray shielded Markey in the only way he knew how. He planted himself between him and the door.

"Don't worry," she said. "Remember what I told you. Nothing bad is going to happen. Go ahead and sit down. I'm not going to leave you, and Pastor Jim will be right back."

They reluctantly did as they were told. She took a hard look at the two. She had assumed Markey was older than Curtis Ray. She now realized the opposite was true. Markey looked about eight.

She strained to hear sounds beyond the room, but the office was sufficiently sound proof. Maybe someone else saw the fight. Or someone saw and recognized the boys.

Jim opened the door and motioned to her. She joined him in the hall.

"You can stop worrying," Jim said. "The officer was checking out a disturbance call. He's gone now."

"A disturbance call? How did they know to come here? I wonder who called it in."

"Didn't say. You're the one with the police connection. Ask your friend."

Not if she could help it. "What did you tell the officer?"

"That a member of my congregation needed some emergency prayer counseling."

She was dubious. "He was satisfied?"

"Didn't argue. He knows me. Attends services here. You probably know him."

For one terrible moment, she thought he was talking about Nelson. But in the next breath he assured her he wasn't Nelson.

"I better take the boys back to Open Palms," she said.

Jim lifted an eyebrow. "Boys?"

"You can't keep them here. Either one."

He looked relieved. "You're right. They both need counseling and medical care."

"We are a full service shelter," she said, barely managing a grin.

They went back inside his office. Curtis Ray stood with his feet parted as if ready to fight. "He won't go with the cops."

"He doesn't have to," Niki told him. "You're both coming with me to the shelter. Markey can have the bed next to yours."

Markey moved away from Curtis Ray and stood next to Jim. "Thanks, Pastor Jim. Guess you saved me." He grinned. "You're bitchin' with a bat, Pastor Jim."

Jim laughed. "Don't tell anyone." In a more sober tone, he added, "Remember, you can see me anytime you want.

The shelter's only a block away. Niki will take care of you."

Curtis Ray turned to Markey and, in a voice that sounded much older than his years, said, "You're with me. We can do this."

"Thanks for all you've done," Niki said to Jim. "And for calling me tonight."

Jim looked out the small window that looked over the strip mall. "It's morning now. Looks quiet, but that won't last. Guess neither of us will get any sleep."

"Oh, well. Sleep's overrated anyway." She smiled weakly and reached to shake his hand. Unfortunately, it was her bad arm and she winced in pain. Jim started to say something, but she cut him off. "I'll deal with it, Jim. I'm sure it's only a bruise, not broken." She turned to the boys. "Okay. My car's out front, if it hasn't been towed."

Her Toyota was intact. Even though the drive to the shelter took no more than two minutes, by the time she parked in the back lot she was biting her lip to keep from crying. Holding her arm protectively against her, she led the boys in through the door next to the kitchen. "You hungry?" she asked.

Both nodded vigorously.

She told them to go wash up. While they were in the bathroom, she found Robert, the night volunteer, and explained about the boys. Vince, the guard normally stationed at the front door, wouldn't be in for two more hours. The same went for Alice. None of the resident teens were up yet.

She walked into the kitchen, wondering if she would be able to cook with one hand. Maybe cereal would suffice. The boys had less sleep than she had. Then she stopped abruptly. Nelson stood leaning against the counter, arms folded, a scowl stitched on his face. She didn't know whether to be glad or angry. When he didn't say anything, just stared at her, she got defensive. "What are you doing here?"

Had Jim lied about the cop at the door? Not a chance. Not Jim. But someone obviously notified Nelson.

"Got a call," he said. "What are *you* doing here?"

"Got a call." She walked up to the fridge, went to open it, and yelped in pain.

"What the—" His dispassionate expression turned into alarm. He rushed to her side. "Did he do this to you?" His voice was an octave higher than usual. "Sit down. No, forget that. I'm taking you to the ER."

Her arm only throbbed now and she could speak coherently. "I don't need the ER. I'll be fine with ice."

"Bullshit," he said. "I'm taking you to the hospital, and you're getting X-rays."

She couldn't think about her injuries now. She needed to protect the two runaways without giving them away. "I've got two terrified boys in the other room whose sleep was disturbed. They're hungry and tired. Who's going to feed them? You?"

"Two boys?" Nelson stared at her, eyelids twitching, right hand fisting. He breathed through his nose, making a noise like a train shooting through a tunnel. "You can't keep covering for Curtis Ray. You know that, don't you?" When she didn't answer, he sighed. "Yes, I'll feed them. I'll even tuck them in bed. Then I'm taking you to the ER."

"Great. One look at you will send them back on the streets again." But she was less sure about not going to the ER as the pain ran up her shoulder and neck.

"If they haven't flown the coop again by now, you can stop worrying." Nelson pointed to her arm. "You got that fighting. I suppose I shouldn't ask."

"No, don't. Did someone complain?" The pain made her irritable.

"A patrol cop found Snake on the street, bent halfway over, muttering to himself. He asked him if he wanted the hospital. Instead of answering, Snake snarled and said he could take care of it himself. Sort of like what you said a few minutes ago. Then the cop asked him if he wanted to file a complaint. Snake repeated his answer."

"I'm not filing a complaint either," she said. "I'll let you take me to the ER if you'll stop asking questions."

Nelson stepped to the fridge. "What should I fix for those two hooligans?"

She racked her brain, trying to recall the contents of the refrigerator. "Eggs and bacon, with toast, if we have enough bread. I better check to make sure they're awake."

"Better see if they're still inside," Nelson said.

She threw him an exasperated glance. She was just as fed up with the subterfuge but had little choice. Her arm still hurt like crazy. Once the boys were taken care of, she'd make a sling. She didn't need the hospital. She'd rather be home in bed than sitting for hours waiting to be treated.

Curtis Ray and Markey were in the game room where she had left them. The television was on. They were sprawled across the couch not moving, staring at a cartoon show, their eyes glazed over as if they had been hypnotized.

"Breakfast will be ready in a couple of minutes," Niki said.

They didn't move.

"Did you hear me?"

One of them, she thought it was Curtis Ray, grunted in reply.

"Okay. Can I have your attention for a moment?" When they didn't respond, she went to the TV and clicked it off.

They blinked and wiggled a little.

"Whassup?" Curtis Ray said, and yawned big and noisily.

Markey slid down on his side and propped his head on his hand.

Her gaze went first to Curtis Ray, then Markey. "Officer Spalonetti is here. Curtis Ray, best you don't speak. We're not telling him you left Open Palms to meet Markey, and I don't want you to lie to him. I haven't told him anything yet, but he knows. We'll all pretend he doesn't. So say nothing. Understood?"

Curtis Ray looked fully awake now. "Why are you protecting me?"

"I don't think you belong in TYC or any other kind of

jail. Lilith is working on getting all charges dropped in your case. But the only reason you're allowed to stay here was on the condition you don't leave without special permission and without supervision. If the judge, or anyone else, finds out what you did tonight, you could be sent away. Is that reason enough?"

He stared at her, finally nodded. "Sorry, Miss Niki." He sat up straighter. "I had to find Markey. I knew he was at the church."

"Next time you have a hunch, you tell me, and we'll check it out together. I don't care if it's in the middle of the night or the heat of the day."

A bell rang—one of those small handheld dinner bells she had bought for the shelter last year. She smiled. "Hope you're hungry. That sound means breakfast is ready."

The boys looked at each other and slid off the couch. On the way out of the room, Markey yanked on the hem of her shirt. She stopped and looked down at him.

"You saved us from Snake," he said. "You're the bravest girl I ever saw. Bitchin' fighter, too."

She knelt down beside him. "Good thing Pastor Jim brought his bat or the fight would've lasted longer. I teach kids martial arts. If you stay, I can teach you some moves to protect yourself."

"I know some stuff," Curtis Ray said.

"Yeah," Markey said. "We can beat the shit out of Snake and put him in the hospital."

She didn't reply. What mattered right now was seeing that these boys would never have to be alone with the likes of Clayton Shamberg or Snake again. They were dealing with years of pent up rage that could easily explode into violence or swallow them up in a cloak of silence. If they stayed at Open Palms under her care, she would face a challenge. It wouldn't be easy, but as the saying goes, nothing worthwhile was easy.

Nelson was in the dining room filling plates with scrambled eggs and crisp bacon. A stack of buttered toast sat between the plates. Both boys treated Nelson like he was from outer space, gave him a wide berth, and didn't look him in the eye. No one spoke as they sat down.

"If you want to say grace, go ahead, the way you usually do at camp," she said.

Curtis Ray raised his fork. "What if we don't wanna?"

"Then don't," she said, keeping her tone light. "This place isn't run by a church. Everyone here has their own beliefs, and we don't dictate to others."

Markey looked confused. "Why? At camp we had rules. We had to pray."

"Yeah," Curtis Ray agreed. "Preacher Capp orders us to pray, and then makes us do bad stuff and more bad stuff just to make him money."

Markey pushed his plate to the middle of the table and laid his head down. Sobs came out like coughs at first, but got loud and forceful. Tears fell freely. Shoulders shook.

"Now look what you made me do," Curtis Ray shouted and hit the table with his fists.

Niki slid next to Markey, with her bad arm on the other side. "It's all right, Markey. Let it out."

Nelson pulled up a chair next to Curtis Ray. "You didn't do anything wrong," he told the boy. "He needed to let go. He'll feel better after this."

Curtis Ray stared at him. No tears fell from his eyes but they were red and watery. His lips quivered but he said nothing. The veins in his temple throbbed and his hands shook. Niki could see it was all the boy could do to keep from exploding. Instead, he held it in. She knew fear and guilt raged inside him, shredding him into fragments. She saw the raw emotion in his eyes, his expression, even in the way he held his body. She'd seen it too often in others.

He would need a lot of counseling. She wanted to cry for him and with him. Help him release the demons that clawed at him. Exhaustion, worry, and finally relief that he found his friend had been too much for one night.

Markey's sobs finally subsided. He looked around him.

His cheeks turned red, and he averted his eyes. He sniffled, stared at hands folded in his lap.

"No need to be embarrassed," Nelson said. "You guys better get some shut eye." He looked ready to give up on the breakfast he had so diligently prepared.

His words, though, had a different affect. Markey raised his head with a look of alarm. He pulled his plate toward him, picked up his fork, and began shoveling the now cold eggs in his mouth. Curtis Ray stared at him then shrugged. He picked up his fork and started eating. The room went quiet, as if none of the drama had happened. The boys finished their meal in silence. When their plates were clean, they scraped their chairs back.

"I'll take him upstairs," Curtis Ray offered. "I'll show him what bed is his."

"I'll come up with you," she said.

"Don't have to," Curtis Ray said.

"Yes, I do. I want to." She smiled at them. "Normally, I don't walk every kid to their room, but in this case, since this is Markey's first night, I want to make sure you have everything you need."

She glanced back at Nelson, who was gathering up the dishes to take to the kitchen. He met her eyes, pointed to his arm, and then at her.

She got the message.

CHAPTER 22

Nelson drove her to the ER, and she cursed all the way.

"I should have taken the bastard," she said. "What good am I teaching kids self-defense when I can't overpower one ugly teenager?"

"Why are you beating yourself up?" Nelson said. "Snake's five times bigger and stronger than you. From what I heard, you were on his back, not engaged in hand-to-hand combat. You're injured because you didn't let go."

"Who told you that?"

He regarded her with a you've-got-to-be-kidding look.

"So when did you talk to Jim?"

"After you left with the boys. The patrol officer called me. He recognized your car across the street from the church."

"Why should he get into my business?" she said.

"He knows me."

"So what? Does someone call you whenever they see my car parked on the street?"

"Of course not, grumpy. He found Snake, who didn't look too good, but refused to go to the hospital. Took an eyewitness report from someone who saw the fight."

"An eyewitness? At that hour?" She found that hard to believe.

"Homeless guy. You doubt it? Look at the neighbor-hood."

He was right, she had to admit. Damn it, everything sur-rounding these boys created more questions than answers.

Nelson pulled into the turnaround at the entrance to Me-morial Hermann Hospital ER. "Get registered, and I'll park the car. Be back in a few minutes."

"You don't have to stay with me. You know it'll be hours."

"Your stepmother would agree with me if she knew. You need X-rays. No arguing. I'll be back so don't get any ideas about calling a cab."

She got out of the car and flipped him off. He waved as he drove out of the circle toward police parking.

Four hours later, Nelson deposited Niki at her doorstep. Before she reached for the knob, Lilith appeared in the frame with the exasperated expression of a mother who had waited up all night for her daughter after the prom.

Lilith's first words were, "Where have you been?" Then she took a closer look and indignation turned to concern. "What—Why do you have a cast on your arm?"

"Mind if I come in first?" Niki said, with an edge to her voice that didn't come close to expressing her irritation. Lack of sleep only added to the bug-crawling restlessness she'd experienced in the hospital waiting room.

"I've been sick with worry," Lilith complained. "I woke up early, way too early, and found you gone. I called Open Palms and was told you'd been in a fight."

All Niki wanted to do was catch a couple of hours of sleep in the privacy of her own home without someone in-terrogating her. "That's all there was to it."

Lilith looked pained. "Don't act like it's none of my business. A mother has the right to worry about her child." Before Niki could object, she added, "Even a stepmother."

Niki formulated a retort but stopped, surprised to see tears in Lilith's eyes. For the first time, she realized how worried her stepmother had been. Maybe she had been selfish in her desire to close the woman off. But Niki didn't want anyone to worry about her, and she didn't want to feel guilty. She was about to apologize when Lilith changed tactics and took the tone of the attorney. "This had to do with Curtis Ray, didn't it?" she said. "That's why you were called? He's my client, Niki. That makes this my business."

Niki sighed in defeat. "Is there any coffee made? Looks like I'm going to need some."

Lilith's shoulders relaxed. Her voice softened. "A full pot. I've been expecting you."

For the next thirty minutes, Niki filled Lilith in, starting with the call from Jim Haynes.

"So both boys are with you now," Lilith said when Niki concluded. "That's a relief. We can work with that. But Snake's another matter."

"I can't do anything about him," Niki said. "He hadn't made a move on the boys before I tackled him. What am I going to charge him with, defending himself? No, I'll figure out another way to get him."

"I hope so. So what's your next step?"

"I want to take Markey and Curtis Ray by Shamberg's house. Markey took the pictures that were on the phone. Maybe he can remember more about where he was when it took them."

"When is this going to happen?"

"I was thinking this afternoon after they wake up."

"And you've had some sleep. I interrupted your plans for catching a nap, and now I've filled you with caffeine."

"Doesn't matter." Niki stifled a yawn. "What I need is a shower."

Lilith pointed to Niki's cast. "Not with that."

"I can manage." At least it wasn't one of those heavy, hard casings. The ER doc told her a soft cast was all she needed but to keep it dry.

Once she got up the stairs she had reservations. She could take a bath or just a sponge bath. While she was making up her mind, exhaustion hit her like a truck.

I'll just lie down for a few minutes. Her bed felt downy soft. Her eyelids felt like lead.

She woke up with a groan. Her arm throbbed from when she had turned on it in her sleep. Her nose had started bleeding again. Her eyes felt like sandpaper, and her head pounded. A glance at her bedside alarm clock showed she had slept for three hours.

"Crap!" Her body felt stiff as she forced herself to sit up. Every muscle screamed in protest. Even while teaching martial arts, she hadn't been in a real fight for over a year.

A sponge bath didn't seem to be enough, and a shower would certainly get the cast soaked. While the bath water ran, she brushed her teeth. Why the hell did he have to injure her right arm? The ER doctor told her six weeks. That's how long she would have to reprogram her left hand to type reports and go through the everyday motions that came naturally with her right. *Damn Snake!* She hoped his balls would turn blue and fall off.

The miracle soap she specially ordered every month from Louisiana worked its voodoo on her muscles and smoothed her skin without the greasy feeling some soaps left. The process felt awkward as she attempted to keep the cast dry. She didn't wash her hair. Already too much time had been spent on her nap and bath. To shampoo with one hand would be too much work. She would let her favorite hairdresser do her tricks if she could spare the time for a visit.

Lilith was gone when Niki finally came downstairs. She checked for a note but found none. She decided her stepmother was getting even. Niki could use that to justify her own actions, she thought smugly. She picked up her purse and dug around for her keys. *Damn.* Her car was still parked across the street from the church. Now what? Call Nelson? Try Lilith's cell? No way! She would either have to walk or call a cab. Walking wasn't out of the question. Driving to Open Palms took only five minutes. Then again, even a brisk walk would take close to an hour. Anger at herself,

and at Snake, rose in her throat. If she called a cab, it probably would take an hour to get to her house.

Her cell phone rang. She saw the call was blocked. She
answered it anyway.

"Miss Alexander? This is Clayton Shamberg."

She stared at her phone. She couldn't believe what she'd
just heard.

"Are you there, Miss Alexander?"

"I'm here." Her voice cracked. She cleared her throat.
"What do you want?"

"To apologize for Snake and find out if you were okay. I
understand you had to go to the emergency room."

"I'm fine. Snake tell you what happened?"

"Who told me doesn't matter. I'll be glad to pay for any
hospital bills if my gardener caused your injuries."

"I don't want your money, Mr. Shamberg. I don't need
your help, period. You can tell your *gardener* he'd better
stay clear of the shelter and any boys on the street, or I'll
have him arrested. Are we clear?"

"On what grounds, Miss Alexander?"

She pictured him grinning. "Don't worry. I'll find something."

"Do you need a ride to Open Palms? I happened to notice you were without your car."

Niki swiped the phone off viciously and screamed her
frustration into the empty house. She took a deep breath and
opened the front door. No cars on the street. No one lurking
about.

"Bastard," she said out loud. If Clayton Shamberg
thought he would get to her by intimidation, he better think
again.

She started to dial the cab company when the door
opened and Lilith appeared. "Oh good, you're awake." She
stopped and peered at Niki's expression. "What's wrong?"

"Where were you?"

"Open Palms to check on the boys. You look angry. Did
something else happen while I was gone?"

Niki told her about the phone call from Shamberg.

"That deranged sonofabitch. I hope you hung up on him. He doesn't know it yet, but his ass is fried. Oh, my dear, that's not all, is it? You thought I left you stranded? I'm sorry. When I realized you didn't have your car, I took your keys. Your car is out front. Come on, I've got the boys with me. We're taking them along for some sightseeing." When Niki didn't move, Lilith said, "What's the matter? It was your idea, remember?"

Niki snapped to and grabbed her purse. "Absolutely nothing is the matter. Let's do it."

Her first reaction was to plant a sloppy kiss on Lilith in an out-of-character show of gratitude, but restrained the impulse. She settled for squeezing Lilith's hand as they walked outside together.

"Did you see Jayme?" Niki asked when they reached the car.

"Yes. She wanted to come along, but I told her it would be best if only the boys came this time. I made her promise not to go anywhere, and we'd give her the whole rundown once we got back. She wasn't happy, but Curtis Ray talked to her and she settled down."

Niki nodded. "Good." She winced in pain as soon as she turned the key in the ignition.

Lilith glanced at her. "Do you want me to drive?"

"No, I know the way. This is easier than giving directions." She decided not to mention the pain in her arm as she drove. She told herself to suck it up.

Curtis Ray and Markey both became quiet when Niki turned down the street where Shamberg had shot Curtis Ray. She slowed in front of the house. The driveway was empty of cars, but that didn't mean the house was empty.

"I came here with Officer Spalonetti," Niki told the boys. "The pictures you took, Markey, didn't match what we saw in the house. Could you have been somewhere else?"

Markey opened the car door before anyone could stop him. Niki jumped out after him, but he slowed as he mounted the stairs leading to the front door. He turned and looked at Niki with a confused expression. His gaze turned to Curtis Ray. Niki waited at the curb, watching Markey descend with knees locked, hitting each stair with a deliberate stomp as if he were testing the shell and concrete mixture.

He looked up at Niki with a solemn expression. "This isn't the house."

CHAPTER 23

Niki let Lilith use the computer in her office at Open Palms to research the holdings of Clayton Shamberg's corporation.

"According to the Harris County Appraisal District, he owns several properties under three different Delaware corporations," Lilith said. "I've printed out the list. You know any realtors? They may be able to show us the properties."

"Felicia Redding was my realtor," Niki said. "But I think there's an easier way."

Lilith looked up from the computer. "How's that?"

"Markey. He took the pictures. He admitted to being in Shamberg's house before, that's why Curtis Ray went there to find the videos. But he was taken to the studio at least once, either by Shamberg or someone else. I don't believe he just forgot where it was.

Lilith leaned back in her chair. "I had the same thought. But why wouldn't he want us to find the place?"

"Wish I knew." She had her suspicions, but hoped she was wrong.

"Give me your realtor's number," Lilith said.

Niki went to her Rolodex and thumbed through the business cards.

"When are you going to catch up with digital?" Lilith said. "You can scan all those cards in the computer."

"I don't have time. It's easier this way, and it's right at

my fingertips." Niki popped out a business card taped on a Rolodex insert and handed it to Lilith. "See?"

Lilith laughed half-heartedly with a slight shake of her head. "You win this round. But think about it. I can scan them in for you."

"Don't you dare touch my cards."

Alice Voss poked her head in the door. "You have a visitor. Didn't know if you'd want to be disturbed."

"Who is it?" Niki was wary. Alice knew she was always available for the kids, so it had be someone from the outside.

"Tara." Alice wiggled her nose as if a skunk had passed through the office.

Niki laughed with relief. "Tell her to come in."

Alice huffed off and her footsteps echoed down the hall. Five seconds later, Tara came in. She wore a Harley-Davidson T-shirt that hung over neon blue shorts too tight for her bulging belly and legs. Two orange braids brushed against her shoulders. She gave a friendly nod to Lilith. "Hey, Mama, whassup?"

"Your spirits, I see," Lilith answered.

"Yeah, Mama, you called it." Tara chuckled. "My spirit's always high."

Tara sobered as she noted Niki's cast. "That bastard do that? I'll cream his ass."

"Who told you?" Niki asked.

"Girl, everyone knows by now."

"Snake?" She couldn't see it, unless he left out the part with the bat.

"Naw. Don't think he'd spread the word and get himself in trouble with the big guy. There's always eyes on the street, girl. You should know that. Anyway, I heard you had him in a chokehold. If the warrior pastor hadn't batted him, he'd of been out."

"Doubt it. I don't think my arm would've held out much longer," she said. The memory sent a message to her right arm and invoked more pain. She winced.

"That's his style," Tara said. "Plays dirty."

Her mind raced. Another plan half-formed in her head. "How well does Ric know Snake?"

Tara looked surprised, then shrugged. "Don't know. Why?"

"I need information from Snake. You think Ric could get it out of him?"

"What kind of info?"

"The houses his boss owns. I'm sure Snake has been to most of them."

"Houses? Like more than one?"

"Those he owns himself or purchased by one or more of his corporations," Niki said. "Snake's all over the place. Maybe he does all Shamberg's properties. Ric owes me a few favors. If he could get Snake to give up some addresses, we could call it even.

"Ouch, you got my head aching, but Snake ain't been talking to Ric. They got into a fight and it ain't over. I'll try, but Ric's stubborn."

"Never mind then. I'll think of something else."

"You always do, girl. Can I see Curtis Ray before we go? Haven't seen him around since before he, you know, got shot."

"Markey's probably with him," Niki said.

"Yeah? The kid you were asking about, right? Cool that you found him."

"They should be in the game room."

When Tara left the office, Lilith turned to her. "Known her long?"

"Years. She and Ric helped me with another case involving a lost boy. She knows how to relate to the younger kids."

"I saw that at the street church." Lilith folded her arms across her chest. "She's not the only one."

"Meaning?"

"You're the psychologist. You're the one who relates."

Niki shook her head. "I'm only a counselor."

"Well, you should get certified. You know more about these kids than most of the professionals in your field, and they get paid more than you."

"I'm not in this for the money." Peals of laughter rose from the game room. "I thought about it, even went back to school for a semester. But this is a full-time job, and I can't spare the time to get certified or earn a degree."

"Listen to yourself. Can't spare the time? How often are you here?" Lilith held up a hand before Niki could argue. "You still think like a cop. Half the time you're out chasing bad guys, instead of counseling the kids here. Am I right?"

Niki didn't want to think about it now. She got up and stepped into the hall, listening to laughter bursting from the game room. "Hold on a sec." She followed the sound.

Tara sat on the floor, arm wrestling with both Markey and Curtis Ray, one on each side of her. An audience of five teenage boys and three girls cheered them on. One of the girls was Jayme, cheering as loud as the others.

Niki returned to her office and said to Lilith, "Tara's building rapport with the boys."

Lilith looked amused. "Who's winning?"

"The boys, of course." She pointed to the computer screen. "Any luck?"

"Not unless you count scores of apartment buildings and condos. I have nothing for another single family residence in River Oaks. But I'll keep looking and expand the area."

Tara popped her head in the room. "I'm going now. I called Ric, but he's not answering. I'll keep trying."

Before Niki could respond, Tara was gone.

"Here's something," Lilith said, tapping on the computer screen with a fingernail. "I brought up the corporation documents. I know one of the attorneys who signed a few. We went to law school together. Dated once."

Niki turned an interested eye on the screen. "Hope it wasn't one of those disaster dates."

Lilith puffed out her chest. "I have never had one of those," she said in a prim voice.

Then she picked up her cell and punched in numbers. Niki stepped out of her office. She walked down the hall to check on Curtis Ray and Markey. They were taking turns on the pinball machine. The bells accompanied a cartoon feature on the TV. Jayme slouched on the couch, arms folded, lips pursed, watching the boys.

When Niki returned, Lilith stood. The computer screen was blank. Lilith wore a gleeful expression.

"I'm having lunch with Tony Ascera," she announced.

Niki grinned. "The attorney? That was fast. Can you call this a date?"

"Be serious, Niki. I'm investigating."

"You're meeting him now?"

"No time like the present." Lilith said, with a jaunty wave. "I'll report back with addresses. You wait and see."

"What happened to attorney/client confidentiality?" Niki tossed back.

Halfway down the hall, Lilith turned. "This is attorney/attorncy seeking prime real estate values." Lilith gave a wicked grin and trotted out the door.

Niki went back into her office. A few minutes later Alice appeared.

"You got time in your busy schedule to visit with some new arrivals?" she said in an accusing tone.

Niki resisted a groan. Maybe Lilith was right. She was spending more time out of the office than in.

"Of course I can see them," she said, contritely. "Are they here now?"

Alice sniffed. "I'll bring in the first one."

For the rest of the afternoon, Niki worked with two girls and three boys. Among them, one had been forced out of his home because he'd stolen money from his older sister. Another had been severely neglected by a single parent addicted to pain pills. One girl's mother died and she had nowhere to go but the street. Two had run away to escape physical and sexual assault.

By five-thirty, Niki felt exhausted, her arm throbbed, and

she was mentally and emotionally drained. She checked her text messages and voice mails. No word from either Lilith or Nelson. She was about to drag her body out of the chair when Jayme appeared.

One look at the girl's face and Niki's stomach tightened in alarm. "Are the boys all right?"

Jayme burst into tears.

Niki drew her into her arms. "Honey, what happened?"

"Curtis Ray won't pay any attention to me. All he wants to do is be with Markey. He doesn't care about me."

Niki's heart went out to her. Jayme had been there for Curtis Ray when he was looking for Markey, helped him break into a house, defended him when he got shot, and now he ignored her for his friend.

"Just like a guy," she said, trying to inject humor into the situation. Jayme wasn't having any of it.

"There's nothing to do here," Jayme said.

"You want to go home? Kaley would love to see you."

Jayme's eyes widened. "No! What if Curtis Ray needs me again? I can't leave him."

This sounded like some people's marriages. Was Jayme taking lessons from her mother?

"You chose to come," she said. "That's not a commitment. You can go home whenever you want. But Curtis Ray and Markey have to stay here."

"They need my help." Jayme's tone was resolute.

"Honey, you're helping by being their friend."

Jayme burst into tears and walked out of the room, leaving Niki to stare after her in wonderment.

CHAPTER 24

Niki slid into the last booth at Charlie's Diner opposite Nelson. "I'm glad you called."

His grin was infectious. "Miss me?"

"What? Yes, that, too." She couldn't help but smile. She reached for a menu from behind the working jukebox. "What's new on the case?"

He looked at her with amusement. "So that's why you're glad I called?"

"One of the reasons." She leaned against the table. "Come on, give."

"Okay, this might interest you," he said. "I had one of the officers pick up Snake and shake him down. He claimed he wasn't doing anything wrong when you attacked him. He's thinking about pressing charges."

"Pressing charges? Against me?" She slapped the menu down. "That lousy sonofabitch! He was stalking those boys. Who knows what he would have done if I hadn't shown up?"

"We had to let him go," Nelson said.

The waitress appeared. Niki leaned back and waited until their orders were taken.

"No chance of arresting Shamberg either, I suppose," she said after the waitress had left.

"No evidence that he's broken the law. We were lucky to get a judge to sign a warrant on the strength of the photos, but found nothing. That just means he removed any videos he put on the web. He uses different computers and laptops. We—"

"What about the shooting?" she interrupted.

"This is Texas," Nelson said, with a sigh. "We've gone over this before. There's nothing we can do. Curtis Ray invaded his house at night. He feared for his life."

"Even you choked on that one," she said. "So he gets away with shooting a minor *and* pedophilia and pornography?"

"We still have to follow the evidence. There's nothing I can do. The sex crimes unit is investigating the pedophile stuff. I want him as badly as you do, Niki."

She gave a sigh of resignation. "I know you do."

Their food arrived. Her stomach growled. Their discussion hadn't hurt her appetite. She tackled her hamburger with relish.

Nelson took two bites of his bacon burger before he asked, "Where's Lilith?"

She swallowed. "Don't know. She's been gone all morning. She had lunch yesterday with the attorney who filed Shamberg's corporation papers. She was supposed to meet with my realtor today. She's full of ideas. If one pans out, I'll be happy."

Nelson looked dubious. "I wish her luck. What else is she doing?"

"Not letting the polish dry on her nails. Spent most of the morning ordering records from the courthouse and the appraisal office."

"And you?"

"I'm still working with Curtis Ray and Markey. It doesn't seem likely that Markey could forget where he took those pictures. All this would be so much easier if he could just lead us to the place."

Nelson peered at her over a glass of milk. "You think he's been lying to you?"

She thought this over. "I think he's one very angry boy.

Not that I blame him. We don't know what happened in that room before or after he took the pictures. My guess is he wound up in one of Shamberg's videos, but he won't admit it." She chewed on a fry. "It makes me sick what those boys went through. I hope Shamberg gets exactly what he deserves. A horrible death."

She pushed her plate away just as the waitress came by to bring the check. "Gotta get back to work."

He wiped his mouth on a napkin and reached for his wallet. "Me too. Luis and I are following up on a few leads."

"Good luck. Why don't you call after you're done? Maybe we can meet Lilith and go to dinner." She slid out of the booth and waited for him to join her.

Outside, the heat made them forget the cold air from the diner. Nelson reached a hand behind her neck and pulled her in for a kiss. She pressed against him, held the kiss longer than necessary, but when they parted, she saw the gleam of desire in his eyes.

"I'll call you," he said, his voice husky.

Ten minutes later she arrived at Open Palms. Jayme was in the game room watching television when Niki stuck her head in. "Where are the boys?"

Jayme stretched her arms over her head and yawned. She gave Niki a bored look. "Taking a rest."

"Upstairs?" Niki backed into the hall. "I better go check on them."

"No." Jayme jumped up. "They're reading the Bible to each other and didn't want to be disturbed. They said they'd be down shortly."

Reading the Bible? Now there was a story she didn't hear every day. Why was Jayme so intent on keeping her from seeing the boys? Niki started toward the stairs and heard Jayme follow her, still protesting.

Niki was interrupted by Darren, one of the new boys she had interviewed the day before. He burst in from the back entrance holding his arm. Blood dripped on the floor. Niki shouted for a volunteer or another counselor. The call went unheeded. None of the volunteers were available. Alice wasn't in her office. A closer look revealed only a flesh wound, but he had to see a nurse. She walked with him while he explained how he had been attacked on his way from the Stop and Shop. He didn't want to stick around until the police came and ran back to the shelter instead.

She assumed there was more to the story. Darren's anger and belligerent attitude often got him into fights. She made a mental note to have extra counseling sessions later. Right now she had to find Curtis Ray and Markey. She returned to the game room, only to find Jayme gone.

Before she could run upstairs to the bedrooms, a police officer arrived to take a statement from Darren, who pleaded with her to stay with him. By the time the interview was over, her skin prickled like tiny needles had rolled over her. All her senses were telling her the boys were in trouble.

Her phone rang as she started up the stairs. Lilith's name came on the screen. She was tempted to let the call go to voice mail. On the fourth ring, she hit the button.

"Niki? Where are the boys?" Lilith sounded upset, even desperate.

Niki felt as if she'd been slugged in the stomach. "Upstairs, according to Jayme. What's happened?"

"You better go check."

"Damn it, tell me what's happened."

"I found Shamberg's studio." A stifled sob choked off the words.

"You did? What else, Lilith? Videos? Pictures? What?"

"Shamberg," Lilith said with slightly more control. "He's been murdered."

CHAPTER 25

Surely Niki hadn't heard her stepmother correctly. "What are you saying? Shamberg's been murdered?" Lilith croaked out a sound, something between a sob and a cough. Her words came out muddled, almost incoherent. "It was horrible, Niki. He got ripped apart. Butchered. So much blood. I think he was castrated. I couldn't look at what someone stuck in his mouth. Couldn't tell how many wounds. I called Luis and then ran out of the room."

Niki closed her eyes but Lilith's words flashed a picture as big as a movie screen. Shamberg was dead? Then, remembering Lilith's first question, she went into panic mode. Where were Curtis Ray and Markey? Jayme's crazy words rang warning bells in her head. *Reading the Bible? Damn that girl.*

Lilith's voice penetrated her thoughts. "Niki? Are you still there? Have you found the boys yet?"

They better be upstairs. "I'll call you back." Niki disconnected and bolted up the stairs. She threw open the door to the boys' bedroom. Empty. She sprinted to Jayme's room. The same.

Her stomach felt like a claw had reached inside and twisted it in knots. She punched numbers on her cell. Lilith answered.

"Not here," she said before Lilith could ask. "Check the streets where you are."

"Oh, fuck." The wail of a siren accompanied Lilith's words. "I'm not going to tell Nelson and Luis that you lost those kids. They better not be around here. I wouldn't show my worst husband what I saw today. What about Jayme?"

"She lied for them. Before I could check out her story, I got interrupted by another emergency. How are you holding up?"

"I'm okay now that I don't have to look at him any-more." Her breath whistled through her teeth. "I'm glad he's gone. He got what he deserved, the prick." She paused. "He had a lot of enemies, Niki. Including me."

"You'd never kill anyone, not even him," she said.

"Thanks for the vote of confidence. You're probably right, but I can understand the killer's rage. I almost feel sorry for him—or her. Whoever did this needs professional help."

Niki never thought she would hear these words from a former prosecutor. "When are you leaving there?"

"I have to stick around until Nelson and Luis show up. The first responders are here securing the scene. I'm out-side, trying not to throw up."

"Good. Give me the address. I'm on my way." Niki came downstairs and checked the empty game room. No sign of Jayme.

"Not necessary, unless you're a ghoul."

"Not to see the body, you idiot. For you."

"Don't bother with me. Shamberg isn't going anywhere but the morgue. Find the boys first. I'll see you later."

"Wait for me. I'm coming to get you. I can tell by your voice you're not in any shape to drive. Give me the address, Lilith. Now."

"You're being ridiculous." Lilith sighed and recited the address.

Niki thought she detected a note of relief in Lilith's voice. She scribbled down the address and stuffed the note in her pocket before she went searching for Jayme.

Several older teens were milling around in the hall.

Some were in the laundry room while others were in the computer rooms.

She found Jayme on the back patio sitting among the rose bushes with a book in her hand. "Where are they?" she demanded.

Wide-eyed, trying to look innocent, Jayme shrugged. "Who?" Then after seeing the look on Niki's face decided to counter with another question. "Aren't they upstairs?"

"You know very well they aren't. Your lies aren't going to work this time, Jayme."

Jayme went on the defensive. "They were sick of being made to stay in all day and night."

"I don't care. Tell me where they went. No more lies, or I'll call your grandmother to pick you up right now."

"I'm not lying," Jayme wailed. "They didn't tell me any-thing."

Niki raised her cell phone and showed it to Jayme. "I mean it. No more chances. Where are they?"

"I don't know. Honest." A cloud of fear dampened Jayme's face. "Are they in trouble?"

"Trouble? The judge agreed to let Curtis Ray stay here as long as he didn't leave for any reason. You want him to go to Juvie? That's what will happen if the police find them before I do."

Even as Niki spoke, Curtis Ray's own words came back to her with dagger-like sharpness. *I wish he was dead.*

"He hasn't done anything wrong." Tears swam in Jayme's eyes. "Markey's with him. They said they'd be right back. I wanted to go with them but they wouldn't let me."

"They give any hint where they were headed?"

Jayme shook her head. Her voice quivered. "They said they had something they had to do, but they'd be back be-fore you knew they were gone. They swore me to silence."

"Five hours ago?"

"Has it been that long?" Jayme asked in a small voice.

"Let's both hope they're walking through the front door

right now." She stood. "Did they take anything with them?"

"No." Jayme looked crushed. "Are you going to send me back? Please don't. I'll do anything—"

Evidently, this had been on Jayme's mind for a while. Niki was angry enough to take her to her grandmother's. Problem was she'd only run away again. "I'll think about it." Niki made it sound like a threat.

Jayme's face crunched up like discarded paper. "Pul-leese? I swear I won't lie to you again. Okay?"

"Tell me everything you know." Even as Niki uttered the words, she feared taking precious time away from the search. Jayme looked lost. Niki sat beside her. "I need your help, Jayme. If you know what their plans were, you must tell me. You're not ratting them out. You might be saving them."

Jayme's eyes widened. "Saving them? Is it bad? You think something's happened to them?"

Niki gave her a stern look. "I hope not."

Jayme caught her lower lip in her teeth. In a small voice, she said, "They said something about pictures that Markey took." Her eyes widened, and she burst out, "But that's all I know. I swear!" Tears swam in her eyes.

Niki took a deep breath. "You stay here. I'm giving you one last chance to obey. Don't leave. I'm going to find them."

She left Jayme sitting on the bench with the setting sun in her eyes. Had Markey decided to take Curtis Ray to the studio where he had taken the pictures? Did they try to confront Shamberg? After all that man had done to them, Curtis Ray had every reason to go after Shamberg. He wanted revenge. He'd said as much to her. But was the boy capable of killing and in such a horrible way? *Were they at the house now?*

She dialed Lilith's number. "Any sign of the boys over there?" she asked when Lilith answered.

"Nothing yet. You still coming?"

"On my way. Keep a watch out for them." Niki explained what Jayme had confided to her and heard Lilith groan.

She hung up and strode quickly through the shelter, passing teens unaware of the drama going on around them. She tried to keep her emotions under control, but the fear of what she might find almost broke her again.

Alice had to be told first. Her response was crisp and quick. "I know you want to see if the boys are there and get Lilith, but you'd better go see Pastor Jim. They might have stopped there."

Jim took the news of Shamberg's murder with a calm she didn't expect. His foremost concern was for the boys. He hadn't seen them but he immediately got on the phone and put out the word. "There are several kids who know Curtis Ray and what happened to him. They've seen Markey with him."

Niki bit her lip, hesitating before she said, "Do you think Curtis Ray could kill Shamberg?"

He looked at her for what seemed to be an eternity, but in reality only seconds passed. "He's angry, for sure, but if you're asking if he's capable, my answer has to be no."

She nodded, grateful he agreed with her. She pulled the note from her pocket and read her sloppy handwriting. She entered the address in her GPS. Her mouth went dry when she realized the close proximity of the studio to the high school. The implication ignited a new anger. How many times did Shamberg watch students play football or soccer? How many boys did Shamberg take from there? How many victims were screaming for justice? She wasn't sorry Shamberg was dead. Not at all. But her heart went out to his victims.

She drove slowly, searching the streets, hoping to see Curtis Ray and Markey. She would have a hard talk with Markey the next time she saw him. He needed to know how his lies put him and his best friend at risk.

When her GPS voice announced their arrival, she found the street impassable. Police cars, emergency vehicles, the crime scene unit, the medical examiner's car and a host of TV vans clogged the entrances to both ends of the street. She turned around, parked a block and a half away, and took off jogging.

When she got closer, she was stopped by a patrol officer who didn't want to listen to her. She took out her cell and realized she had four missed calls, three from Lilith and one from Nelson. She called him first, but heard his voice mail. She tried Lilith next and was rewarded when the line picked up.

"Niki? Thank God. Where are you?"

"Trying to get past the cops. They won't let me through. Where's Nelson?"

"I'll get him for you." Lilith sounded tired. Niki realized she hadn't asked about the boys. Not a good sign. That should have been Lilith's first question. She rubbed the ache that started at the back of her neck, ran down her spine, and settled in her lower back. Her arm throbbed. Nelson came on the line, and Niki told him the cops wouldn't let her through.

"Let me talk to the officer in charge there," he said without preamble.

She handed the phone to the officer. He returned the phone to her and waved her in. She thanked him and followed a path between the vehicles.

Nelson was waiting for her. His expression revealed nothing. She looked around for Lilith.

"Niki." His tone warned her. "An officer found the boys."

Her breath caught in her throat. He pointed to a police car. Curtis Ray and Markey sat in the back seat. Markey's face was ashen. Curtis Ray stared straight ahead, face tight.

"No!" she whispered hoarsely. "They didn't do this."

"They were across the street. When the officer saw them, they ran."

"Of course they did. They were scared."

Lilith stepped out from behind a car and joined her. "I told him the same thing."

Niki's eyes never left Nelson's. "Are they under arrest?"

"We have to question them."

"But you haven't charged them with anything?" she said to confirm.

"Not until we know more."

Niki shook her head to clear the buzzing noise. *This was all a bad dream. Two young boys overpowering a big man like Shamberg? No way.* "What have you learned so far?"

"Niki, I can't talk about this with you. You know that."

"You're going to put them in Juvie?" Niki said.

Lilith rested her hand on Niki's shoulder. "Leave it to me. Unfortunately, Open Palms may not be an option since they escaped twice."

"Can I talk to them?" Niki asked.

"I have to take their statements firs—," Nelson answered.

"I'm their attorney," Lilith interrupted. "I can talk to them."

Nelson shrugged. "Go ahead."

Lilith took Niki's good arm. "I want Niki with me as their acting counselor," she told Nelson. "To listen only. I'll do the talking."

Nelson nodded with only a moment's hesitation. Niki slid in the back seat next to the boys. Lilith took their other side.

Niki's throat felt like an ice cube was stuck there, waiting for tears to melt it. Both boys looked so scared and small.

"I want to hear your side of the story," Lilith began.

Both boys glanced at each other. Curtis Ray spoke first. "Markey remembered the house. He wanted to show me."

"You finally remembered?" Lilith shook her head. "The detectives aren't stupid, Markey. They'll want to know why you kept this information from them. Don't make the mistake of lying to them again."

Markey pressed his lips together in an expression of studied indifference.

Lilith watched them for a long moment. She finally spoke in a firm but sympathetic tone. "After what you've both been through, you had every reason to want him dead. I want an honest answer. Did you have anything to do with his murder?"

Curtis Ray's lower lip trembled, but his voice was surprisingly strong. "I never got the chance."

Lilith nodded. "I know you boys didn't kill him. His killer would be covered with blood. I don't see a lick of blood on either of you. That's the only reason you haven't been arrested."

Curtis Ray moved his hand toward Markey, but stopped before he touched him. "Then can we go back to Open Palms?"

Lilith sighed and glanced at Niki. "Not this time. You ran away. Twice. After the judge ordered you to stay at the shelter and not leave. Not smart, Curtis Ray. They want to talk to you first, see if you know who *did* kill him. Maybe you had something to do with it. Maybe you led the killer or killers to the house. Will they find your fingerprints inside?"

The two boys glanced at each other. Niki's heart sank.

It was Markey who finally spoke, in a voice so soft Niki had to lean toward him to hear the words. "We were only there a few minutes to show Curtis Ray where I took the pictures. We didn't see Clay though. We didn't see anybody."

"What's going to happen to us now?" Curtis Ray asked.

"You'll be held at Juvie," Lilith said. "Curtis Ray, you still have a charge of attempted burglary hanging over you. Markey, you have just admitted that you both broke into his house today."

Markey leaned forward, stopped only by the cuffs on his wrists. "I didn't break in. I had a key."

"How?" Niki blurted out.

Markey's doe-brown eyes gazed at her. A slight tremor

went through his slight body. "Clay gave it to me. He told me he needed a new assistant, and he wanted me. But I said I didn't want to. He said I would change my mind. But I didn't."

"You still have the key, Markey?" Lilith asked.

He nodded, pulled a small object out of his pocket, and held it up for her.

Lilith slipped the key into her pocket. "I'll have to turn this over to the police."

The boys exchanged fearful glances, but didn't speak.

"Did you see anyone else going into that house or coming out?" Niki asked.

"We heard someone," Curtis Ray said. "That's when we got out of there and hid across the street." He pointed at Lilith. "We saw you."

CHAPTER 26

Two hours later, after Nelson picked up the boys, Niki drove Lilith away from the murder scene. Neither spoke as they headed to Lilith's rental car.

Lilith broke the silence first. "I was checking an address I'd discovered in the corporate filings," she said in answer to Niki's unspoken question. "He was already dead when I went inside."

Niki's hands were white-knuckled to the steering wheel.

"I saw more than his body," Lilith continued, looking straight ahead. "He had pictures on the wall and photos in his desk of nude boys in every kind of position."

Niki's fingers tightened. "What did you do with the key Markey gave you? Did you give it to Nelson?"

Lilith stared straight ahead. "What key?"

Niki sighed. "That's concealing evidence."

"I'm representing the boys. I'll present any necessary evidence when I feel the time is right."

"Who really killed Shamberg?"

"Watch where you're going," Lilith said as the Toyota swerved dangerously close to parked cars.

Niki steered back into their lane. "Times like these, I wish I was still a cop. I feel so helpless."

Lilith made a sound somewhere between a cough and a laugh. "Honey, from what I hear, you never stopped being a cop."

"That's not true." Niki paused, considering Lilith's words. "It may seem like I'm crossing the line sometimes, but not really. If I'm in a position to help a child in trouble with the law, I take it. I'm fully aware this is Luis and Nelson's case."

"Right. But that's not going stop you, is it?"

Niki wasn't sure if Lilith was encouraging her or being sarcastic. "I'm not going to let the law *railroad* innocent children."

"Now you're getting into my territory," Lilith said. She pointed to a gray Lincoln. "There it is."

Niki pulled up next to the rental.

Lilith didn't move to get out right away. "Let me do my job. Leave the murder investigation to the cops. Let me defend the innocent in court. You took on the care of a young girl. Jayme is at Open Palms right now, terrified, miserable, probably feeling like she betrayed her best friend. Do what you promised her mother. That's all I've got to say."

Niki felt a flush of heat spread over her face. As usual, her stepmother had nailed it.

The older woman paused before getting out of the car. "You knew all this already."

Twenty minutes later, Niki parked in front of Open Palms. She found Jayme in the game room in front of the television where a news brief showed the two boys being led away.

"They didn't do it!" Jayme screamed. "They didn't. It's a lie." She rushed into Niki's arms.

Niki pulled her close. The girl clung to her, sobbing. When the sobs turned to short intakes of breath, Niki said, "I know they didn't do this."

Jayme looked up at her, lower lip trembling. "How did you find them?"

"The police found them. By now, they're downtown, giving their statements."

"Markey just wanted to show Curtis Ray the house, that's all." Fresh tears filled Jayme's eyes.

Niki lifted a tear-streaked face to search the girl's expression. "You knew that all along, didn't you?" she said, fighting to keep the irritation out of her voice.

"Sorry," Jayme whimpered.

Niki sighed and sat down next to her on the sofa. "You probably thought you were helping them. Don't lie to me again. I won't leave you, Jayme. I promised your mom. I'm here for you whenever you need to talk. Okay?"

Jayme bit her lip and nodded. "When are they coming back?"

"They won't be. You have to understand. They weren't supposed to leave, and now the boys will have to find another place."

Jayme's face puckered up once again.

Niki dug for a tissue in her purse and dabbed Jayme's eyes. "Is there anything else you forgot to tell me?"

Jayme shook her head.

Niki hated to leave the girl alone. "You can stay in here, but I'm changing the channel. Want something to eat?"

Jayme sniffled and nodded. She took the tissue and blew her nose.

A man's voice, loud and demanding, rose over the everyday noise of the shelter. They both turned toward the sound.

"Change of plans," Niki told Jayme. "Go upstairs and stay there until I come for you."

Jayme hesitated, but Niki's stern look gave no room for argument. Jayme moved to the stairs, hesitated and glanced toward the front of the building.

"Go," Niki said. She watched until Jayme disappeared up the stairs and around the corner.

The man continued to bellow in a voice Niki didn't know. She heard Alice's commanding tone override the man's. Seconds later she recognized the man she first met in the hospital, demanding to take Curtis Ray home with him. Webster Capp lumbered toward her. His coarse gray hair stuck out from under his hat. The seams on his weathered face had deepened into craters since the first time she saw him. As he drew closer, the smell of whiskey and cigarettes assaulted her.

"You," he shouted. "Yeah, you're the one I want. Where's my boy Curtis Ray?"

"Mr. Capp, keep your voice down," she instructed. "You have no business here. You need to leave right now."

"Don't give me orders, lady. I know my rights. You've taken my boy, kept him from his home at the camp, and I'm taking him back."

"You're in the wrong place. He's not here."

Capp's face reddened. "You're lying."

Niki kept her voice neutral. "Take off your hat, Mr. Capp, if you want to talk to me."

His watery eyes grew round, but he paused and slid the hat off, revealing a sunburned bald spot on top of his head.

"I guess you haven't heard the latest," she said.

He blustered, taking a step into the laundry room, then back into the hall. Next he peered past the half-closed door of the chapel. Finally, he faced Niki with narrowed eyes. "What you mean?" he said in a low gravelly voice.

Niki folded her arms across her chest. "Let's discuss this privately. In fact, I've been cooped up in here far too long. I need some fresh air. Why don't we go out back? It's not too hot and there're plenty of shade trees."

As she'd guessed, Capp wasn't an indoor type of guy. His bluster petered out once they were outside. She felt better with no teenagers around to be intimated by him or to overhear their conversation.

The late afternoon heat was accompanied by a slightly cooler breeze, making the path almost bearable.

She spoke first. "I thought you were going back to the camp."

His chest puffed out. "I wasn't going to leave my boy to be treated like a criminal."

"You keep calling him 'your boy' when, in fact, he couldn't be your blood relative."

He gave her a look of pity. "They are all my boys, Mrs. Alexander."

Niki bit back an angry retort. Instead, she said, "I assumed you've heard the news about Shamberg's murder."

"'Course I have. That's why I'm here. The cops think Curtis Ray did it. They're wrong. Why, that boy couldn't kill anyone."

"We agree on that. Who do you think killed Shamberg?"

Capp shrugged. "Must have been a robbery gone badly. Clayton was a generous, benevolent man. He donated the land for the camp. He's helped hundreds, no, thousands, of boys. Don't know why anyone would hurt him, let alone want him dead."

If he kept defending Shamberg, Niki was afraid she'd lose control and punch the man. Instead, she concentrated on the squirrel that was running up the tree on her right. She didn't speak until her breathing returned to normal. Then she leveled her eyes at him. "He shot Curtis Ray. Did you defend his actions then?"

"An honest mistake," Capp protested. "He saw a black kid running out of his house at night. He thought the worst. Who wouldn't? He was within his rights. Do I condone what he did to Curtis Ray? 'Course not. But that kid shouldn't have been in his house. What the hell was he doing there?"

"So you blame Curtis Ray for getting shot?"

"Well, shit! No, not really. You're putting words in my mouth. I'm sayin' the kid shouldn't have been there, but that don't mean he went and killed Clay for it."

"But you still think Clayton Shamberg is a kind and benevolent man. I heard he had *invited*, if that's the right word, Curtis Ray into his house on different occasions."

Capp's small, watery blue eyes became slits under puffy lids. "Whaddya mean?"

"You said Shamberg donated the camp land. But he owns it, and you pay rent to him, or his corporation."

"That money you call rent is put in a trust to sustain the

camp if anything happens to him. It's meant to protect us." He ran a brown hand over his chin stubble. "He's a very astute businessman."

"You've seen the paperwork regarding this trust?"

"I don't need to see it. Clayton told me his lawyers took care of it, and I believe him."

"Do you pay him in other ways?"

He scowled. "What do you mean?"

"Do you send boys to him?"

"I don't appreciate what you're saying. You think he took Curtis Ray into his house for some illegal business? No, ma'am. He wanted the boys to become men and support themselves. I sent boys to him at his request, sure. To work, to intern. So they could learn the business. There's nothing wrong in that, lady."

"If that truly was the case." Before he could argue, she continued. "You've known him a long time, I take it."

Capp stared at her. "We come from the same small town," he answered with some hesitation, as if sensing a trap.

"What town was that?"

Capp mentioned a place she was vaguely familiar with and waved his hand dismissively. "You probably never heard of the town. Hardly anyone has."

"You were friends?"

Capp's cheeks deepened in color. "Well, I wouldn't say that, exactly. He was a loner, didn't mix with the rest of us. He warn't rich growing up, just the opposite, but he acted like he was better than anyone else."

"But now you're important in your own way. You're a preacher. You're in charge of a successful wilderness camp, which means you have a mission to teach and guide and counsel these boys. Isn't that right?"

"Um, yeah, that's right." he said, as if expecting the punch line he knew would follow.

"So what you do is even more important than what Clayton does. Excuse me, I mean did."

Capp didn't say anything. His brow wrinkled.

"What about the boys who didn't come back to the camp?" she persisted. "The ones who ran away or disappeared?"

He looked wary now, his eyes flicking to the gate that led to the street.

"Did you go look for them?" she asked. "Send someone else to find them?"

"Don't know what you're talking about," Capp said, his voice getting louder.

"Sure you do," she said, with a smile meant to catch him off guard. "You already admitted to sending certain boys to Shamberg for *training*. Isn't that what you called it? No, wait. It was projects given to them. Projects, like home movies?"

Capp straightened his spine and planted his feet apart. "I don't like what you're implying."

"I'm trying to get at the truth. I don't believe you are so ignorant and blind that you didn't see or know what was going on at Shamberg's house. Maybe you even participated. Do you get your kicks fondling naked boys, Mr. Capp?" For a moment she wondered if she'd gone too far.

His eyes widened. "What kind of sick shit you saying?" A deep red infused his neck and colored his face. He raised one fist and shook it at her. "Fuck you, lady. That's bullshit. Take back your blasphemous words. I never hurt those boys that way. Why, I love those boys."

Love? How many times had she heard those same words coming from pedophiles? She didn't bother to hide her contempt. "I'm not a cop, Mr. Capp, or I'd have had you arrested a long time ago. You're not even a real preacher. Tell me, did you get rich on the boys? Did Shamberg give you a cut from the profits of the movies? Did you get your jollies watching them?"

He sputtered and poked a finger at her chest. "Go to hell, lady."

"Stop with the theatrics, old man," she said. "I'm not

your audience. You knew what Shamberg was doing to those boys. They came to you, crying and begging you to stop him. But you didn't. You couldn't. He paid you too much money. You had to keep the gravy coming. The boys be damned. Did you soften them up before you turned them over to him?"

Capp raised his hand. For a moment she believed he intended to strike her. But she stood her ground and watched him open his mouth and close it again, like a fish gulping air. His arm shook and seemed to lose strength as he let it fall to his side. He turned abruptly and stalked toward the back door.

"Do not open that door," she ordered loudly. "Go out the back gate."

He stopped and turned to stare at her. Waves of hate wafted from him, as did a stench of fear.

The impact of the odor made her nauseated. She wanted to punch him. Hit him with all her strength. She wanted to kick him in the balls and make him suffer. She ached to hurt him. *Come on. Try something. Anything.*

Capp's jaw clenched. He didn't move. "You're wrong, lady. You can't prove any of that. If Clayton did those things, I would've known."

"You knew. You did nothing to prevent it."

He stepped toward her until he was inches away. "If I knew, I would have killed him myself."

She met his gaze. "Maybe you did."

"You want to know who killed him? Look who was closest to him. That's all I got to say." Capp turned his head and spat a wad at the ground before he headed for the gate.

A sound like divine thunder punctured the air as he slammed the gate shut.

CHAPTER 27

Niki and Nelson left Café Laredo's and decided to walk off their dinner. Not yet dark, the evening was balmy, a dying summer redolent of the spices that flavored their tortillas. Mosquitoes buzzed around them. They swatted at them as they strolled down the tree-lined sidewalk.

By mutual agreement, they had decided not to talk shop while they ate. Now she felt free to discuss her surprise visitor who had been on her mind since he'd left. First she asked her usual, "What's new with the case?"

"Nothing. Dead ends all around," Nelson admitted. "Depending on who we talked to Shamberg was either a farsighted genius or a giant claw, greedily chewing up the land for his own gain. We took the computers we found at both houses and his offices. The experts are taking apart the hard drives. If there's anything linking Shamberg to the videos Curtis Ray was looking for, they'll find it."

Would Shamberg have left evidence behind? He'd been so clever and elusive while alive. All they had was speculation and the unlikely possibility he might have become careless before he was murdered.

Or the murderer found what he was looking for. In which case, all bets were off.

"I got a visit from Webster Capp a couple of days ago," she announced.

He gave her a sharp look. "Why didn't you tell me before?"

"Remember our agreement? No shop talk while eating. Besides, you've been so busy with the case I haven't been able to talk to you. I did try to reach you but you didn't return any of my calls."

Nelson exhaled. "What did he want?"

"Curtis Ray, again. I told him he was in custody and not allowed visitors."

"He believed you?"

"I certainly wasn't going to tell him the boys were with Lilith. He believed me. He's not going to check." A bus rumbled by, and she waited until it reached the next block before she spoke again. "We had an interesting talk."

His nostrils flared, but he waited for her to continue.

"I asked him about his business with Shamberg. At first he said nothing we didn't already know. So I asked why he sent boys from the camp to him. He claims it was a work program. The boys who showed the most potential were to be interns in Shamberg's corporations. Can you swallow that one?"

"Not without holding my nose," he said with a derisive laugh. "Funny you should mention Capp. I got a warrant to subpoena his bank records and we went over them today."

"He's a serious suspect?"

"Everyone's a suspect," he said curtly.

Was Nelson angry that she talked to Capp? "He came to me, Nelly. Not the other way around."

Nelson didn't say anything for a few moments. Finally, he let loose a sigh. "I know. This case has us all in knots. I'm not upset with you." He took her hand and gave it a gentle squeeze. "We brought Capp in for questioning yesterday after we did a background check. He's tied up with Shamberg in a dozen ways. They grew up together. Don't know which one came up with the idea for a boy's camp, but it's only logical to assume they worked together from the beginning."

"That's the impression I got," she said.

"Capp pays the rent on the camp out of his business account to the tune of twenty-five hundred a month. That's pennies compared with what the land's worth. Why so cheap? He didn't explain the automatic monthly deposits of ten thousand dollars from one of Shamberg's corporations into his personal account. The last payment doubled. Twenty thousand. For what? He didn't have an answer for that one either."

"You said they grew up together. So it must be a joint project. But Shamberg's payments to him don't sound right." She hopped over a fallen tree branch in her path. "Capp had a parting shot to me before he left. He said look at whoever was closest to the man."

"Hmmm. That would include him. Who else?"

She hesitated. "What about Snake? The boy worked for him, ran his errands, worked more as a bodyguard than a gardener. Wouldn't doubt he was one of Shamberg's toys. Maybe he finally turned on his boss."

"We're already looking at Snake," Nelson said. "Did Capp ask about Markey?"

"No. Maybe he thinks Markey really disappeared."

"Maybe that's what the twenty thousand was for," he said.

"To get rid of Markey?" An ugly thought, but she wouldn't be surprised if that turned out to be the case.

"It crossed my mind," he said.

"Luckily, Markey escaped," Niki said.

"With a motive to kill," Nelson added.

She shook her head. "Not him. Not those boys."

"Took a lot of hate." Nelson paused. "I'm not saying they killed him. No evidence to suggest that. But they might have led the killer or killers to him."

She couldn't see them doing any of that. "Who else have you questioned? What about the condos Shamberg's company was building in the Village? He got death threats over that property."

On less troublesome ground, Nelson's tone became more assured. "The people Shamberg worked with described him as being demanding, friendly, punctual, kept his own hours, calm, hot tempered, and, well, you get the picture. Everyone had a different take on the guy. His office manager, a guy named Henry Watts, painted his boss as driven. When Shamberg wanted a building or a plot of land, he let nothing get in his way. Death threats didn't faze Shamberg. We checked them all out. Didn't go anywhere."

They stopped at an intersection and waited for the red light to change to green.

"What about personal relationships?" Niki asked, thinking of the pictures she'd seen in Shamberg's house. She remembered the beautiful blonde with Shamberg and how happy they looked together.

Nelson nodded. "Didn't I tell you? He was engaged. They were together for years. The woman came from wealthy construction money. I remember thinking it was a match made in concrete heaven."

She should have guessed. "That's big, Nelly. How could you forget to tell me?"

"It didn't occur to me. They broke up weeks before he was killed. We talked to her and let her go."

"What did she say?"

"She's devastated. Can't believe anyone had motive to kill him. She describes Shamberg as charming, exciting, and generous. She's never suspected her fiancé of being anything other than how he presented himself."

"And you believed her?" Niki said.

"The woman sounded sincere."

She shook her head in disbelief. "Men. You'd believe any woman with a beautiful and innocent-looking face. Not just you, all men. I saw her picture in Shamberg's house. If she thought he was so great, who decided to break it off?"

The light changed, and he didn't speak again until they had crossed the street. Dusk brought a rosy tint to a passing cloud and left a trail of pink smoke.

"She wouldn't go into details," Nelson said. "Only that it was a mutual decision. Before you ask, she had an alibi for the time of the murder."

"I'd like to talk to her."

"You're kidding."

"No, I'm serious." She gazed pointedly at him. "You're a man and a police investigator. She's not going to confide in you. I want to know what happened to make her leave him."

"Why would she talk to you, Niki? Get real."

"I'm trying. Look at this another way. She's still hurting this close after the breakup and now she's dealing with his murder. She needs someone to vent her feelings to, some-one who would understand how she's feeling." She shrugged. "Won't hurt to ask."

"No way. Not in a million years." Nelson wore a smug smile. "May I remind you once again that you're interfering in my case? Besides, I may want to talk to her again."

She bumped his side with her good arm. "You can have her after I'm finished."

"After what's left, you mean."

"Give me her name." When he hesitated, she added, "I can look it up. I bet she's on Facebook or Twitter." She held up her hand before he could protest. "I'm not interfering, as you call it. Civilians can and do help the police solve crimes. For your information, I've met the captain who heads the Crime Analysis Command Center, and he told me civilians work with his officers twenty-four/seven. I'm a civilian working with you to solve this crime." She grinned. She'd won this round. Maybe.

Nelson laughed. "Those civilians get paid and are trained."

"So? Thank me for doing this for nothing. You can't say *I* haven't been trained." She stopped and turned to face him, forcing him to stop as well. Her arms encircled his neck. "Let me do this for Curtis Ray and Markey."

"I've already overstepped my boundaries by letting their

attorney ad litem take them into her custody," he said sourly. He removed her arms and continued to walk. She quickened to catch up with him.

"I meant to thank you for that," she said. "Lilith is taking good care of the boys."

Niki's stepmother had used part of her inheritance from her last husband to rent a residential suite in a small hotel located downtown. It seemed the best way to go since it was no longer safe for the boys at Open Palms. The first step was getting the judge to agree after Lilith made the decision to keep the boys with her.

"Can I get the ex-fiancé's name now? Save me time. You can pay me when we get to my place." She winked at him "Nobody home but me."

He gave a sigh of defeat. "Payment will be exacted," he promised. Though he tried to look stern, a grin split his face.

CHAPTER 28

On a warm Thursday evening, Chloe Sanders entered Palazzo's with the air of confidence only breeding and money could maintain. Her patrician features were more luminous than in her pictures with Shamberg. She wore an expensive-looking pink summer suit that flattered her slim figure. Her feathered blonde curls framed an unsmiling angular face dominated by a model's cheekbones and thin red lips.

Niki stood by the corner table next to the south window. Chloe acknowledged her and threaded her way between seated lunch customers.

"Thanks for meeting me." Niki extended her good arm to Chloe who touched her hand lightly.

Chloe perched in the chair opposite Niki like a bird ready to fly away at the first sign of an upwind. Despite her tentative position, her voice held a note of determination. "You said you had information concerning my ex-fiancé's murder."

"I'll get to that in a moment," Niki said with a smile that she hoped would put Chloe at ease. "First let me say, I'm sorry for your loss. It must have been a terrible shock."

"It was," Chloe said stiffly.

"What was he like?" Niki said, trying to sound interested, much as a television interviewer might be.

Chloe regarded her with a speculative gaze. Instead of

answering, she said, "You're the counselor for Open Palms, the shelter for runaway teens. I understand that boy who broke into Clayton's home is staying there. A little young for that shelter, isn't he? I would think he belonged in Juvenile Hall."

Niki stiffened. It wasn't so much that Chloe didn't use Curtis Ray's name that bothered her, but that she referenced him as the boy who broke into Shamberg's home, not as the boy he shot. "In case you're wondering, that boy, as you call him, didn't kill your former fiancé. He's been cleared."

"I'm glad to hear that," Chloe said. "I didn't believe for a moment that the boy was guilty. I don't understand why anyone would do such a horrible thing. Do the police have any suspects?"

"They're still investigating," Niki said. "You understand I'm not at liberty to divulge anything the police have uncovered."

Chloe stared at her without speaking. Only a tell-tale muscle that twitched under her left eye revealed any sign of discomfort.

Niki decided to get to the point. "You were engaged for a long time. I saw the pictures of both of you in his house. You made a very handsome couple. One of the investigators said it looked like a match made in concrete heaven."

Chloe expelled a breath and pursed her lips together. Her expression made it clear to Niki what she thought of the analogy.

"Sorry," Niki said, "Bad joke. He was, of course, referring to your family's construction business and its association with Clayton's real estate holdings."

Chloe flicked a speck of invisible lint off her jacket. "There is no association," she said. "The two businesses have little in common. The only time my father worked with Clayton was during the building of the Village condos."

"Did he and your father get along?"

Chloe hesitated as if considering how to answer. "They

were civil to each other around me. They weren't close. What does their relationship have to do with Clayton's murder?"

"I take it your father didn't exactly approve of your engagement?"

"His approval, or lack of it, had nothing to do with our breakup."

Their waiter approached. Chloe seemed to welcome the interruption and ordered a dry martini. Niki asked for iced tea.

"The police look at everyone who knew the victim," Niki said. "I met Shamberg. I didn't have a clue he was going through an unhappy breakup. Maybe that explains why he seemed so angry." She paused, letting her words have their effect on the other woman.

Chloe didn't respond. Not even another muscle twitch.

Niki continued. "It must have been a double shock to hear he was murdered after you called off the wedding."

Chloe's eyes flickered to the bar area and back to Niki. "You're assuming I was the one who called it off."

"Didn't you? If I learned my fiancé shot a child, I wouldn't want to have anything to do with him. Curtis Ray was only twelve."

"Oh? I heard he was really thirteen." Chloe flushed. "I was devastated and so was Clayton. You say you met him, but you obviously don't know him, or you wouldn't be so judgmental. He was terribly upset to learn the boy's age. What was that child doing? He shouldn't have been there in the first place."

Same rationale that Capp had expressed earlier. Blaming Curtis Ray for being shot while defending the shooter. Chloe didn't seem the type of woman who stood by her man regardless of what he did. After all, she had broken off their engagement. Or had she?

The waiter came with their drinks. Chloe almost snatched the martini out of his hand. Niki waited until he was out of earshot before she spoke. "Did you ever ask yourself if there was another reason Clayton shot Curtis Ray, a child who hadn't stolen anything and was running away?"

"What do you mean? What other reason?" Chloe said, her tone guarded.

"I'm asking you. Ever see them together? Did Curtis Ray spend time at his house?"

Chloe raised her martini glass to her lips, but then lowered it inches from the table. "What do you mean? Clayton barely knew the boy. I don't like what you're implying. What would he and a thirteen-year-old have in common?"

"I don't know. Think about it. Curtis Ray claims to have been looking for something that rightfully belonged to him. Something he left behind the last time he's been there as Shamberg's guest."

Chloe shook her head. "I never heard Clayton mention Curtis Ray."

Niki didn't argue the point. "You and Clayton were together for several years. You knew him better than anyone else, but he obviously kept secrets. Secrets that could motivate a killer. Do you know of anyone who hated him that much?"

Chloe didn't answer right away. Her cheeks turned a deep pink. Niki couldn't tell if the drink or the question was responsible.

"Nobody in his position gets through life without making enemies," Chloe said finally. "You're asking who hated him enough to kill him. From what you just said, that boy could have had a motive."

Niki put her hands under the table and doubled them into fists. "Curtis Ray is not a killer."

Chloe met Niki's direct gaze, but her bravado didn't last and she lowered her eyes. "No, I don't believe so either. It would take the strength of a grown man who knew how to wield a knife and had the guts to use it that way."

"That's how the police see it." Niki reined in her temper before changing the subject. "How did you two meet?"

Chloe's hand shook slightly, and a few drops of her martini spilled before the drink reached her lips. She drank half before carefully setting it down. She seemed grateful for the change of subject and took her time answering. "We met at a theater opening. After a few dates we saw that we had much in common. I remembered that his father used to work for my father. I didn't know him then, of course. His family came from a small town and they didn't have much money."

Chloe's story of Shamberg's humble beginnings substantiated what Capp had told Niki.

"What I admired about Clayton was his drive to overcome adversity," Chloe continued. "That may sound like a cliché but, as with most clichés, in this case, it was true. He was self-made and proud of it. I wouldn't be surprised if he stepped on a few toes on the way up, but don't most successful men? I don't know of anything he did that would make an opponent angry enough to kill him."

Niki waited for her to go on, but Chloe looked satisfied with her answer. She took another sip of her martini.

"If you were so in love with the man and he with you," Niki said, "why the break up?"

Chloe waved to the waiter and pointed to her near empty glass. "The reasons aren't relevant. I'd rather not discuss it."

Niki let the subject go for the moment. "Tell me about Clayton's land deals. I'm especially curious about the boys' camp on his land. Maybe you didn't know that Curtis Ray lived there."

Chloe visibly stiffened then tried to hide it. "No, I didn't know. I was never involved with his business. Clayton's corporations own several properties. I heard about the camp, but only in vague terms."

"So you never speculated that Clayton's business, or his land deals, might be somehow connected to his murder?"

"I told you, I'm not aware of any enemies, business or otherwise."

"You must have stayed at his houses on occasion," Niki said.

Chloe didn't seem fazed by this new direction.

"We spent time at his River Oaks home. Why all the questions?"

"Old habits. I used to be with HPD before I became a counselor. Detectives and counselors tend to be more inquisitive than others." Niki sipped her tea. "We were talking about his houses. There's the one in River Oaks and then there's the one in which he was found."

The waiter returned with a fresh martini. This time Chloe's hand shook a little more when she tried to pick up the glass. Niki took note of her difficulty in keeping up the crumbling façade of the uncaring ex. Chloe reached for the menu and hid her face behind it. "Give me the Caesar salad without the chicken," she told the waiter when he appeared. "And bring another martini when you bring the salad."

The waiter turned to Niki.

"I'll have the same but without the martini," she told him.

Not about to let Chloe off the hook, Niki said to her, "You were going to tell me about the second house."

Chloe waited until the waiter left. "I only know of the one. I was never in Clayton's studio, if that's what he used the second house for."

"Weren't you curious?"

"About something he didn't share with me? No. That's his business." Chloe took another drink. "Was his business."

"Odd," Niki commented. "What kind of business would he have in a studio? Was he an amateur photographer or painter?"

Chloe slammed her glass on the table so hard it tipped over. Gin and vermouth spread out in a circle on the tablecloth. "Why are you badgering me? I told you, I don't know anything about other houses or what he was doing there. I'm sick of your questions. I just want to be left alone." She waved to the waiter who hurried over and dabbed at the spill.

Chloe fumed and pushed back her chair. Niki was afraid the woman would stomp off and she would never get this chance again. "I understand, Chloe," she said in a soothing tone. "I do. I'm sorry to have upset you." She waited until Chloe's breathing returned to normal. "Like I said, I've met the man. The circumstances weren't great, but I didn't know him like you do. It's very helpful to get the perspective of someone close to him." She paused and gauged Chloe's posture. The women appeared wary, but Niki was reasonably certain that she wouldn't flee.

Chloe waved to the waiter, signaling him to bring her another drink. A good sign that she would stay.

Niki continued to press her advantage. "What about his gardener? You must have met him. What's his name? You know who I mean."

Chloe blinked and rubbed her temples. "Why would I? I didn't concern myself with his help."

"Why not? The gardener lived above the garage at his home where you said you often stayed with Clayton. I was under the impression he was more than a gardener. A bodyguard, for instance. Do you know why Clayton needed a bodyguard?"

"No." Irritation sharpened her tone. "I know nothing about Snake."

Niki smiled. "I didn't mention his name. Snake, is it?"

Chloe gave her a frosty look. "I knew he existed, but that doesn't mean I knew him personally. I'm not blind or deaf. I'm sure I've heard Clayton mention him."

"What other employees or friends visited regularly?"

"I was there to be with Clayton, and he rarely entertained."

"Did you meet many of the boys from the camp? I understand he used several as interns in his office."

Chloe shifted uncomfortably. "On occasion, yes. He also had a few live at his home. He liked working at home, and he needed someone to type contracts and answer the phone. Basic secretarial work. Most of them didn't work out. But there was one who lived with him for a few years and was highly intelligent and versatile. Very efficient typist. Clayton used to brag about him. His name escapes me at the moment. Then there were the boys from the camp. I'm assuming they were the interns you were referring to."

"Did you notice anything unusual about the boys? It's my understanding they were all about the same age, starting about twelve."

Their food and Chloe's third martini arrived. Chloe drank first and ordered another before the waiter left. She stabbed at the salad. "I don't know what you mean by unusual."

"Did Clayton have a special affinity for twelve-year-olds? I mean, did he treat them special, buy them gifts, take them to movies, that sort of thing?"

Chloe refused to look at Niki, and her fork jabbed viciously at a tomato wedge. "I didn't notice."

"You must have had a thought about how young they were," Niki persisted.

Chloe's head shot up and she spoke in clipped tones. "I said, I didn't notice." She dropped her fork on the table and took a deep breath, forcing her shoulders to relax. "I don't understand where you're going with these questions. Clayton has always tried to help others less fortunate than himself. You have to know about Clayton's family to understand him. His father was a day worker on a construction crew, and his mother an office worker."

Niki listened with renewed interest. "So you knew him back then?"

"N—not really. I mean, we didn't actually m—meet then," Chloe said, stumbling over her words. "I would see him from afar when I visited Daddy. Clayton sometimes came to work with his father during the summer until his accident."

"Clayton had an accident?"

"No, his father did. He caught his arm in a saw. Took it right off. I saw it happen." She shuddered, and her hand curled around the stem of her martini glass. "Later, I learned his father started drinking and got laid off. Clayton's mother left them a year later. That's when his father sent Clayton to a boys' camp. I suppose that's why he wanted to build one himself. He said it was his way of giving back." She lifted the glass to her lips and drank.

"How old was Clayton when he was sent to the camp?"

Chloe shrugged. "He wasn't a teenager."

"About twelve, do you think?" When Chloe didn't answer, Niki pressed further. "Did something traumatic happen to Clayton while he lived at the camp?"

"He never talked about those years," Chloe said, setting the empty glass down. "Whenever I broached the subject, he cut me off or got angry. He used to have nightmares when we first got together."

"You must have met Webster Capp. He's from the same town as you and Clayton."

Chloe's eyes widened. "Web? Of course. Web's older than Clayton, but I believe he attended the same camp. Might ask him if anything happened to Clayton during that time."

The waiter came back with two more drinks, a fresh martini for Chloe, and another iced tea for Niki.

"You said you used to see Clayton when he came to work with his father. Did you become friends at that time?"

Chloe looked out the window, as if seeing a time and place from long ago. A whisper of a smile played around her mouth. "Clayton never noticed me, or if he did, he didn't let on. He was such a handsome boy. I used to dream about him, imagine meeting him again when we were both grown up." Her eyes hardened and she turned to Niki. "When we did meet again, years later, he had become very successful and very rich. I had gone through a brief marriage and was doing the society fund-raising expected of my father's child. I was bored out of my mind. When Clayton

moved to River Oaks, we ran into each other. He didn't recognize me. I never mentioned how I used to watch him. I
didn't think he'd want to be reminded of those years." She
gave a self-deprecating laugh. "But for me, I thought my
childhood fantasy had sprung to life."

Chloe's story disturbed Niki on many levels. Chloe had
yet to describe Clayton as anything other than the man of
her dreams. "Chloe, I need to know what happened that
caused you to break up with him."

"Why?" Chloe finished her martini in one gulp. "Look,
nothing happened. We grew apart. That's all."

"No, that isn't all," Niki said, capturing the woman's
gaze. "You can't stay in denial forever, Chloe. It will destroy you, and I don't want to see that happen. You're a
good person. I can see that. You fell in love. But something
happened to force you see the truth about Prince Charming.
I can't believe you didn't know about his studio. Didn't you
wonder what went on there? Or why he kept boys at his
house? Help me, Chloe. I'm trying to save a boy's life.
Please. Help me."

Chloe stood, scraping back her chair. "Help you do
what? Convict Clayton? Smear his memory? You brought
me here on false pretenses. You said you had information,
but instead you're trying to use me to destroy the reputation
of a dead man. I don't have to listen to you. I don't have to
answer your questions. I should never have agreed to this
meeting." Her body shook, but still she didn't move away
from the table. Tears swam in her eyes

"Please, listen to me. I didn't lie to you, but I needed to
get your story. We'll both leave in a minute."

Chloe's shoulders shook and she covered her face.

"Talk to me, Chloe. How did you find out about Clayton?"

Chloe squeezed her eyes shut and turned away. "Please,
leave me alone."

Niki extended her arms toward Chloe without touching.
"You have to face the truth, or you'll be hurting worse. It'll

all come out in the trial." She took Chloe's hands in hers. "Think about the boys, the survivors, Chloe, and what they are going through."

"Why are you doing this to me?" Chloe cried out.

Others in the room turned to look at them.

Niki felt Chloe pulling away and tightened her grip. She kept her voice low. "I'm sorry to be so hard on you. But lies will only destroy you. Lying to yourself is even worse. All the martinis in the world won't erase the truth. Children are suffering because of what Clayton did to them."

Chloe's hands went limp in Niki's. With her makeup running and her face becoming a distorted mask, she whispered, "I didn't know." A sob broke from her. "Not for years. Then one day I came across a tape." Her voice hardened and she stiffened. "I threw it away. It was so disgusting. I didn't want to think about it. But I kept on thinking about it and seeing those movies in my head. I began noticing other things, the boys who visited. So young. I wanted to kill him. I really did. I knew if I stayed with him another day, I would castrate him myself. I'm glad he's dead. I feel sorry for his murderer because I know what he must be going through." Tears spilled over her cheeks and she looked away.

Niki felt the energy run out of her like the last ounce of gasoline on a long, dark road. She had what she came for, but it didn't make her feel any better. "I'll get the check, and we'll get out of here. I'm so sorry, Chloe."

Chloe used her napkin to pat her face, which now looked carved in granite. "No, you're not sorry. I'm ready to get out of this fucking restaurant before someone I know comes in and sees me this way."

Niki settled the bill and followed Chloe outside. The sun was obscured by a dark cloud. The smell of approaching rain filled the air. "Chloe, I know you're hurting. I know someone you can talk to if that would help."

Chloe turned on her. Her eyes were rimmed with red streaks. "A shrink? Thanks, anyway, but I'm already seeing one on a regular basis since I broke up with Clayton. I suppose I should have expected this to happen when I agreed to meet with you. Should I be grateful for being forced to face what I haven't been able to all this time? Well, I'm not. Right now, if I ever see you again, it would be too soon." She wheeled around on her heel.

The last Niki saw of her was her backside disappearing into a waiting black BMW.

CHAPTER 29

Niki gave Nelson a quick summary of her luncheon with Chloe Sanders as they sat in his office at Travis Center.

"Guess your meeting didn't go the way you planned," he said.

"Not exactly," she replied, her face heating from the memory. "In the end, Chloe thought I was trying to help her instead of the other way around. With some people, it's all about them."

"You got it." He leaned forward and rested his elbows on his desk. "Now that you've had time to think, did Miss Sanders kill him?"

Niki rubbed her temples. "First, she defended him, then she admitted she wanted to kill him. I think she needed an excuse for staying with him as long as she did and ignoring the signs. In the end, it doesn't matter why Clayton Shamberg became a sexual deviant and preyed on young boys. Maybe he felt abandoned by both his mother who left him, and by his disabled father who sent him to a boys' camp. Maybe he had been molested by someone at the camp. That doesn't excuse him. At the same time, it provides Chloe Sanders a motive."

Nelson picked up a pencil and chewed on the eraser end. "You didn't see his body."

"No, and you didn't see her face. She found a tape. I believe she used the word castrate."

Nelson tapped the pencil against his chin. "I don't see a woman like Chloe Sanders killing him with that kind of force."

"A woman like Chloe?" she repeated. "That's the most sexist remark I've ever heard from you."

"Any woman then." He flipped open the file folder in front of him. "Do you agree?"

"Yes," Niki said, relenting. "You're right. That's not the way a woman would ordinarily kill. But she could have hired someone."

He shook his head. "No. This was overkill. Not the work of a paid killer. This was rage—pure and simple."

She crossed her legs, letting the silence between them stretch out. She stared blankly at the file in front of him as if reading the contents inside through the cover. She focused on her own thoughts.

"Snake knew what Shamberg was doing," she said, looking up. "He followed his boss's orders. He cleaned up Shamberg's messes by going after Jayme and the DVD. I'm sure Shamberg took care of him in his own special way. I'm willing to bet he's as much a victim as the boys he delivered to Shamberg."

"I agree," Nelson acknowledged. "Snake's a possibility, but right now he's in the wind. Until he shows up and I can get his DNA and talk to him, we can't prove anything."

"Did you ever find the DVDs at Shamberg's studio?" she asked.

"Not a one. I assume they're in the hands of whoever killed him."

"Let's hope they're not in tiny pieces at the bottom of a land fill." A second later, she smacked her forehead with her palm. "Damn it! I almost forgot about the DVD Jayme lost in the library. I'm going to take her with me and we're going to look again."

Nelson looked up. "Don't forget the killer also knows

one is missing and is looking for it. It's the one piece of evidence that proves Shamberg's a pedophile. It also exposes whoever was videotaped with him."

She stood and started for the door. "That's what I'm counting on."

Luis Perez brushed past her on his way in. He looked weary. Beads of sweat rolled down his forehead from his hairline. He squinted at her and motioned her back into the room.

"I've been talking to the FBI," Luis said without preamble. "They're closing down the camp. I don't know what they're going to do with all those boys. It's a nightmare."

Niki leaned against the wall. *The FBI finally caught up with Webster Capp*, she thought. *About time*. "The feds arrested Capp?" she asked.

"Not yet. When they find him, he'll be charged with child trafficking and fraud," Luis said.

"When you find him?" she repeated in dismay. "What if he comes back to Open Palms? What if he threatens the kids?"

Luis frowned. "What do you mean *comes back*?"

"He came looking for Curtis Ray last week," Niki said.

"It's in my report," Nelson said, not looking at Luis's reddening face.

"Capp told me he was leaving for the camp. He intended to take Curtis Ray with him," Niki said. "I told him Curtis Ray wasn't going anywhere."

Nelson was on his feet. "He might still be in the area. He must know by now that the feds are on his ass, so he'd be laying low."

"How long have the feds been involved?" Niki said.

"Their investigation has been ongoing starting last year." Luis glanced up, his gaze shifting from Niki to Nelson.. "Lindsay Marks is the Special Agent in Charge. Remember her?"

Niki groaned. "You've got to be kidding."

Nelson gave a wry chuckle. "That's the breaks."

Marks's involvement in a previous case, involving the Mexican cartel, left Niki with a sour taste in her mouth over the FBI's habit of holding back information from the local police.

"Hope we don't have to deal with her this time," Niki said.

Luis looked perplexed. "What do you mean, *we*? You aren't involved."

"By association, I am. Curtis Ray is involved. Markey is involved. They are my responsibility, for now, since they were assigned to Open Palms. You said the feds are shutting down the camp that was their home." She glared at Luis. "Am I missing something?"

"Only that you aren't a cop anymore," Luis said.

"You better call Lilith and warn her," Nelson advised.

She nodded and reached for her cell phone, but stopped as another question occurred to her. "Did the feds have an informant inside the camp? They must have."

Luis glanced up from the file. "They're pretty closed mouth about their informants, but I've learned they're working with the Brookshire cops."

Brookshire? She had been in Brookshire not too long ago. "There was a cop who helped me when I was looking for Jayme."

"Yeah, I remember. You had lunch with him," Nelson said, casting a look at Niki that she couldn't read. "Russ Baker, wasn't it? He told you he transported a couple of boys to the camp on a judge's order."

Luis frowned. "Who?"

"Patrol cop who went through the academy same time as Niki and Mike," Nelson said, his gaze not wavering from hers.

"He remembered my husband. I don't think he knew I existed at the time. And don't give me that look, Nelly."

Nelson gave a slight shrug. "What look?"

"The one you get when you're trying to read my mind."

He turned back to the file in front of him. "Don't know what you're talking about."

Luis gave a short cough. "All right, kids. Enough already. Niki, maybe another Brookshire visit is due. Have a little chat with Officer Baker. See what you can find out."

"Good idea," she said with a gotcha smile at Nelson. He gave her a slight head shake. She ignored him and turned back to Luis. "So now what happens to the boys at the camp? Where will they go?"

"They'll be sent back to their parents," Luis said.

"And if they don't have families?" She was thinking of Curtis Ray, Markey, and others like them.

Luis sighed. "CPS will take over. DePelchin Children's Home is a possibility. Foster care. Whatever the judge decides." He gave her a sympathetic look. "I don't like it any more than you do. It sucks."

"Capp could be even more dangerous now," Nelson said. "With the camp under siege by the feds, his livelihood gone, he may feel he has nothing to lose."

"He might even go after Curtis Ray and Markey," Niki said.

Luis frowned. "He would know the boys could testify against him." Before she could protest, he added, "Curtis Ray or Markey might not be called. Sounds like the feds have enough on Capp already."

His words didn't make her feel any better. She wasn't taking any chances. She fished out her cell phone and rang Lilith. When Lilith answered, Niki told her about Capp and the feds. "Stay in the room. Don't let the boys out for any reason. I'll call you when it's all clear."

Lilith's response was not to ask questions, but to remain calm. Her answer was brief and decisive. "You got it."

Niki hung up and started for the door. She paused with her hand on the knob and turned back to the men. "You think Capp killed Shamberg?"

"He's a prime suspect," Nelson replied.

"But you have no proof yet, and he's an awfully good liar," she said.

"His whole persona is a lie, Niki," Luis said. "We haven't found any record that he was ever ordained. He never preached in a church. Calling himself a preacher only serves to give him credibility to the boys and their parents."

She nodded. "He didn't fool me."

"You've seen worse," Luis reminded her.

"Have I?" She hadn't seen Shamberg's home movies and hoped she'd never have to. The DVDs that might have convicted him had disappeared, if they'd ever existed. They only had Curtis Ray's word, and the reason he gave for searching Shamberg's house. The reason, he claimed, that Shamberg had shot him.

The DVD Curtis Ray had given Jayme to hide could be the one piece of evidence that proved his story.

She felt suddenly energized. "I have to go," she said to the men. "Call me if you find Capp."

"Hey," Nelson called, "where're you going?"

"The library, to find the missing DVD." She hurried out to the elevators.

CHAPTER 30

Thirty minutes after she left police headquarters, Niki parked in front of Open Palms. She hadn't spent much time with Jayme since Shamberg's murder. While Niki was investigating, Jayme had been left to the volunteers and Alice Voss. Not a bad idea, but not the same as Niki counseling her.

When she walked through the door, she saw Jayme arguing with Vince, the guard.

Vince greeted Niki with a stern expression. "I caught her trying to leave."

Jayme turned to Niki. "I'm going to the library. You can't stop me. I can take the bus."

"I know why you want to go," Niki said. "We'll both go."

Both Jayme and Vince looked startled.

Jayme broke into a tentative smile. "For real?"

"I planned on taking you even before I got here," she said. "You're the one who put the DVD in the library. Who else would I bring? Maybe this time we'll get lucky. Or you'll remember."

Jayme's smile was more coy than open. "I've been thinking about where it could be."

"I'll bet you have," Niki said.

Ten minutes later, they arrived at the Freed-Montrose branch of the library. Situated on one side of a brick-lined courtyard that catered to three popular restaurants, parking was at a premium. Rather than find a spot in the covered garage behind the courtyard, Niki circled the block until she saw a car back out of a spot in front of the Black Lab Restaurant, famous for its English pub décor and menu. Niki pulled in just as another car came up behind her and honked. Niki ignored the angry driver. Jayme glanced at her, but said nothing.

Niki locked up the car and took Jayme inside the two-story library. Niki watched her make a preliminary pass around the room. Even as she suspected Jayme's ploy, Niki wondered if she was reliving that day when, after witnessing her friend getting shot, she emerged from her hiding place in River Oaks and walked all the way to Montrose. Jayme had been hot, sweaty, and traumatized, and she would have been relieved to find a cool, dark place to hide. The library had been the perfect place to rest and exhaustion would have quickly overtaken her. Afterward, the idea must have come to her that this was the perfect place to hide the DVD.

Jayme opened her eyes and stopped at the rack of DVDs. She ran her fingers over them. As though hypnotized, she went to the stairs, climbed to the second floor, looked around, and then continued to the alcove where she had slept that night. Jayme turned to the shelves of reference books behind her.

Niki's skin tingled at the back of her neck. Hair rose on her arms. She felt other eyes staring at them. Looking down the rows of books, she noticed the guard at his post. His head was bent over a stack of papers. She turned back to Jayme and caught her staring at the various encyclopedias and dictionaries. With a quick motion of her hand, Jayme pulled out a thick volume and let the book fall open. She shook it and a single DVD dropped out. She caught the disk before it hit the floor. Holding the DVD in her hands, she looked triumphant.

The girl had put on a great show, Niki acknowledged. It

wasn't hard to guess what really happened. Sometime after their initial fruitless search, Jayme had returned to the library and found the missing DVD. It didn't matter because, by then, Curtis Ray was safely out of the hospital and at Open Palms. The chances were good he wouldn't go to jail for stealing the disk, so Jayme decided to hide the DVD again until it was needed. Now that Shamberg was dead, his secret life could be exposed without putting Curtis Ray in danger. Niki wondered if Jayme came up with this plan, or if it had been hatched by Curtis Ray. Was Curtis Ray on this disk? Was that the reason he felt compelled to break into Shamberg's house?

"Well done, Jayme," Niki told the girl as they reached the door. "We'll hand this over to the police. The FBI will be interested, too."

Jayme's eyes widened. "FBI?"

"They're closing the camp. Curtis Ray and Markey will never have to go back there."

A smile spread across Jayme's face. "For real?"

"Yes, for real."

"Awesome. Can I tell Curtis Ray and Markey?"

"We'll call them when we get back."

Niki pulled open the door and held it for Jayme who stepped out into the bright sunlight. A second later, someone plowed into them with enough force to knock both Niki and Jayme against the wall. He ripped the DVD out of Jayme's hand and raced toward the street.

Niki shoved Jayme back inside the library and took off after their attacker. She recognized Snake's bald head as he dove between two cars, barely missing being hit. Cars honked as she followed him into the street, dodging more cars in her path. She reached the other side, but saw no sign of Snake in either direction.

Jayme had come back outside, wailing loudly for all to hear.

CHAPTER 31

Niki spent most of the afternoon consoling Jayme, though she knew no words could take away the anger and frustration the girl felt. Curtis Ray had trusted her to keep safe the very item for which he risked death. In her mind, she had failed him. Niki tried to convince her otherwise, telling her no one could have foreseen Snake snatching the DVD from her hands. But Jayme was no longer listening.

Finally, in a desperate move, Niki called Lilith at the hotel. After she explained what happened, her stepmother was all too willing to have her bring Jayme to stay with her and the boys.

"Will she tell Curtis Ray?" Jayme wailed. "He'll hate me."

"No, she won't say anything," Niki assured her. "That's up to you."

They gathered Jayme's meager belongings and headed to the Harper Arms Hotel, an older six-story brick building that looked incongruous, squeezed in among the steel and glass high-rises. Lilith welcomed them in the top floor suite. The simple furnishings were meant to look like a home, and the strewn clothes, toys, books, and games strengthened that impression.

The smell of garlic and other Italian seasonings in a slow cooking tomato sauce filled the suite. Lilith greeted them with a warm smile. Her face was flushed and her dark hair was swept back. She pointed to Curtis Ray and Markey who were sitting on the floor playing an X-Box game on the TV.

"Hey, kid," Curtis didn't even look up from the screen. "Come see this cool game."

Markey, busy pushing buttons on his own control, added, "Yeah, it's bitchin'! Hey, wanna play?"

Jayme hesitated.

Curtis Ray picked up a third control stick from the floor and held it out to her without looking away from the TV screen. His other hand kept shooting bad guys. "You can be Princess Leila." He scooted closer to Markey to make room for her.

After a few moments of hesitation, Jayme crept over to the boys and sat cross-legged next to Curtis Ray. She took the control stick from him and studied the screen briefly before leaning forward in concentration. In minutes, all three were engrossed in the game.

There was no mention of what had happened to the missing DVD.

Lilith brought Niki into the kitchen, which was warm from the pots cooking on a full-sized stove. She spoke in a whisper. "You were right to call me. They need each other right now."

"Does Curtis Ray know?"

"I didn't tell him. If Jayme wants to, that's up to her. But there's nothing to be done about it now. Shamberg's dead and whatever is on the DVD is best destroyed if it shows up again. More important is Curtis Ray and his recovery."

Niki glanced back into the other room. "Jayme was so upset, and now look at her. The boys accept her without question."

"The gift of innocence and youth," Lilith said. "Even though adults try to snatch it away, there is resilience in some that can't or won't be destroyed. The strong survives somehow."

"I see that at Open Palms. It amazes me every day," Niki said.

"But some don't survive," Lilith said, lowering her voice even more. "They anesthetize themselves with drugs, and when one medication doesn't help, they look for the harder stuff, whatever will take away the pain that won't allow them to live a normal life, or whatever they consider normal. They ignore the pain suffered by those who love them. The more guilt they feel, the more they anesthetize. A vicious cycle. Some end up in a mental institution or in jail. Others take their own lives because they can't live with themselves anymore."

"You've seen this close up," Niki commented.

"More than I cared to," Lilith said.

Niki waited for more, but Lilith gave a small shake of her head. "Why don't you stay for dinner? The kids will love that. So will I."

Niki stayed. The incident of the DVD was never brought up that night. Jayme's occasional furtive glances toward Curtis Ray went unnoticed.

"It's best that way," Lilith told Niki over their after-dinner coffee. They watched while the three kids went back to playing their game.

"It really bothered her," Niki said.

"That was then. This is now. She doesn't want to hurt Curtis Ray. That's clear enough. His attitude toward her shows he has accepted her unconditionally. How can we question a child's way of showing friendship and love?"

"You're right," Niki said, listening to their laughter. It made sense in a way that most adults wouldn't understand.

The night sky was a dark blue without a hint of clouds when she arrived back home. Her cell phone rang as she sank into an easy chair.

It was Nelson. He sounded grim. "Thought you'd want to know we found Snake."

She straightened. "Good. Where is he?"

"Next to a dumpster off Montrose. He's dead, Niki. Been murdered."

CHAPTER 32

Niki pushed to her feet at Nelson words. Snake murdered? "How?"

"Same as Shamberg," Nelson said. "Multiple stab wounds."

"Same?" she repeated.

"Well, his genitals were intact, and he wasn't shot. Stab wounds were similar."

She paused before asking, "The DVD?"

"Wasn't on him."

She thought about Jayme. "Thanks for telling me."

"I'll be here all night," he said.

"It's going to be a rough one, isn't it?"

"Yeah. How's Jayme holding up?"

"I took her to be with the boys and Lilith. She's fine now."

"Good."

She took a deep breath. "I'm taking Luis's advice and going to Brookshire tomorrow. I want to find out for myself what the Brookshire cops know."

"I see," he said. "You mean, what your friend Officer Baker knows."

Did she detect a little jealousy in his tone? "He's not my friend. I told you. He knew Mike and me from the Academy. I didn't even remember him. He helped me when I was looking for Jayme and, if he's helping the FBI, I can try to get information to help you guys. I'm convinced that the murders of Shamberg and Snake are connected to the camp." She paused, but heard only silence on the other end. "I need to feel useful, Nelson. Everything's quiet at Open Palms. Robert and Alice have the place under control. And I could use a change of scenery."

"A change, huh?" His tone was wary.

"Oh, you know what I mean. I'll call you when I get back."

"Be careful," he said.

"You, too." She disconnected.

Nelson's attitude was getting under her skin. She didn't ask for or need his approval for anything she did. It was Luis who suggested she go to Brookshire. So why the sarcasm she heard in Nelson's tone? He couldn't be jealous of Baker. Was he upset that she was working the case without consulting him?

She suddenly craved a drink. The enormity of what evil humans were capable of made her feel covered with slime. What Curtis Ray and the other boys had been through filled her with rage that had no outlet. A nice bottle of Scotch would come in handy right then. *Yeah, that's all you need,* said the voice in her head. On top of everything was Nelson's new attitude. Why was she letting him upset her so? Was it because their relationship was getting claustrophobic?

The word love had never come up between them. The sex was always great. She felt comfortable hanging with him. Maybe Nelson wanted more. The thought scared her more than the idea of facing a mugger with a gun.

Yes, she definitely needed a change of scenery. More than that, she needed to vent her anger out on someone.

Sleep came fitfully with dreams of faceless children being herded into a dark cave by giants who looked like Snake. In their midst, an angel of vengeance attacked with swords that produced no blood.

She awoke sweating and kicking off the covers. Her arm

throbbed. She had discarded the cast days ago when her skin began to itch, and she couldn't reach the area to scratch. A shower made her feel almost human again. She put on jeans and a T-shirt and made a pot of coffee. As she finished her first cup, she rang Lilith, who assured her that all was well. Room service had brought up breakfast for all of them and now the kids were playing more video games.

Niki let Lilith in on her plans for the day and was rewarded by her stepmother's nod of approval. At least someone thought she was doing the smart thing.

She decided to call before making the trip to Brookshire in case Baker wasn't on duty that day. He sounded glad to hear from her.

It was close to noon by the time she parked outside the Brookshire police station. She greeted the officer on the front desk who told her Baker was expecting her. He directed her down a short hall behind him. She arrived at an open cubicle where Baker sat at an L-shaped desk. His back faced her, and she heard tapping on a keyboard. A half-full coffee mug fit in a spot not covered by paperwork.

Niki leaned against the doorframe. "A boring job, as I remember."

At the sound of her voice, Baker swiveled around. A warm smile revealed brilliant white teeth as he rose to greet her. "Ms. Alexander, glad you could come. Be right with you."

"Niki, please." She glanced at her watch. "There's no hurry. Since it's almost noon, let me buy you lunch. You bought last time."

"I'll take any excuse to get out of here, and you must call me Russ." He shuffled the papers on his desk into a neat pile and shoved them into a folder, which he placed on the right corner of his desk. "There's a new place down the street. We can walk, if that's all right with you."

"I enjoy walking." *Just not in the heat.* But she didn't protest when he led the way out of the station.

The walk wasn't as unpleasant as she'd anticipated. An

afternoon breeze came sporadically enough to cut through the muggy air. In contrast, the restaurant felt frosty on her skin when they first entered. She looked around. Burly, sun-tanned men filled several tables. Niki guessed they were the truckers whose big rigs were parked across the street at the filling station.

"Isn't this the same place we ate before?" Niki asked, remembering the truckers and the location. The inside of the diner hadn't changed either.

Russ glanced around. "Hey, you're right. I haven't been here in a while. The place has new owners. I heard the food's better. I'll let you be the judge."

He led her to a booth against the back wall. As he slid in, she couldn't help comparing Russ to Nelson. They had similar builds, but they shared more than that. The two de-fining features she admired most on Nelson were his strong jaw and warm dark eyes. She saw these features in Russ Baker. She looked down at his ring finger and saw that it was occupied by a wide gold band. *You can stop worrying, Nelly.* She smiled to herself at the thought.

A waitress appeared and handed over menus. Niki glanced at hers. Same menu as before. She ordered her usu-al hamburger, fries, and iced tea. Russ echoed the order.

After the waitress left, Russ settled back and turned seri-ous. "It's funny you called when you did. I was going to call you. I got your message that you found Jayme."

"Thanks to you."

He shrugged. "I didn't do much."

"Sure you did. You helped me find Kaley."

He cracked a smile. "So I'm guessing she was able to help you to find her friend. Is Jayme okay? I drove past Rhonda Taymore's house a few times. Didn't see any sign of her granddaughter."

"Jayme's staying at Open Palms," she said.

"Is she in trouble?"

She leaned her elbows on the table. "I understand your concern as a policeman, but why would she be in trouble?"

Russ picked up a napkin and folded it over absently. "I get the news. When I heard that Clayton Shamberg shot a boy and there had been a young girl involved as well, I was shocked. The news didn't name the kids." His hand closed over the napkin. "Was the girl Jayme?"

"That's a big leap, Russ, from being missing to being involved in a B and E. Why didn't you check with the Houston cops? They'd talk to you."

"I've been busy here. One of those 'could've, would've, should've' excuses. By the time I thought about calling…well, I had other matters to worry about."

"You said Shamberg's name like you knew him."

He looked momentarily startled. "Like I said, I heard the news. His name stood out."

Their iced tea arrived and he seemed relieved at the interruption. He shook packets of sugar into his glass and stirred.

His answer wasn't the one she was looking for, but Niki let it go and sipped her unsweetened tea. "I don't know how you put it together, but you're right. Jayme was the girl. I kept her from being arrested. Rhonda agreed she should stay at Open Palms."

"And the boy who was shot?" he asked. "How is he doing?"

She was surprised to read the intensity in his eyes. "His name is Curtis Ray." At that moment, she knew the reason for his questions. It had nothing to do with Jayme. "Shit, you already knew that."

His eyes narrowed. "How bad is it?"

She hesitated, not sure how much she should tell him. His shoulders were tight around his neck. His concern was obvious, and it seemed out of context. She hoped her answer wouldn't bite her in the ass later. "If you mean is he physically all right, he's still sore. The bullet hit one kidney but the doctors were able to save it. He has trouble sleeping. Has frequent nightmares. So now it's your turn. How do you know him? Is Curtis Ray related to you?"

Baker's look of surprise threw her off balance. "Related?" he repeated. A short laugh that sounded like a bark underscored the word. "Okay, I can see why you thought that. My wife says he even looks like me. No, my interest goes deeper than that."

"Deeper?"

The waitress stopped at their table and refilled their glasses.

Russ waited until she left. He shifted forward and put his hands on the table between them. "First, tell me, is he still staying at Open Palms?"

"I'm not saying another word about him until I hear how you knew Clayton Shamberg."

He looked surprised. "He owns land around here."

"Yes, he owns the land and the camp where Curtis Ray was staying," Niki said. "You already knew that, but not from the news. It was never mentioned. Did you know him personally?"

"Never met the man," Russ said. "I wanted him investigated for land fraud, but that was out of my jurisdiction." He drank more tea and looked down at his glass. "Enough about him. I appreciate the way you've taken care of Curtis Ray. And Jayme. I knew you would. Thanks for coming."

"That's not why I'm here," she said, unable to hide her growing anger. "We're not done. Why are you so interested in Curtis Ray? What's your connection?"

Before he could answer, their hamburgers arrived. After the waitress left, Niki pushed her plate aside. "I'm waiting."

He glanced at his hamburger, picked up a French fry, stared at it as if in a trance, and dropped it back on his plate. "Five years ago, I was called to the scene of a horrific accident. The car was wrapped around a pole. Both the driver and the front passenger were dead. The smell of whiskey was so strong I could have gotten drunk just inhaling the air. The boy in the back seat miraculously survived. He must have been sleeping at the time of the crash, probably what saved his life. He looked to be around six. He later told me he was eight."

Her chest constricted. "Those were his parents in front?"

"That's what I assumed. He told me he was Curtis Ray Johnson." Russ's jaw muscles twitched. "The dead woman was his mother. The driver, a man, had been staying with them, but wasn't his father. I asked him if he knew where his father was. He answered that he'd never met him."

He picked up his hamburger, took a bite, and set it back on his plate.

Niki watched him. "You locate any other family?"

"We looked. Curtis Ray had been living with his mother not far from here on one of the country roads. A shack is all it was, on land where nothing much grows anymore. I looked over county and state records for relatives. As you might guess, there were lots of Johnsons, but none turned out to be related to Curtis Ray."

"Did you call social services?" Niki asked.

"Not right away," he admitted. "I—I let him stay with me. He was a good kid. We got along great. My wife loved him. But, finally, social services came to my door. I wanted to put him in school, but he didn't have any records. He told me he was home schooled. When I checked on him later, I was told he had run away before he could be placed with a foster family. Later, I heard the Reverend Webster Capp had picked him up and claimed to be distantly related to him. I wish he'd never laid eyes on that camp or Webster Capp." He stared out the window as if he could find answers somewhere on that dusty street.

"Was that the last time you saw him?"

When he turned back to her, she saw misery in his eyes. "No. Last year, the county judge ordered a couple of rowdy teenagers to be sentenced to a year at the camp. I volunteered to drive them. It gave me an excuse to look in on Curtis Ray." He drank the rest of his iced tea and set the empty glass down with a thump. He picked up the rest of his hamburger but didn't eat. "He recognized me, but wouldn't speak at first. I was shocked. He had changed from a sweet, kind-hearted boy, a good-natured boy, to an angry rebellious ten-year-old. Before I left, he begged me to take him out of there."

"You couldn't."

Russ stared bleakly at her. "No, I couldn't. I had no authority. No right. Not a relative. I had to tell him to stay there. 'Suck it up,' I think were my words. The hate in that boy's eyes curdled my stomach."

"Did you ever go back to the camp?"

"Several times. I tried to find out what was going on that made Curtis Ray so angry. He didn't trust me. That hurt the worst."

"What did social services say?"

"One person I talked to said Webster Capp seemed righteous. From what I've seen he's a religious zealot and a charlatan. I begged them to investigate. What could they do? Social services in this part of the state is underfunded and understaffed. I'm sure they didn't put any effort into finding another home for Curtis Ray."

"How did Capp get away with claiming he was related to Curtis Ray?" Niki asked.

Baker gave a short, humorless laugh. "Yeah, that got to me, too. Don't know what Curtis Ray's pappy was, though. Could've been white for all I know. Maybe he *is* related to Capp somehow, but I doubt it. I think he claims to be all those boys' uncles. I'm talking about the ones who don't have families. My mother's half white, my father black. Curtis Ray is light-skinned like me. Hell, I might even pass for his father, though I sure never slept with his ma. My wife would divorce me in a second. *I'd* divorce me." He tried to laugh, but the sound didn't leave his throat.

Niki pushed away her plate and rested her elbows on the table. "Let me get this straight. You think Capp stole Curtis Ray and other boys like him?"

His eyes were as hard as black stones. "Yeah, for a purpose. I think he was farming out boys who had no families to pedophiles like Clayton Shamberg. But I haven't been able to prove it. Yet."

"That's how you knew about Shamberg," Niki said. "I was right. You are working with the feds."

His eyes widened. "What?"

"Don't worry, I won't blow your cover," she said.

"You think I'm doing *what* again?"

He wasn't a very convincing actor, Niki decided. "You're a CI. My ex-partner in Homicide dropped that bomb on me. I hope you nail the bastard. I don't want Curtis Ray or Markey ever going back to that camp."

He studied her for a long moment. "I'm the one who called the FBI. I suspected they were abusing the boys. They don't use cops as confidential informants. Yes, I looked into the land records and found out Shamberg owned the land. On paper, he rented the camp to Webster Capp and his so-called church. Later, I realized the huge profit Capp was making by farming out the boys to the highest bidder. I told the feds I would hand over any proof I could dig up during my trips out there. After I found out what Shamberg did to Curtis Ray, I wanted to kill the man myself. "

"You're not the only one," Niki said.

He crumbled his napkin into a tight ball. "Curtis Ray and his friend, Markey, aren't killers. I know those boys. I've been worried sick about them, wondering if they were all right."

"Don't worry, they're staying with my stepmother," Niki said. "She's been appointed as Curtis Ray's attorney ad litem. She's very good at what she does. You can trust her." As an afterthought, she added, "Jayme's now with them, too."

Russ gave a weak smile. "Well, I'll be damned." He put several bills on the table and stood. "Want to take a ride?"

Niki slid out of the bench seat. "Where?"

"You wanted to see the camp for yourself, right? Let's go now. Once the feds close it down, we won't be able to get near it."

CHAPTER 33

They were too late. That's what Niki thought when Russ's patrol car pulled up to the entrance. Summer-scorched grass surrounded the barbed wire fence. An eerie quiet lay beyond. Niki noticed that the gate was locked together by a heavy chain and bolted from inside.

The sound of another engine made Niki look up. A black Lincoln approached them from the other side. "I do believe we have a welcoming committee," she said to Russ.

"Special Agent Kent Willis," Russ said.

A man emerged, wearing a vest displaying the letters FBI. He took his time getting to the gate. Niki couldn't read any of the signs she usually detected from law enforcement. Nothing behind the agent's dark glasses or the grim set of his mouth told her what to expect.

The man's tone was more casual than his appearance. "Good morning, Officer Baker. We weren't expecting you today."

"Mornin', Kent," Russ said. "I talked to Special Agent Marks last week. At that time there were still a few boys here. Has the camp been closed down already?"

"As of yesterday," the agent said. "There're about eight boys left. We're expecting they'll be picked up by the end of the day. Agent Marks is leading a team to go over the grounds."

"Will you let her know I'm with a youth counselor? I'm

sure she could use some help with the boys until their rides get here."

Willis used his phone and, a few minutes later, he swung open the gate. "You know where to go." He got into his car and backed out of the way.

Niki settled in the passenger seat of the patrol car and aimed the air vent on her face. They rumbled along a narrow dirt road, past the watchful agent sitting in the Lincoln, though she couldn't see him behind the darkly tinted windows. Russ briefed her on what to expect. Looking out the window, the panorama took in tall green and yellow grass tilting toward healthy pines. Buildings in the distance began to take shape. Up ahead, rolling hills and more trees reached to where the sky met earth. They passed a spot of blue far off to her left, maybe a lake or a pond.

The rambling buildings became visible as they drew closer. Niki was impressed with the brick and rough timber that made the main structure look sturdy enough to last the next hundred years. The trees that surrounded the building were sparse in number. She saw an old tire hanging from a crooked branch by a frayed rope.

Russ pulled up in front of the porch next to a line of official FBI vehicles. "You can see the cabins from here," he told Niki and pointed to a row of small buildings behind the main house. "They each sleep four. You probably spotted the man-made lake over there." He turned slightly to his right. "Stables are over there, what's left of them. The horses have been removed and sent to a farm. Riding trails go over that hill and circle behind the lake."

Niki eyed another building near the main house. "What's in there?"

"School and wood shop." His tone turned wistful. "Don't know what will happen to this place now."

Russ cut the engine and they both got out of the car. Heat enveloped Niki as if she'd stepped into a sauna. Her exposed skin took on a sheen of moisture. She shut the car door, decrying the loss of air conditioning, and noticed the erect figure on the front porch. Niki recognized Special Agent Lindsay Marks even before Russ introduced her. Niki steeled herself when she saw the expression on Marks's face. The memory of the last time she had to deal with her still burned. Special Agent Marks had kept vital information from her and, as a result, Niki almost lost a child in her care. This time Niki would be ready.

"I should have known it would be you," Marks said by way of greeting.

"Where there are teenagers in trouble, you will find me," Niki said dryly.

Marks didn't react. "What's your interest in this camp, Ms. Alexander?"

"Two boys who managed to escape from here. I want to know why. Officer Baker was kind enough to suggest I take a look around. I see now I should have come earlier."

Russ mounted the stairs and intervened. "This was fast work, Lindsay. Kent said you still have some boys here. I'd say our timing was good. Niki can talk to the boys and do what she can to calm them or prepare them for what's coming."

Marks shook his hand. "Glad you're here, Officer Baker. The preacher who runs the camp apparently abandoned the place early. We have one counselor who stayed after the others took off." A trickle of sweat dripped down her face. "Make yourself useful. I need to get back to my men."

The gaze that Marks turned to Niki held no warmth.

"I'll do whatever I can," Niki said.

She wondered if the boys were inside the main house, but the approaching sound of stomping boots to the right of the building dispelled that idea. Voices raised in a cadence became louder.

When they were fully in view, she realized the ragtag band was less than a dozen straggling boys. Their leader looker older, and she thought she recognized him. The others differed slightly in height, weight, and age. One boy looked almost as young as Curtis Ray, and Niki placed the others as being close to sixteen and up. All wore shorts and T-shirts, as well as boots.

Marks explained they were coming from a swim in the lake.

Niki squinted, trying to make out their leader. "Isn't that Davey Tanner?" So he did make it back to the camp without Webster Capp.

Marks looked surprised. "I didn't realize you knew him. He's the counselor I mentioned. Those boys are the remaining campers."

"I saw Davey in Houston a couple of days ago," Niki said. "He led us to believe he was coming here with Preacher Capp."

"He came alone," Marks said.

"Where are the other boys from?" Niki asked.

"Two are from Austin. Their parents have been notified and are on their way here. One lives in Dallas and was ordered here by a judge. He'll be sent to Juvie unless the judge decides differently. The rest are from surrounding areas, Belton, Temple, and one is waiting on a constable from Midland. He left Midland at four in the morning. Should be here in another hour or so."

The boys scrambled up the porch, and Niki backed out of their way. The heat had dried them off during their march from the lake, and she caught a whiff of lake water and rank body odor as they passed her. She answered their curious glances with a friendly smile that wasn't returned. They all knew Russ, though, and acknowledged him with a nod or a wave.

Russ touched Niki's shoulder when the door shut after them. "I'll be inside. Come in when you're finished here."

Niki turned to Marks. "Anyone who doesn't have family members to pick them up?"

Marks regarded her with a slight smile. "That's a strange question to ask."

"Not really. Curtis Ray and Markey Lockner have no known relatives. They are orphans as far as the law is concerned. Are there others in the camp records who don't show families?"

"I can't reveal that information," Marks said tersely.

Frustrated, but hardly surprised by Marks' attitude, Niki said, "Why are you here? I thought it would be the local sheriff or the state police, not the FBI."

Marks gave her a look probably reserved for bothersome reporters. "The sheriff and the state police have been out here numerous times on disturbance calls. We were brought in to investigate possible charges of interstate child trafficking and pornography. There's enough evidence to take both Webster Capp and the landowner to trial. Unfortunately, someone decided not to wait for the wheels of justice to spin and took out Shamberg. As a result, we're missing some vital information."

"Any idea who that someone could be?"

"You know as much as we do," Marks said.

Niki doubted that.

The sound of a barking dog coming from a grove of trees startled her. She turned and saw several agents emerge from the forest. She counted three German Shepherds with them. "Dogs? What are they doing here?"

"Sniffing out evidence," Marks said shortly. "If you'll excuse me, I need to check on my men."

Niki swallowed hard and watched her join the agents. She didn't like the feeling of foreboding that came over her. Only one reason for the dogs came to her. She didn't even want to consider that answer. She turned away and went inside the house to look for Russ.

She glanced around the large room—spacious with high, exposed beams. Built-in bookshelves were only a third filled. An empty fireplace was the focal point in the wall on her left. Several worn sofas were placed seemingly without a plan and empty chairs surrounded tables that held random books and papers.

Davey Tanner entered the room. He stopped short when he saw her.

She greeted him with a smile. "Hi, Davey. Remember me? We met at the hospital."

"Yeah, I remember," he said, not returning the smile. "Why you here?"

"Checking out the camp. When did you arrive?"

"Why?" His tone was defensive.

She kept her tone light. "No reason. I thought you'd be with Webster Capp."

"No. Why would you think that?"

"He was looking for you." She hesitated in the face of his hostile attitude. "I just assumed you rode together."

"Did you come here for me?"

Surprised at the question, she said, "No, but I know the police had some questions concerning Mr. Shamberg."

His jaw clenched and then loosened. When his light blue eyes met hers, she felt the invisible force of his anger stab through her. She stiffened.

"Fuck the pigs and Preach." His upper lip curled in a snarl. "You think I wanted to stick around H-Town after Clay got knocked off by some crazed burglar? The only real friend I had in this fucking world is gone. He took me off the street, lady. Now what I'm supposed to do? This was my goddamned home. Where am I supposed to go?"

"Davey, I can see you're angry, and I don't blame you. You've been dealt a harsh hand. You came back here, not only because this is home, but you knew the boys needed you. You've been their counselor and they rely on you. You're the only one left who cares."

His eyes widened in surprise. After a moment, he gave her a nod of approval as if she'd finally got the correct answer. "Effen' right."

Russ came into the room. After surveying the scene, he approached them.

Niki acknowledged him with a quick nod and turned back to Davey. "What makes you think it was a burglar who killed Clay?"

"Ha! Everyone knew Clay had big bucks with stuff lying

around for the taking. Like those thieves, Curtis Ray and his buddy. I'm not saying they did it, but they had no trouble stealing my camera and breaking into Clay's house. If I'd stuck around, I'd have told that to the cops."

"The boys have been cleared, Davey," she said. "The cops are still looking for his killer."

"Not if I find him first," Davey said, the words spitting out.

"Calm down, Davey," Russ said, moving next to the boy.

Davey whirled on him. "Don't fuck with me. I got my rights. You ever lose someone close to you, officer?"

"Yes, I have." Russ said, keeping his voice even. "I can't know everything you're feeling, but I've experienced loss, and the pain can be almost too hard to bear. It doesn't go away. It stays with you, but someday you'll be able to handle it better."

"More bullshit." Davey waved his fist under Russ's nose. "I got nobody and nobody gives a rat's ass."

"Take it easy, son." Russ started to put an arm around the boy's shoulder. Davey cringed, and Russ quickly dropped his arm.

Davey's eyes widened and without warning, laughter pealed from him. He laughed so hard he bent over holding his stomach. In the next second, his laughter cut off. He stood a foot away from Russ, his body twitching, a grin splitting his face. "Had you there for a minute, didn't I, Officer Baker?"

Russ looked taken aback. "Take it easy, son."

Davey jerked his head up. Anger fused his face. "Son? I ain't your son. I ain't nobody's son." He swung an arm around the room. "The boys? They're *my* boys. I'm responsible. I'm in charge. Preach ain't coming back for them. They're going to lock his sorry ass up and swallow the key."

"Why would they do that?" Russ said.

The tension left Davey's face as quickly as it had appeared. He leaned toward Russ with a conspiratorial glint.

"Don't you know nothing? They'll get him for what he did to them."

Russ's expression showed nothing. "What did he do?"

"What Clay paid him to do. Isn't that enough?"

"What do you mean, Clay paid?" Niki interrupted. "For what?"

Davey looked at her, lips curled back in a snarl. "You know. For the boys—*his interns*—whatever he called them—to work for him. That was the line he gave them. Hah. A business don't have paid interns, they work for free. But Preach got paid. Plenty."

"How do you know all this?" Russ asked.

He laughed—a harsh, angry sound. "I was there in his house, wasn't I? I did his books, man. I got eyes. I saw everything. I know everything."

Niki felt sick at the thought of what this implied, but she forced herself to go on. "Did that include his production company?"

Davey stiffened. "What?"

"I heard he used the boys as actors, and put movies online, and even kept DVDs for himself. Those DVDs are missing."

Russ squeezed her arm, as if trying to convince her to pull back and not push Davey. Under other circumstances, she would agree. But this was her last chance at getting the information she needed, no matter how much it hurt.

Davey stared back at her. After several seconds of dead silence, he wagged a finger at her and grinned. "Naughty thoughts. Shame on you."

Dismayed, she continued, despite the feeling she was losing him. "You've said you were close to him. Didn't you live with him for a few years after he rescued you?"

Davey looked at her warily. "What of it?"

"You want to talk about it?"

His skin tightened around his eyes. "Nothing to talk about."

"Okay," Niki conceded, feeling desperation closing over

her throat. "Who do *you* think killed him?" As soon as she asked the question, the air around them felt several degrees colder.

Davey's eyes became dull. "Why ask me?"

She felt Russ's warning hand on her sleeve. "I figure it had to be someone he trusted enough to let in his house. You knew him best. Who did he let in, who did he get close to? You must have an idea or two."

Davey raised his hands and, this time, physically backed away from her. "Fuck you. You want me to rat someone out? Fuck that. Go on back to H-Town, lady." He turned to Russ. "Tell her, Officer. I ain't no rat. Even if I knew, I wouldn't tell you."

For emphasis, Davey jammed his forefinger to her chest and leaned into her. For a moment she felt his eyes penetrate through to her soul. She couldn't move. Russ's voice came from a long way off but she couldn't make out what he was saying. Then the spell was broken. Davey spun around and slammed out the door.

Niki felt shaken, as if an invisible giant had lifted the house and dropped it. She stared after Davey in confusion. "Does he know?"

"He's clearly unstable," Russ said, watching her reaction. "Maybe he knows something, or maybe he's playing with us, and that was all an act."

"I'm worried about him," she said. "Who decided to make him a counselor?"

"He was too old to stay on as a camper. They had nowhere else to put him. I'm worried about him, too. I'm not sure what they have planned for him after today."

"I suppose he'll go back to Houston, but to what?"

"Someone needs to keep an eye on him once he's out of here," Russ said. "You all right?"

She nodded. "I'll be glad when this is over."

"Right. Come on, I'll introduce you to the others."

The community kitchen held industrial appliances, and the counters had room for dozens of meals. However, the camp's cook had long disappeared. Two teenagers were in the process of making sandwiches. They were still in their shorts and T-shirts. Both tall and lanky, they could have been brothers except for their color, and one of them had shoulder-length dreadlocks as compared to the other's spiky blond hair. They gave Niki a curious stare.

"Cato, Danny, I want you to meet Niki Alexander. She's a counselor for runaways in Houston. Cato and Danny are both from Brookshire."

Cato, the one with the dreadlocks, leaned his elbow against the counter. "Give me ride home, Officer? Mom's car's in the shop. Again."

Russ raised an eyebrow. "I'll have to get an okay from the feds, but we'll figure it out."

Cato shrugged. "Danny don't have no one to pick him up either."

"Is that right?" Russ said, looking at Danny.

"No big deal." Danny swabbed mayo on his bread.

"Sure, it's a big deal," Russ said. "Where're your folks?"

"They're separated. Haven't seen my dad since he left. Mom's working at the diner. She can't get off."

Russ glanced at Niki before responding to Danny. "I don't see a problem taking you, too. I'll have to clear it with Special Agent Marks. Where're the others?"

"Might be in the school room," Cato said. "Can't go swimming any more. Nothing much going on but waiting."

"Borr-ing," Danny said.

"Hopefully not for too much longer," Niki said.

They left the kitchen and went back into the front room. In their absence four boys had claimed a table and were playing a card game. Poker, Niki guessed, glancing at the cards. An older boy was slouched in his chair holding an unlit cigarette.

He yawned noisily. "Whassup, Officer Baker?"

"You tell me, Wally," Russ answered. "I want to make sure all of you have rides home."

"Not home. Back to freaking Midland and Juvie when

that officer gets here. Why don't you take me instead, Officer Baker? Bet you can swing it if you wanted to."

"Afraid that's not possible," Russ replied. "But you might catch a break. I'll speak to the constable. Maybe when you go up in front of the judge, he'll let you off with time served." He turned to Brian, one of two dark-skinned boys at the table. "How about you, Brian?"

"Mom said she's coming with my aunt," Brian said.

"Nobody's coming for me," said the boy sitting next to Brian. His eyes were moist and dark and he kept blinking. His lips trembled, but the pulse at his temple throbbed and there was anger in his tone.

Russ leaned toward the thin teenager. "Jeremy? Where're your folks?"

Jeremy shrugged. "Got none. Preach found me on the street and drove me here."

"I thought you'd been here almost a year," Russ said.

"Yeah, I just turned fourteen last month." He looked down at his hands. "So where am I going now?"

"I'll talk with Special Agent Marks. You won't be left behind. You can be sure of that."

"And me?" said the boy next to him. "Preach found me a couple of months ago after my mom died. Got no other family."

"You're…" Russ scrunched up his face as he tried to reach in the air for the boy's name.

"Nate," the boy provided. His face split with a crooked grin.

"Yes," Russ said with uncertainty. "I don't remember seeing you."

Nate's answered with a smirk. "That's 'cause Preach didn't want you to."

Russ didn't respond. Instead, he turned toward a fifth boy who just entered the room. He was taller than the others, and Niki guessed his age at sixteen or even seventeen.

"What about you?" Russ asked him. "You're Kit, right? You got a ride?"

"You bet, Officer," Kit said with a drawl. "Y'all makin' a list and checkin' it twice?"

"That's right, son. Don't want to miss anyone. Where's Timothy? You seen him?"

"School house," Kit said. "Just came from there myself."

"You guys sit tight. We'll be right back." Russ nodded to Niki, who rose at the same time he did.

He didn't give her a chance to question the boys. She wanted to know if any of them, but particularly Jeremy and Nate, had been sent to Shamberg. They both were the right age. Maybe they'd been spared by the older man's murder.

"This is not the time," Russ said once they were outside and blasted by the afternoon heat.

Her jaw dropped. "Are you reading my mind now?"

"I saw it in your face. We'll get answers when we have more information."

"I know that," she said. "They weren't ready. Give me some credit. I've been at this counseling gig for a long time."

"I need to talk to Lindsay," he said. "But first I want to find Timothy."

They headed to the schoolhouse. The simple one-story structure had a wide porch and built more economically than the main house, but for the same reason wouldn't last as long. The simple design had a bathroom and two connected rooms. They found Timothy sitting at a table filled with school books that looked outdated. He had one of the math books open and a blank sheet of paper next to it. He was thin and looked lost in an oversized shirt and baggy pants.

They sat down as Russ made the introductions.

"Yo. Heard about you from Davey," Timothy said to Niki. "He don't like you much. This guy says you're okay. I'll take his word over Davey's any day."

"That suits me." Niki gave him a smile which wasn't returned. "Officer Baker vouches for you, too."

She was about to say more when shouts and barking

dogs stopped her. The sound brought all three to their feet.

Niki felt a knot twist in her stomach. She remembered the dogs. *The cadaver dogs. Oh shit.*

Russ was already at the door when she caught up with him. He held up his hand to stop her from going out. "Take Timothy back to the main house and keep the boys inside."

"Where are you going?"

"To find Lindsay. I'll let you know."

Movement to their left caught their attention. Three boys sailed off the porch of the main house. Four more started down the stairs.

Russ ran forward and ordered them back. They might have ignored him, but the sight of two federal agents jogging toward them and waving at them to turn around gave more weight to Russ's orders.

When Niki showed up with Timothy, an uproar of complaints filled the room. Why were they being treated like children? Why couldn't they go out there and see for themselves?

She squeezed next to them at the large front window that looked out toward the trees. Too far away to see what was happening, she barely made out the cluster of men and heard the high pitched whine of the dogs.

Niki's hands trembled. There was only one answer that made sense.

They had found a body.

CHAPTER 34

Within hours of the gruesome discovery, the camp dissolved into chaos. Word spread through the house that someone had been buried outside, and they were searching for more victims. Feds and dogs were combing the area. The medical examiner and CSU were notified and were on their way from Austin. Soon, the state police and the local sheriff would arrive. Meanwhile, no one would be allowed to leave.

Trapped inside the main house and congregated in the living room, most of the boys seemed to have an opinion as to who was buried. Names were mentioned. Questions arose. For a while they all stood by the window. Finally Russ and Niki retreated to a round table. Timothy joined them.

"Could be Quincy," Timothy offered. "He kinda disappeared."

"Disappeared?" Niki said. "Did you know him well?"

"Not really. He kept to himself."

"What makes you think it's Quincy?" Russ asked.

Timothy rested his elbows on the table. "No one's seen him lately. We just thought he ran off."

"Were his folks notified?" Russ asked.

"Don't know. Nobody visited him. He never talked about his folks."

"Had he run off before?" Niki said.

"Umm…well, we thought so, but then he showed up and said he'd been in Houston. Wasn't the same after that. Wouldn't talk about it."

"How did he act?" Russ asked.

"Got in fights over nothing. Real moody. Slept a lot. One thing, he peed the bed a lot. He tried to hide it, but we could all smell it. We thought he was sick. Flu or something. One day, I realized we hadn't seen him in a while. Didn't know if his folks showed up and took him."

"When was the last time you saw him?" Niki asked, a knot twisting her stomach that had started when Houston was mentioned.

"Weeks ago, or maybe a month." Timothy's eyes darted from Russ to Niki then to the window. "I'm not saying he's the one out there."

Niki followed his gaze. Davey stood at the window, apart from the others, ignoring attempts at conversation. A statue.

She turned back to Timothy. "Do you remember if anyone else disappeared around that time? Or any other time?"

His eyes widened. "Guys come and go. Don't mean they're buried out there."

"No," Niki amended quickly. "I didn't mean that." Even as she uttered the words, she realized the idea of more bodies had occurred to her. The cadaver dogs were still searching. The prospect made her shudder. She felt Russ's disapproving gaze. *Not in front of the boys*, his look conveyed.

She sat back. "How did you come to be here, Timothy?"

He gave a short laugh. He seemed relieved at the change of subject. "I cussed out my English teacher. She was a bitch. You want to hear some crap? I get picked up for cutting school and the judge fines my ol' lady. How's that for justice? We got no money. Fucking judge put my mom in jail and sends me here. System's fucked, man. Kids miss school 'cause they don't feel good, and they go after the parents."

Davey showed up at their table. He glared at Timothy. "You spreading lies again, nigga?"

"Go fuck yourself," Timothy snapped. "Bet you could tell them who's buried out there. You probably carried the shovel."

A smirk curled Davey's lips. "Yeah, right alongside you, bro."

Timothy pushed back his chair and stood. He spread his feet apart, and his chest rose and fell. "Yeah?"

"Cool it, fellas." Russ intervened, rising and inserting himself between them. He addressed Timothy. "Let's get a soda from the kitchen."

When they left, Davey's eyes glittered after them. Niki could feel the tension radiating from him. "Davey, you're upset. Take a few deep breaths and relax. This whole situation is hard on everyone." Her words seemed to wash over him without any affect. "You don't like Timothy?"

Davey raised his brows in mock surprise. "Tim? Hell, we're best buds. He's like my little brother. You didn't see that?" He swung his leg over the chair Timothy had vacated and sat with his arms hanging over the back.

Niki ignored the sarcasm in his tone. "Do you know who's buried out there?"

An amused expression crossed his face. "Now why would you ask me that? How would I know? You think I buried them?"

"I wasn't accusing you. What I meant was, you've been here a long time. You pay attention to what's going on. As a counselor, you'd know if someone suddenly disappeared for no reason."

"They all disappear sometime, don't they? Cops come get them, their folks take them. Don't mean nothing to me."

"Or you take them to Houston," she said, watching his reaction.

"Yeah. No big deal." His eyes narrowed and he leaned slightly toward her. "Never seen anyone get buried, though."

"Who would do such a thing? No idea?"

"Nope. Say, how's ol' Curtis Ray? Ever get my camera out of the evidence bag?"

"He's doing okay." She wasn't surprised at the change of subject. Only that it hadn't happened earlier. "You'll still have to wait for the camera."

One leg jiggled. "Guess he's still at Open Palms?"

How did he know Curtis Ray had been staying at Open Palms? But, of course, Webster Capp would have told him. "Why? Are you worried about him?"

"Not anymore." He stood abruptly, knocking the chair over. "Tell you who you should be worried about. Kit. He carries this badass army knife. For real. Maybe you should talk to him." He turned and walked away.

She stared at his retreating back. If Kit really had a knife on him, he could get into real trouble if Lindsay or any other feds found it.

She spotted Kit coming out of the kitchen and heading toward the back of the house. She intercepted him.

"Davey says you have a knife," she said quietly. "If you do, and you get caught, it will go worse for you when you go back."

He started to deny it then looked around to see if anyone was watching them.

She spoke carefully. "Normally, I wouldn't say this, but given the unusual circumstances we find ourselves in, I'll give you a break. I won't say anything to anyone if you give me the knife now." She held out her hand. "It will be our secret. This is your one and only chance."

He hesitated, eyes steady on hers. Wordlessly, he reached into his back pocket and handed over a Swiss Army knife. She nodded as she accepted it and slipped it into her own back pocket. He walked away, tightlipped.

When she went back to the table, Russ rejoined her, carrying two cans of soda. He handed one to her, glanced around the room, surveyed the scattering of boys, put the chair in an upright position, and straddled it. "Everything all right?"

Must be a guy thing, she thought, watching him. "Not really. I'm worried about Davey. Is Timothy okay?"

"He blew it off. He can handle himself."

"Who's Quincy? Did you ever meet him?"

"Once, if he's the kid I'm thinking of. Fifteen, or so. About the same age as Tim. I didn't know he was missing."

"There must have been a search, though. Someone noticed. Wouldn't you have heard?" Niki persisted. "A missing child is a big deal."

"Nobody, until now, mentioned Quincy as a possible victim," he said. "Maybe his folks picked him up. I'll check with Lindsay and the locals."

"You don't find this strange? There has to be records of some kind. What kind of camp is this when a child goes missing, and nobody knows anything or seems to care?"

He stared at her. "What do you mean, nobody cares? Why are we here? Lindsay Marks cares. I care."

"Yes, now that we're here and digging up a body. But what about back then? When a child goes missing, I would certainly have questions right away, not a month after he's been gone. Where are his parents? Have they been notified? Has anyone looked for him?"

"I don't have the answers." His voice raised in anger. "Give me Webster Capp and I'll force him to tell me. If nobody reported Quince missing, then something *is* very wrong. Whether he turns out to be the body out there or not, I'll find out what happened to him."

"A little late," Niki said.

"Yeah, you're right." He grimaced. "I've been too busy being a cop in Brookshire to be notified every time a troubled boy disappears miles away at this camp. My bad."

"Sorry," Niki said. "I know it's not your problem."

"Of course it's my problem. It's everyone's problem when a kid goes missing."

"I meant, I'm not blaming you."

"Oh, that makes everything okay, doesn't it?" He was silent for several moments, his face drawn and miserable. "This day has set my teeth on edge. The feds, the dogs, these boys, and what they've been through. The medical examiner will be here soon, and CSU." His gaze met and held hers. "I don't know what you want from me. No one even hinted to me that Quincy went missing. I never expected there'd be a body buried here."

"I know," she said.

"I was investigating child pornography and trafficking of minors, not murder."

"I'm not accusing you of anything."

He slid off the chair. "I'm going to see what's happening outside."

Niki watched him. As much as she wanted to go with him, she couldn't leave the boys alone. Maybe if she asked Davey, he could watch them. On the other hand, was he stable enough right now? She didn't trust him. What had he expected her to do after telling her about Kit?

She stood and stretched. A brisk walk around the house showed the boys in different stages of unrest. Most sprawled in chairs or on the floor, quiet as if waiting for a shift in the atmosphere. The specter of death hung in the air.

She saw no sign of Davey. Timothy wasn't in any of the rooms either. For some reason she couldn't name, her uneasiness grew. A few nails of panic pricked her.

The calm broke with shouts that pierced the air. She rushed to the window. The wind had picked up, sending a dust cloud around the site where the feds were working. She needed to get closer and stepped outside for a better view. The dogs were barking again. Men with shovels were digging at a different site than the first. Another body?

The ground rumbled under her. Her attention was diverted to the dirt road by trucks and cars arriving through more dust clouds. Niki recognized the CSU van and the medical examiner's SUV. Constables from the sheriff's department drove up followed by the state police in their black and whites.

Six boys stepped out on the porch and crowded around her. She searched their anxious faces, silently naming them.

"Anyone seen Timothy?" She tried to make her voice sound natural. Not panicked. Not yet. "How about Davey?"

A few grunts answered in the negative. Her chest felt tight. "All of you need to go back inside." No one moved. She raised her voice. "Now."

With great reluctance, they shuffled through the door, heads straining to look behind them. Their silence was louder than words. They congregated at the window, tight, anxious faces plastered against the glass.

Her stomach twisted in knots. Russ Baker's patrol car wasn't parked in front anymore. She dug around her pockets for her cell. *Damn!* She must have left it in Russ's car. A patrol car pulled into the space where Russ's patrol car had been. More lined up until the front of the building was a parking lot.

Where did Russ go? Had she gone too far with her accusations? *Face it, Niki.* Russ Baker, his car, and her cell phone all had disappeared. And where were Timothy and Davey?

CHAPTER 35

Anger at Russ turned to panic when he didn't show up. Did he take Timothy and Davey? His patrol car was gone. Had she made him so angry that he would leave her? No, he wouldn't do that. But then, she didn't really know him.

She went back inside to confront anxious faces.

"We'll have to wait and see." She could tell by their expression this wasn't what they wanted to hear. She sighed. "You know more than I do. Probably more than the FBI. You've seen what's been happening during the months and years you've been here."

"Like what?" Kit asked. "You mean, like a body being buried? Sorry, lady, we didn't even see anyone die."

She couldn't blame them for being cynical. "We need any information you think might help."

"Why should we help?" Cody said. "We're outta here. Fuck this place."

His attitude seemed to be felt by all the others. "You think by leaving, you're done with this place? It doesn't work that way. Whoever put those boys in the ground will do the same or worse to others if they're not stopped. You don't want that on your conscience, believe me. I understand you're angry. You have every right. Running away won't get rid of the nightmares. Doing nothing won't bring justice."

After a lengthy silence and furtive glances between them, Wally spoke up. "Nobody believes us anyway."

"The FBI will. Why do you think they're here right now? They know why you were sent here and they know about the abuse you or your friends endured. Maybe a victim died and was put in that grave. Whatever you're holding back, you don't have to be silent anymore. The men responsible will be charged for their crimes. Your stories can help put them away and prevent others from being hurt. Even more importantly, talking about it will start the healing process for *you*. Please, tell someone. If not me, then Special Agent Marks, or Russ Baker, or anyone you might feel you can trust." She searched their faces. Eyes that should have been clear were hard and far older than their years. "Think about what I'm telling you."

The door flew open. Lindsay Marks, not Russ, walked in. She looked tired and anxious.

Niki took her aside away from the boys. "What have you found?"

"Two bodies. They're still combing the woods for more. Where's Russ?"

"He took off," Niki said, not hiding her irritation. "I'm not sure where. I couldn't call. I think I left my cell phone in his car."

Marks stared at her. "What do you mean, he's gone?"

"I haven't seen him or Davey. I can't find Timothy either." A wave of anger anchored her. She strode to the door. "Look for yourself. His car isn't out front." *To hell with Russ Baker. If he harmed either one of those boys, I'll shoot him myself.*

Marks followed her outside. She slipped on her sunglasses and surveyed the yard. After a second, Mark's expression changed. She pointed in the direction of the lake. "Take a look."

Niki stared at the man and boy walking toward the house. Shock, relief, and another surge of anger hit her fast. They were chatting away, oblivious to the anxiety they had

caused her. Russ looked up and frowned as if sensing tur-
moil ahead. Timothy looked like a younger version of the
man, grim-faced and solemn.

"What's wrong?" Russ said when they reached the
porch.

Timothy ducked his head and took the porch steps two at
a time. Marks followed, leaving Niki alone with Russ.

"Where's your car?" she demanded.

His eyes widened at her tone. "I had to move it to make
room for the emergency vehicles. I took Timothy with me.
He needed a chance to talk in private. Why?"

"You could have said something." She cursed herself as
soon as the words came out. She sounded like a whining
wife.

Russ's jaw went slack. "You thought I'd left you? Seriously? Guess I haven't made much of an impression."

"I didn't know what to expect. One minute you were
here and the next you and Timothy were gone. I'm supposed to trust you? I don't know you that well, Officer
Baker."

"Okay, you've made your point," he said. "So why
didn't you call?"

"I left my cell in your car." Her cheeks burned. "You
didn't find it?"

"No, didn't see it, but I wasn't looking for it. We can
check now if you'd like."

"That's okay. Did Davey go with you?"

Russ's gaze went to the door. "He's not here? I haven't
seen him."

Marks rejoined them in time for her to overhear them.
She held a manila folder. "What about Davey?"

"He's acted erratic ever since we got here," Niki said.
"Now he's missing."

"Are you sure?" Marks said, with an undertone of sarcasm. "Maybe he thought he wasn't needed anymore."

"Well, he wasn't with Russ," Niki shot back. "He's not
inside either."

Russ pointed to the folder. "What's in that?"

Marks's expression turned grim. "Capp kept pictures of all the boys in his office. We'll try to identify the bodies by these photos. The deaths are recent and there are no visible injuries that should hamper identification. The bad news is they might be digging up a third body."

Russ grimaced. The agent faced away from them but not before Niki saw the professional mask crumble.

Marks wiped her forehead with her sleeve and pulled herself together. "I've got to get back to the men."

"I'll go with you," Russ said. "I've met most of the boys on my visits here. I can help with ID."

Marks paused in front of Niki. "Don't worry about Davey. He'll show up. Have you checked to see if his motorcycle is still here?"

Niki's jaw dropped in surprise. "He has a motorcycle? What does it look like?"

"Bright yellow. That's how he gets to and from Houston. I thought you knew." Marks turned to Russ. "Coming?"

Russ hesitated. "Go ahead. I'll meet you there." He turned to Niki. "Come on, I'll show you where he keeps it."

They walked around the house to the back where Russ had moved his patrol car. He pointed to a lone oak tree. "He usually parks it right there in the shade."

The space was empty.

"You're right. He's gone." He sounded surprised.

"Back to Houston? Without a word? So much for being responsible."

"Nothing we can do about it now." He winked at her. "Davey will be all right."

"Are you sure about that? I'm not."

"There's nothing we can do. At twenty, he's not a juvenile, and we don't have jurisdiction over him. From what I've been told, Davey comes and goes. He can take care of himself."

"He's unstable. We've both seen that." But Russ had stopped listening. His gaze was focused on the edge of the trees and the grave site. She gave up. "Never mind. Can we look in your car for my phone while we're here?"

"Sure." He switched his attention back to her and opened the passenger's door.

"You don't lock it?"

He shook his head. "Didn't think we'd be staying this long."

It only took a glance to see her phone on the passenger's seat. She picked it up and tried to turn it on. The battery was dead.

"Well, at least it's here." She pocketed the phone, but again he'd turned away from her and wasn't listening. "You all right?"

"I will be," he said, attempting a smile but failing miserably. "Go back to the house and stay with the boys. Don't let them out."

She watched him as he strode toward the trees. She knew how he felt, that he didn't have a choice. It wasn't a job she'd wish on anyone. Sweat dripped off her hairline and her face felt tight. She went inside where the air didn't seem as cold as before. She counted heads. Some were slouched on the sofa. Others watched out the window. All accounted for, except Davey. She walked past them into the kitchen. Water from the faucet slid down her throat like a cool, refreshing wave. She returned to the main room. Tension electrified the air. Idle stares went through her. She took a deep breath and sank into a chair at the round table.

She reached for the deck of cards left behind earlier and shuffled them. "Anyone for poker?"

CHAPTER 36

As the late afternoon sun dipped behind a cloud and spewed pink flames across the sky, Niki joined Marks and Russ on the porch. Marks shook off her black jacket. Her skin shone with a layer of sweat and the wet ends of her blonde hair stuck to her neck.

Niki carried three glasses of ice water on a tray. Marks and Russ each took one. Niki sat the tray on the ground and eased into the empty chair between them. She sipped her water and waited for the news. From the expression on Marks's face, Niki knew it wasn't good.

"Three boys," Marks said, holding the frosty glass against her forehead. "Timothy was right about Quincy. He was the second body we found. The files from the office have them listed as families unknown. One thing I can say about Webster Capp is he kept good records for all the boys. All up until they died. Missing are the death certificates for them and the medical report. All three will have to be autopsied."

"Did you find paperwork on Jeremy and Nate?" Niki asked.

Marks didn't look surprised. "Minimal. We've got their names, dates of birth, and where they were found. I've asked Russ to transport them to Houston. I put in a call to CPS, and they'll put them in the system and take them to a shelter."

"I have a better idea," Niki said. "Let Russ take them as far as Brookshire. My car is there and I can take them on to Houston. CPS can meet us at Open Palms."

"That's fine with me," Russ said, "if the FBI agrees to turn custody over to me. I can then grant the necessary permission to Niki so she can follow up."

Marks gave a brief nod. "Settled then."

Niki felt a sudden urgency to get back home. There was nothing left for them to do here. The officer from Midland had left half an hour ago with Wally. Parents arrived to pick up their sons. Only the four remained.

The screen door to the house creaked open and Cato and Danny appeared, followed by Jeremy and Nate. The latter two looked resigned to their fate. Niki knew better. That attitude was only a mask to cover fear and insecurity. It made her resolve for change that much stronger.

The boys were squeezed in the back seat with their backpacks tossed in the trunk. Niki slid onto the front passenger seat and Russ took the wheel. She picked up her cell.

"Can I charge this in your car?" she asked.

"Sure." Russ grinned. "Better call that boyfriend of yours. Here, you can use mine."

"Thanks." But Nelson's phone went straight to voice mail. She left a brief message saying she was on her way home and would call upon arrival.

Niki twisted in her seat to observe the boys. Their thin bodies didn't take up much room. Jeremy and Nate stared straight ahead, their expressions somber. Now that they were really leaving this place, they looked somewhat lost and scared, but their eyes also held enough curiosity and hope for the future to contain them through the journey.

Cato and Danny spoke little but their silence differed from the other two. They knew where they were headed. They had family and familiar surroundings.

Her thoughts turned to the dead, now on their way to Austin. She settled in her seat and closed her eyes, listening to the chirp of Russ's police radio. She craved the all too elusive sleep. When she checked again on the boys, three were asleep. Only Jeremy stared out of the window, alone with his thoughts and dreams. Niki left him alone, sensing he didn't want to be disturbed.

It was Davey who kept Niki awake. She didn't agree with Russ's assumption that the young man would be all right. Clearly he was troubled. Why had he left without telling anyone? Was he running away, or was he hurrying to meet someone?

CHAPTER 37

The return journey to Brookshire seemed to go faster than the drive to the camp, although the distance was the same. It was still daylight when Russ pulled up in front of the Brookshire police station. The boys in the backseat roused and peered uneasily at their surroundings.

Russ removed Niki's cell phone from his charger and handed it to her. "Well, this is it. Where did you park?"

Niki pointed across the street to where her dusty Toyota was slotted in a diagonal space a short distance from a hardware store. She slid out of the patrol car and opened the back door to let out Jeremy and Nate. "Here's where we get out. The rest of the way won't take long."

With an awkward exchange of hand signals and grunts, they said their goodbyes to Cato and Danny, who would stay in the car until Russ delivered them to their respective homes.

Jeremy and Nate both stretched and looked uneasily at the police station. Russ went to them and shook their hands. "If you boys have any questions or need to talk, you know where to find me. Don't hesitate. In the meantime, you're in good hands with Niki."

Niki nodded and mouthed her thanks. "We need to get moving. Anyone for a pit stop before we go?"

Jeremy stared at the police station for a moment and shook his head. "Not me."

"Let's just go," Nate said, turning away.

Russ tapped Niki's shoulder. "Don't be a stranger. Maybe next time you come this way, you can have dinner with me and my wife."

"I'd like that," she said. "You'll meet Nelson when you get to Houston. I assume you'll be testifying against Webster Capp."

"You got that right," he said. "Have a safe trip."

Once Jeremy and Nate were settled in her backseat, she started the engine and turned the air on high, letting the hot stale air blow out the opened windows. While she waited for the interior to cool, she punched numbers in her cell. Nelson answered on the second ring.

"Where the hell are you?"

"Excuse me?" The anger she heard in his voice put her immediately on the defensive. "I'm fine, thank you for asking. I'm in Brookshire, heading home."

"You've been in Brookshire all this time?"

"No, of course not. We visited the camp. Didn't you get my message? I left a voicemail." She paused, swallowed. "To hell with it. I'll explain when I get back."

"I tried to call you," he said before she could disconnect. "You didn't pick up."

The words sounded like an accusation. "My battery died," she replied with equal coldness. "Anything urgent?"

"Nothing that can't wait."

"Good. Did you find Webster Capp?"

"He was spotted leaving town this morning, but managed to elude us. He didn't show up at the camp?"

"I didn't see him. If he had, Lindsay Marks would have arrested him." She paused and lowered her voice, mindful of the boys listening from the backseat. "They found bodies."

"I heard. It's all over the news."

"Already?" She shouldn't be surprised after seeing the news vans invade the area.

"I guess you saw the graves?" He sounded grim.

She became aware of restless movement from the two teens. "Look, I'll talk to you when I get to Open Palms. I have a delivery." Before he could ask what kind of delivery, she hung up and put the phone on vibrate before tossing it on the passenger's seat. She raised the windows and backed out into the street.

Traffic wasn't heavy on I-10. If it stayed that way, she could make the trip to Houston in under an hour. She tried to relax and tuned the radio to 90.9, the jazz station. She refused to think about Nelson and his sucky attitude for the rest of the trip. She had other concerns and priorities. Jeremy and Nate were now fully awake and they had questions. What was Open Palms? What kind of kids were there? How long would they be able to stay?

She answered the first few questions. Their anxiety over what would happen, when CPS picked them up, rose. Where they would go would depend on CPS and if there were shelters that had room for them until temporary foster homes became available.

What unimaginable acts were these boys exposed to that they hadn't yet confided to another person? They would require years of counseling. Limited government resources didn't offer enough help. Whoever took over their care would need to have a special understanding of how to treat them. Because the foster home contingent was privatized, the state funds didn't always provide the right kind of home environment. Supervision of foster care was minimal. Deaths had resulted. Abuse had gone undetected. Niki had little hope for their success unless someone changed the system in Texas. That seemed unlikely.

The roar of a motorcycle engine jolted her. She glanced over. A bright yellow Yamaha, the same kind Mike had taught her to ride on his off hours. Marks told her Davey rode a yellow Yamaha. She looked closer but all she saw was a slender form leaning forward, a full helmet concealing his features. The motorcycle's engine roared and the bike sped away.

She glanced at Jeremy and Nate through the rearview. Their heads were straining to see out the window.

"Was that Davey?" she asked them.

"Kinda looks like Davey's bike, "Jeremy said.

"Yeah, I think it is," Nate agreed.

Davey left hours before they did. If he was headed to Houston, he should already be there. "Wonder where he's been?"

"Probably stopped to eat," Jeremy suggested.

"That must be it." The mention of food made her stomach rumble. The day had been long and hard on everyone. If she was hungry, she knew the boys had to be ravenous. Shopping malls, restaurants, and fast food places appeared on either side as they grew closer to the city limits. She found a Sonic and pulled into a space. Jeremy and Nate might have been nervous, but their appetites hadn't waned. Triple-deckered cheeseburgers and extra-large orders of fries were devoured and washed down with Cokes before they were back on the road.

Even with the approaching dusk, the heat and humidity sapped her strength when she parked her car in front of Open Palms. The boys were the first out. Robert, the night volunteer, let them in. A glance through the glass window of Alice Voss's office showed the supervisor still at work.

"You won't get past that lady without her seeing you," she told Jeremy and Nate, who were both staring into the office. "She rules this place. Nobody comes in here she doesn't talk to first."

Her cell phone vibrated. She checked the ID and saw Nelson's name. She pressed reject. He'd have to wait until she finished here.

Alice came out of her office to greet them in the hall. The boys looked awestruck. She was as dark as fine chocolate, with a heart as warm as apple pie straight out of the oven. But she was no pushover. She protected "her kids" like a mama lioness with her cubs.

"Who've you got there with you, Miss Niki? Good

strong helpers looks like to me." She appraised them honestly with a nonjudgmental acceptance so typical of her. Whoever took advantage of that openness was sorry afterward.

Niki said. "Jeremy and Nate came from the camp that Webster Capp ran."

"I figured as much," Alice said. "Heard the feds took over. A little late from what I've been hearing on the news. Did you eat on the way?" When Niki nodded, Alice smiled. "That's good. It's still early, Niki, so why don't you do the intake and then show these boys around and get them comfortable. When you're finished, I want to see you."

Niki led the two teenagers to the intake section. Getting their family history and vitals recorded were the necessary first steps before accepting any child who came through their doors. With the paperwork completed, she led them through the shelter with the thoroughness of a teacher. By the time the tour was finished, they knew where to use the bathrooms, find food and drink in the kitchen, do their laundry, sleep in their assigned beds, and pray or mediate in the chapel. Several residents filtered in to check out the newcomers. Niki left Jeremy and Nate to exchange names and get acquainted. They would soon learn they had much in common with the other kids.

Niki advised Robert to stay with them while she talked to Alice. She went into the office and shut the door.

Alice lifted her head from a mound of paperwork and leaned back in her chair. "The feds let you take them?"

"Jeremy and Nate have been signed over to me. Capp picked them up off the street. They didn't have a home, and they weren't enrolled in school. I'm supposed to deliver them to CPS. Actually, CPS is to pick them up from here. Have they called?"

"Not yet. They won't have anyone available tonight. I'd be surprised if they send a social worker this week. Don't worry me none. It won't hurt those boys to stay here and get needed counseling."

"I'll work with them," Niki said and waited for more. Something about Alice's subtle change in attitude made her suspicious.

"Considering CPS's workload, it might be a month or longer." She drummed two fingers on the desk. "You call Nelson yet?"

"I talked to him before I left Brookshire. Right now all I want is a shower and a change of clothes." As if on cue, her cell vibrated again. "Speak of the devil."

"You'd better take it," Alice said with a laugh. "He won't stop. You know he's been worried about you."

"Worried about what?" Niki retorted. "I was surrounded by the feds and with a policeman. He doesn't think I'm capable of taking care of myself?"

"Don't get yourself all in an uproar, girl. Maybe he was thinking about that Officer Baker. Sure is a mighty good-lookin' police guide."

"And married," Niki said, her irritation growing. A jealous boyfriend was the last thing she needed. "Forget it. I need to go home and then check in with Lilith. Have you talked to her?"

"She's called, too," Alice said. "Jayme's doing okay with Curtis Ray and Markey. They're all fine, but she wants you to call her."

"I will. I'm heading to the house. Tell Robert if there're any problems with Jeremy or Nate to get a hold of me."

Fifteen minutes later, Niki opened her front door, wanting relief and solace to wash over her. Didn't happen. The weight of the day's events crashed down on her. She took out her cell and called Luis.

He told her that Capp was still in the wind. "He was seen along I-10, but he eluded the state police and the constables. Do the feds suspect him of killing those kids and burying them out there?"

"Lindsay would tell you before she would tell me," Niki replied. "Won't know how those boys died until the autopsies are done. Do you think Capp could be guilty of killing Shamberg and Snake?"

"There's no evidence that puts him at either scene. Right now the DA has filed charges against him for child trafficking, sexual abuse, and fraud. That's enough to put him away."

"When I saw him last, he told me you should look at whoever was closest to Shamberg. That fit Chloe Sanders, but she has an alibi. He could also be pointing to himself."

"We're working the cases," Luis said, as a gentle reminder to her. "Leave it to us. Are you at home?"

"Just got here," she said.

"Have you talked to Nelson?"

"Briefly." Why was everyone so concerned about her and Nelson?

"Good night, Niki. We'll talk later." The line disconnected.

She walked upstairs like a sleepwalker. Didn't want to think about buried children, Capp, or even Nelson. The grime and dirt of the camp clung to her.

In her bedroom, she stripped off her clothes and ran the shower. She let the hottest water she could stand beat on her. She lathered soap and scrubbed her body and hair. The steaming water stung and pounded the back of her neck muscles until the soreness eased.

When she emerged she felt revived and wide awake. While she dressed her conversation with Chloe Sanders came back to her. Something Chloe had said niggled at her, but she couldn't find a handle for it, only that it seemed important. No matter how hard she tried, she couldn't grasp the elusive message.

She glanced at the clock. Outside the sun was setting. There was still some light outside at eight o'clock. Too early for bed, and she felt restless. Questions pressed her further and wouldn't let go. She got back into her car, went through the drive-through of a What-A-Burger and bought a large Coke. Not that she needed the caffeine, but it wouldn't hurt either. Answers. She needed answers, and her search led her to Chloe Sander's house.

Niki rang the bell. She fully expected Chloe to slam the door in her face. Sure enough, when Chloe opened the door and saw Niki, she started to close it.

"I have one last question, then I'll leave you alone," Niki said before the door shut all the way.

Chloe was dressed casually in a cream-colored pantsuit with a pink silk blouse as if she were expecting a date. She glared at Niki. "We already covered everything there was to be said."

"I'm not here to go over your relationship with Clayton Shamberg," Niki said. "It was something else you said that I need to clarify. I won't take up much of your time."

Chloe held her resolve for several moments before relenting. The hard stare softened briefly. "I'm expecting a friend shortly, so I can only spare you a few minutes."

"That's good enough," Niki assured her.

Chloe showed Niki to a sunroom in the back of the house and offered a seat on the curved green sofa.

Niki perched on the edge. "You said Clayton often employed older boys to run errands, answer phones, take messages, those sorts of duties."

Chloe's lips pursed as if recalling the conversation. "You mean the interns from the camp? We discussed them already."

"No, not them," Niki said. "I'm talking about the young men who lived with him as house boys or secretaries. You mentioned he seemed particularly fond of one. This young man lived with him for a few years. I don't think you mentioned his name."

Chloe gazed out the window. "Yes, I think I know who you mean. Clayton picked him off the street when he was fourteen, as I recall. He'd been kicked out of his house for dealing drugs. Clayton got him clean, taught him skills. Said the boy could make him laugh and even forget work for a day. He was impressed by the boy's intellect, had high hopes for him."

"What happened to him?"

Chloe shrugged. "Clayton finally tired of him, like the others. When the boy turned seventeen, he sent him off to camp to be a counselor. Forgot about him until he needed him again to transport his replacements from the camp to Houston."

Pretty cold, Niki thought. That would make any boy enraged. Going from feeling loved and needed for the first time in his life to being rejected and feeling used, the resentment he felt must have built up each time he made that trip. Niki felt bile rising in her throat. "Do you still deny knowing what Shamberg did to those young men before discarding them like used toilet paper?"

Chloe's face lost color. All the air leaked out of her. "You think that boy…"

"Killed him? I don't know, but I'm beginning to believe it's possible."

Chloe closed her eyes. When she opened them again, they were shiny with moisture. "I refused to see it at the time. God, I forced myself to be blind to everything." She put her head in her hands.

Niki stood, unmoved by her display. "Chloe, do you remember the young man's name?"

Chloe swallowed. "I'll never forget his name or the look on his face the day Clayton sent him away. Davey Tanner."

The words confirmed what Niki already knew in her heart. She turned away from Chloe but heard the sharp intake of breath that followed a sob.

"Thank you, Chloe. I won't bother you again."

Niki let herself out. She sat in her car with the engine running and the cold air blowing. The sight of the yellow motorcycle flying past her on the highway came back to her. Where was Davey Tanner now?

Her cell phone rang. Lilith. Niki answered, feeling a pang of guilt. She had meant to call her stepmother when she got home. "I'm back in Houston," she said. "Are you all right? The kids?"

"We're all well. Saw you on the news. Relieved you're back." Despite her attempt at cheerfulness, Lilith's voice sounded strained. "Did you get my messages?"

"I haven't had time to check." Her cell phone had been on vibrate.

"The concierge called up and said a young man wanted my room number."

The hairs on the back of Niki's neck rose. "What young man?"

"Davey Tanner. But I thought he was at the camp."

"Lilith, listen to me. Don't let him come up. Whatever he says, he's lying."

"Lying about what? What's going on, Niki?"

"I think Davey may have killed Shamberg and Snake."

Lilith gave a low whistle. "He may have some issues, but a killer?"

"I just talked to Chloe Sanders. Davey lived with Shamberg for years until he was dumped when he reached seventeen. But then Shamberg made it worse by making him bring Davey's replacements to him. That young man has had years to build up hate. He might be responsible for those boys who were buried at the camp."

"Niki, you must be mistaken." Lilith's voice rose. "This is crazy. Are you saying he could be after Curtis Ray and Markey?"

"I'm not taking any chances. I'm calling Luis. Stay there. Warn the hotel staff and tell them not to give out your room number to anyone."

She started to hang up, but Lilith said, "Niki, I think he's already got my room number. How did he know where to find me and the boys?"

Good question. How indeed?

Then she knew. Her disappearing cell phone, of course. Davey must have found it in Russ's unlocked patrol car before he left. She had stored both Lilith's cell number and the hotel's. He must have copied them then tossed her cell back on the seat.

"Call Nelson. He'll just give me crap if I call. Tell him I'm heading over to your hotel right now and for him to meet me there." She went to disconnect, but Lilith's voice stopped her.

"Niki, someone's at the door."

CHAPTER 38

Niki sped north on Kirby. The setting sun struck her rearview mirror and hit her eyes while she swerved around rush hour traffic. She flew past the multi-million-dollar homes lining the streets and roared onto Allen Parkway that led her to the edge of downtown.

She kept going over Davey's bizarre behavior at the camp and what his sudden departure meant. Lilith's last call changed everything. Davey Tanner had found Lilith and the children.

Niki swore aloud when a red light stopped her. She used the time to call Lilith again. No answer. She found the number for the hotel and rang the desk. The clerk didn't answer either. Something was definitely wrong. She banged the steering wheel with her fist. The damn light was still red. She rang Nelson. He picked up at once. Without waiting for his greeting, she said, "Going to the Harper Arms. My mother and the boys are in danger. Davey's there and I think he's the killer.

"Hold on," Nelson said. "What are you planning to do? Niki? Answer me."

The light turned green. She disconnected and rammed the gas pedal. No time for lengthy explanations.

The one-way downtown streets with timed signals at every corner inhibited her speed. She swore at every red light. As she grew closer to the hotel, the sound of sirens sparked another stroke of panic. She parked in a loading zone, jumped out of the car, and ran the rest of the way.

As she got closer to the Harper Arms Hotel, the unimaginable came into view. Smoke billowed out an open window. That explained why the clerk hadn't answered. Had Davey used fire to get to Lilith and the kids?

A crowd of onlookers had gathered around the building. Niki pushed through them to get to the front. A yellow Yamaha leaned against the side of the building.

A fireman blocked her way inside. "Stay back, please."

She raised her voice over the noise of the burgeoning crowd. "My mother is in there with three children. I have to get to them."

He barely glanced at her. "Everybody's out of the building."

"You don't understand. There's a killer with them. They're in danger."

The fireman looked skeptical. "Ma'am, I'm telling you, everyone in the hotel has been escorted out. Have you told the police about your suspicions?"

"This is real. You have to let me in."

"Sorry, ma'am. Can't do that."

She tried to see behind him through the smoky haze of the hotel's interior. "What started the fire?"

"One of the trash cans on the fifth floor blew up in flames. But it's all been contained. Nobody got hurt. Every room was evacuated. Until the chief determines the building is safe, nobody gets in."

Fifth floor?

Lilith's room was on the sixth floor. A mass exodus from the building provided a perfect cover for an abduction. Davey was disturbed, but not stupid. She glanced again at Davey's motorcycle.

Another siren signaled there was more help on the way. A van with Channel 2 News printed on the side angled to the curb. A newscaster trotted toward the building followed by a photographer and a TV camera.

Niki heard her name being called. The voice was unmistakable. Nelson.

She turned and, at the same time, saw Lilith's rental car speeding out of an underground parking garage. She couldn't see who was driving through the tinted glass. She took out her phone and punched in Lilith's number. The call went straight to voicemail.

The key was in the ignition of the Yamaha. She made up her mind and knew there was no turning back. She couldn't wait for Nelson. It had been years since her husband taught her how to ride a motorcycle. She told herself it was like falling off a bike and getting back on again.

Nelson shouted her name again. She jumped on the Yamaha without responding. When she turned the key, the engine roared like a hungry tiger. She had one objective— overtaking the car.

Once on the street, she concentrated on keeping the car within sight. For a moment, she almost lost control. The front wheel wobbled until she picked up speed.

Did Davey have a gun? Shamberg was killed with a knife. So was Snake. Thoughts of him using a knife on the children or Lilith made her stomach sour. She suddenly remembered the Swiss Army knife she had taken from Kit at the camp. She had put it in her pocket. With luck it was still there. She didn't like guns, not since she'd had to kill with one. A knife could cut a branch from a tree or slice through a tough steak. The short blade could wound but unless it sliced a main artery, the chances were good it wouldn't kill anyone. It might stop a killer.

Lilith's car charged through a red light, barely avoiding being hit by oncoming cars.

Niki slowed and weaved until she saw an opening then sped through the next intersection. Horns blared behind her, tires skidded, irate drivers shouted curses. She followed when the car turned on Lamar, crossed Bagby onto Allen Parkway.

Without the restraint of signals, the car sped up. Niki

revved the Yamaha's engine and kept the car in sight. Where the hell were they going?

They were almost to the busy intersection of the Parkway and Shepherd, when the rental swerved into a turnoff at the edge of Memorial Park and came to a sudden stop. This unexpected change made Niki brake suddenly into the turn. She lost control and the Yamaha jumped the curb onto grass, wobbled, and dropped sideways. She stuck out her leg to brace herself and barely managed to jump off and roll away to avoid being pinned under the bike. The engine sputtered and died. She got to her feet and whirled to face the street. Relief flooded through her when she saw the car hadn't left.

Her relief was short lived. Davey jumped out, fell on his knees, and scrambled up again. He took off, running down the grassy slope—away from her. She needed to believe Lilith and the children were in the car and safe. Meanwhile Davey was getting away. She had only a split second to decide. Go after Davey or check on Lilith and the children.

Niki yanked the Yamaha upright and jump started the engine. The bike sprang to life again, chewing chunks of grass and dirt as she raced after the young man.

Davey glanced back as he darted back and forth, ducking behind trees to avoid her. Niki slowed on the steep incline, squeezing the brake. She barely avoided a tree and felt branches scratch her face. She reached the bottom of the hill and brought the bike to a full stop. About thirty feet from her, Davey was bent over and breathing hard. She got off the bike and approached on foot. He turned his head, saw her, and took off again.

Niki yelled at him to stop and sprinted after him. She caught up to him and tackled him. The impact forced out what little breath Davey had left. He gagged when she got him back on his feet. His face was as red as a bloody steak. Mud streaks furrowed a path down his cheeks. He struggled to speak, coughed, and bent over, holding his stomach. He glanced sideways toward his bike but didn't move.

Niki grabbed his collar. "They better not be hurt. I swear to God, if they are—"

He raised his head. "Me? It's Preach! He tried to kill me. He's got Curtis Ray and Markey. Look!" He coughed out a sob. Dry heaves racked his body.

Niki turned toward the street and stifled a scream. Lilith and Jayme were stumbling out of the back seat of the car. Webster Capp, his dirty hat askew on his head, emerged from the driver's seat and looked over the hood. From the passenger side window, Niki saw a terrified Curtis Ray and Markey straining to look out. Capp shrieked Davey's name. As he got back into the car, he shouted, "This is on you, Davey!"

A second later, Capp revved the engine and the car took off.

CHAPTER 39

Niki stood, rooted in stunned silence as the rental car sped away. Before the tail lights were out of sight, Lilith and Jayme were running down the hill.

As soon as she found her voice, Niki turned on Davey and demanded, "Where's he taking the boys?"

Davey cringed. Instead of answering, he whimpered like a lost, hurt child and retreated away from her.

"Don't play that game with me," she shouted. "Tell me now."

Lilith reached them, panting hard. "He's not playing, Niki. Look at him, he's going into shock."

Niki didn't waver. "Davey? I know you're stronger than you act. Help me save those boys. What's Capp planning to do?"

Davey took a step toward the bike and faltered. "I can show you."

"Not on the bike, you won't," Niki said. "Tell me where he's going. Stop wasting time."

Jayme stumbled behind Lilith. Sobbing, she took Davey's hand and tugged. "Where are Curtis Ray and Markey? Where's that man taking my friends? Will he hurt them?"

Davey looked down at her. Something changed in his eyes. Fear. He whispered the words, "Clay's studio."

Niki's chest tightened. Not the answer she wanted to

hear, but she wasn't surprised. She jumped on the bike, blinking back sudden tears. Of all the places Capp might have taken the boys, why did he choose the studio where Shamberg made his movies, where he had been murdered?

Before the bike's engine caught, Davey shouted a final warning. "He's got a gun."

Shit. Anger fueled a new surge of adrenaline. There wasn't time to think of anything but the danger facing the boys. She looked back to where Jayme clung to Lilith. Davey looked ready to bolt. Where were the goddamn cops when you needed them?

"Go, Niki!" Lilith yelled. "I'll call Nelson. Hurry!"

Niki revved the engine, and the bike shot up the hill. The ride to Shamberg's second River Oaks residence seemed to take forever. She had been there only once, when Shamberg's body had been found, but she knew the area and followed her instincts. She recognized the outside of the house at once, but didn't see Lilith's rental car in the driveway. She parked close to the back gate, which stood open, and jumped off the bike.

She stopped short when she saw the rental car parked halfway on the grass. The rest of the back yard looked ominous. The yard had been dug up. Two deep holes were empty and waiting. A shovel was stuck in the ground. Niki grabbed it.

The sliding back door was glass. It was locked, as she expected. No time for lock picks. She swung the shovel like a bat aiming for a home run. With four tries, she shattered the glass and unlocked the door. She dropped the shovel on the porch and rushed inside. She heard no sound. Desperation fueled the adrenaline racing through her veins. After checking the main living area, she darted down a long hallway, kicking open doors until she reached the last one. She barely acknowledged the white walls and the twin-sized bed in the corner with cameras on tripods next to it. Her focus was riveted on the figures in the center of the room.

Webster Capp stood with his back to her and didn't react

as she stepped inside the room. He had known she would come. Expected her. Didn't try to hide. He seemed to be lost in a trance. When she looked beyond him, her stomach clenched and roiled.

Curtis Ray and Markey had been placed back to back on a wooden plank that didn't look very sturdy. Their hands were tied behind them. Their legs tied together. Tape covered their mouths from which emitted anguished sounds. Their eyes were like those of wild animals caught in a trap.

But what terrified Niki most was the rope that encircled their necks in a figure eight noose. Niki followed the taut rope to an exposed beam in the ceiling. It came down to wind around a pulley operated by Capp. His hand clenched on the handle.

As soon as she made a move toward the boys, he cranked the rope tighter around their necks. Their moans cut through Niki like a saw.

"Stay back," he warned. "I'll string them up before you reach them."

She stopped. "Let them go, Preacher," she said, her voice cracking. "They're just children."

"They are doomed," Capp said in a flat voice. "This is the only way out for their souls. Can't you see? I'm saving them from destruction."

"Listen to me," she said, trying to keep her voice level. "I'm taking Curtis Ray and Markey out of here alive. Don't make this any worse for yourself. The police will be here any minute. Let go of that handle."

Capp turned his body slightly so she could see the gun in his other hand. There was a strange glint in his eyes. "So you are the devil come to take them home?"

She stared at the gun then forced her eyes to focus on Capp. "I am taking them home. You'd better believe it. Taking them unhurt and alive. Do you understand? Put down the gun. Shooting me won't help you. Give up before it's too late."

"It's already too late," he said in a thundering voice. "All

I need to do is crank this handle a few more times, and the boys will rise to heaven. Don't move."

Niki spread her hands, beseeching him. "Why? What have they done to deserve this? The boys are just children. They can't hurt you." She stepped closer, desperate to find a way to reach the boys before it was too late.

He pointed the gun at her. "Stay back. One more step and you'll be God's witness."

She dropped her hands to her side. "Okay, okay. I'm doing what you ask." She had to keep him talking. "Is this what happened to the boys you buried at the camp? Were you trying to save them, too?" She turned slightly to shield her right side. Carefully, she slid her right hand to her back pocket and felt the Swiss Army knife.

"Ah, they found my poor boys, did they?" Capp's eyes went out of focus, but only for an instant. "They were sick. They didn't want to eat. Always trying to run away. Just like Curtis Ray and Markey."

She eased the Swiss Army knife upward. "Tell me what happened. How did they die?"

He cranked the handle of the pulley a half revolution. The noose tightened on the boys, whose whimpers turned to a chocking sound. Capp's voice deepened. "You think I killed them? I saved them. What kind of life would they have had after Clayton spoiled them? Oh, I know what he did to them. There was only one way to cleanse them. I had to make them clean again."

Clean how? Poison? She couldn't think about that now. She saw what the rope was doing to the boys. She swallowed, an automatic response. "Did you save Shamberg, too?"

His lips curled into a snarl. "Shamberg," he spit. "He was evil. I didn't see it at first. Evil is like that. Evil wears a cloak of innocence and then destroys. But I didn't kill him. Haven't you figured that out yet? It was Davey. Davey killed him and Snake. I told him that it was wrong to let his anger and hate rule his hand."

"And what you're doing isn't wrong?" Keeping her gaze focused on him, she inched closer to the boys. She noticed that Curtis Ray was trying to work his wrists free of the rope while watching her every move with eyes that bulged with strain. Every time his body twitched, the plank under him wobbled. Markey was shaking and blinking rapidly. She tried to warn them with her eyes, but Capp saw her and turned the handle another notch. She turned back to him.

"I'm saving these two," Capp said. "That's different from murder." He narrowed his eyes at her. "Not another step or I'll shoot them right now, starting with Curtis Ray." He turned the gun toward the boy. This brought more whimpers and muffled screams from both boys.

Niki heard a door slam in the distance. Shouts from the police. Capp jerked his head toward the sound and pointed the gun at her. With his other hand, he cranked the handle of the pulley another half rotation, stretching the rope tighter.

Frantic, she tried to think. She pulled the knife from her pocket. Who could she reach first, the boys or Capp? At the same time, she had to alert the police where to find them.

"Don't scream," Capp warned, as if reading her intentions. "I'll shoot you and then the boys."

"It's too late, Preacher," Niki said quickly. "That's the cops coming through the door. Davey told them what you plan to do. Drop the handle. Save the boys and yourself." She had the knife pulled out, and she tensed, ready to rush Capp if necessary.

He closed his eyes and opened them again, staring first at the boys and then up at the ceiling. Without warning, he turned the gun so the barrel touched his lips. "Then we'll all go out together." He shoved the handle down as he pulled the trigger.

"No!" she screamed. She lunged and slammed into him, realizing at the same time that the gun hadn't gone off.

The force of her body made him let go of the handle, and he toppled to the ground. He roared in fury. She spun the handle in the opposite direction so the rope would spin free.

She turned back to him in time to see him raise the gun and aim it at her. She kicked at him, but missed. Instead of the gun blast she expected, there was only a click.

Her surprise was matched by the stunned expression on Capp's face. He fired again. Nothing happened. He bellowed in rage. Niki whirled away from him to free the boys.

Instead of a slack rope, the boys were choking. She looked up in horror to see the rope caught on the ceiling beam. The noose was tight around their necks. She rushed to them, pulled out the knife, and slashed at the rope above their heads. She frantically sawed until the ends frayed and split apart. Next her fingers worked to pry the rope away from their necks while she watched their flushed, panicked faces. Their eyes bulged, and her efforts increased at a maddeningly slow pace.

She ignored the sounds behind her as she managed to get the rope loosened and pulled free. She peeled the tape off their mouths. They sputtered for air, half choking, hands touching their necks. Before she had time to wonder who freed their hands, she saw Nelson on the other side of the boys, taking the rope from their legs.

She sucked in deep gulps of air as she helped Nelson get the boys down from the plank. For the first time, she became aware of the uniforms who surrounded a howling Webster Capp.

All she could say was, "The gun. It didn't go off."

Webster Capp sputtered incoherently as he was handcuffed. Niki couldn't make out his words but it sounded like blasphemy to her.

Nelson remained mute, even as she helped him lay the boys down on the floor. Both Curtis Ray and Markey were having trouble breathing. Nelson applied CPR on Markey, while Niki helped Curtis Ray. They didn't have long to wait before the paramedics arrived, lifted the boys onto stretchers, and carried them out. Capp was led away in cuffs, cussing and screaming.

"Aren't you going to talk to me?" she asked Nelson, while the forensic team went to work.

He didn't answer. She followed him out of the room and into the hall, surprised to see Davey standing there. His wrists were handcuffed behind his back. His eyes were jumpy and he giggled inappropriately. She wondered how much of this persona was an act.

"What is he doing here?" she asked Nelson.

It was Davey who answered. "Duh, I had to show him where you were, didn't I?"

"Shut up," Nelson said.

Niki's gaze flashed from Davey to Nelson. "Where are Lilith and Jayme?"

"Waiting in the car." Nelson's tone was hard and angry.

"I'm not sure if you're angrier at me or Davey," she said. "I had no choice. Even you can see that. If I hadn't gotten here in time, they would be dead. So please don't give me shit. I'm not in the mood."

Davey giggled again.

Niki whirled on him. "What are you laughing at?"

"At Preach. Stupid old fart." Davey laughed out loud. "Clay always said Preach would come apart someday. As soon as I saw the gun, I knew where he got it. I knew it wouldn't work. That's why I jumped out of the car. I knew he wouldn't shoot me or anyone else."

"Oh, yeah?" Nelson said. "How?"

"That gun belonged to Clay. The last time I saw that gun was the last time I saw Clay. That's when I removed the firing pin."

CHAPTER 40

Niki hadn't expected to see Officer Russ Baker again before Webster Capp's trial. But on the second Thursday in October, she saw him emerge from Alice Voss's office. She couldn't hide her surprise. This must be a casual visit since he wasn't in uniform. Her curiosity heightened.

"Are you here for me?" she said by way of greeting.

He grinned. "Always a pleasure to see you, Niki. Actually, I came to visit Curtis Ray and Markey. I've met Mrs. Voss and we had a very nice conversation. She reminds me of my first grade teacher."

"She can be rather intimidating." Niki said, smiling. "The boys are playing video games as usual. They'll be glad to see you." She stepped aside to let him pass.

His toothy grin widened. "I got permission from Mrs. Voss to take them to the Museum of Natural Science. When Curtis Ray was younger, he expressed an interest in dinosaurs. I bet Markey's never been there either. You're never too old for dinosaurs."

Niki laughed. "Alice doesn't usually let someone walk in and take out one of our kids. Not without a background check on them. Did you pass a verbal and written test? I'm impressed. All kidding aside, I know the boys will be thrilled."

The looks on the faces of Curtis Ray and Markey

touched Niki. The one man in Curtis Ray's life he'd trusted as a small boy now came to him on his fourteenth birthday, the best possible present. Markey was wide-eyed, though somewhat more reserved than Curtis Ray, but Russ soon had both of them hanging on every word as he explained their venture back to the dinosaur ages.

CHAPTER 41

The weeks passed quickly after that day. November arrived with cooler weather. It was a rainy Wednesday when Lilith dropped by Open Palms and offered to take Niki to lunch in her new car, a Honda Accord.

They arrived late at El Tiempo, their favorite Mexican restaurant. Lilith ordered a margarita for herself and an iced tea for Niki. Lilith finally seemed to relax after being unusually quiet on the way over. She plunked her menu down and placed her elbows on the table.

She started the conversation in a deadpan voice. "I don't know what's going to happen to Curtis Ray and Markey after what they experienced at that studio. They'll have emotional and mental scars that may never heal. They'll probably never have a regular family life. I wish I could do more for them. You can't keep them at Open Palms. They're too young. You've done wonders with Jeremy and Nate getting them into that special school. I wish I knew where CPS will place Curtis Ray and Markey—"

Niki raised a hand, stopping her tirade. "You can stop worrying. You met Russ Baker the last time he was in Houston visiting the boys. He wants to adopt both Curtis Ray and Markey. Actually, he's already started the paperwork. If he and his wife get approved, and I don't see anything standing in the way, both boys may get the help they need."

"That's wonderful news. What does his wife do?"

"She's a social worker. Very nice woman."

"Very lucky boys." Lilith sipped her drink. "I'm sorry I've been so scarce these last few weeks. I've been so busy at my new office I haven't had time to breathe. How's Jayme?"

"She's back home. Her mother is up for parole, and I think she'll get approved this time. Jayme and the boys text each other, and we arrange visits. They'll be neighbors once the adoption goes through." Niki settled back in her chair. "What about Davey? Whatever made you decide to defend him?"

"Who better? I'm a damn good lawyer, and don't you forget it. Look, here's the thing about Davey. He's never admitted to killing anyone. Claims he can't remember. What the DA has is mostly circumstantial. The weapon was never found."

"Wait," Niki said, dumbfounded. "You think he's innocent?"

Lilith paused, as if considering her answer. "I don't know. I don't want to know. But if he did kill them, I think Webster Capp goaded him to violence while Davey was at camp, drumming in his head Shamberg's rejection and betrayal."

"That's a stretch," Niki said.

"No, I don't think it is. I had Davey evaluated. He's been diagnosed with bi-polar disease and schizophrenia. He hears voices. His mood swings got worse in jail, and he had to be hospitalized. Davey never had a chance. No father, an addict for a mother who kicked him out when he was thirteen because he showed gay tendencies. When he was fourteen, he had the misfortune to meet Clayton Shamberg, who seduced him, used him, and brutalized him. When Shamberg got tired of him, he sent him to camp. Then Webster Capp got hold of him and used him for his own twisted plans."

"There's his motive. You saw Shamberg's body. Only someone filled with rage and hate could do that," Niki said.

"I agree. That makes all of Shamberg's victims potential suspects."

"So what's your plan? Put Shamberg on trial?"

Lilith smiled humorlessly. "Now there's an idea."

"Most schizophrenics are nonviolent," Niki said. "But a majority of convicts are probably bi-polar. That's not a defense for murder. What's your plan?"

"I'm trying to work a deal with the DA's office," Lilith said. "If I can't get them to find for diminished capacity, then I'll try to get the charges reduced in exchange for his testimony against Webster Capp. I don't want to put him through a trial, but a jury might find him not guilty when they get all the facts. People hate pedophiles. They'd like to see all of them dead.

"Davey's a good man at heart," she continued. "He cared deeply for those boys who died at the camp and for all the boys Shamberg and Capp abused. He needs long-term treatment, not prison."

"I wouldn't doubt that your passion could win over a jury." Niki laughed and put her hand over Lilith's. Their eyes met. In a more serious tone, Niki added, "I'm glad you're here, Mom. I've missed you all these years. I just didn't know it until you came back into my life."

"I've missed you, too. More than you'll ever know. You are my daughter, and I plan to stay this time."

Their waiter arrived and took their order. When he left, Lilith sat back and studied Niki. "It's none of my business, I know, but what's happening between you and Nelson?"

Niki took a long sip of her iced tea. "We've both been busy."

"Don't be evasive. Have you two broken up?"

Niki smiled. "This is the real reason we're having lunch, isn't it?"

Lilith grinned, unabashed. "I've tried not to pry, but both of you are so stubborn, and you belong together."

"Mom," Niki began.

"No." Lilith put up her hand. "Let me have my say. I'm

buying lunch, remember? That man is hurting, and so are you, even if you don't want to admit it."

"I can't deal with a man who doesn't trust me or recognize my abilities."

"You really believe that? My dear, Nelson is so proud of you it pops his gut when he's around you. He's just afraid of losing you. When you take it in your head to plunge into danger, that about kills him. Because he loves you."

Lilith's words stuck with Niki the rest of the day. She didn't want to admit even to herself how much she missed Nelson. She was better off without a man in her life. No one to tell her what to do or not to do. Maybe she should get a dog. No, she was gone too much. A cat? They pretty much took care of themselves as long as they had food, water, and a litter box.

She did miss the sex, though, how his arms felt around her afterward, and how they could discuss cases until dawn broke.

She arrived home early that night, made a simple dinner for one, and turned on the TV. During a commercial, she switched on the porch light. She made a cup of tea, turned off the set, and opened the new mystery she had bought earlier in the week. But she couldn't concentrate.

When the knock on her door came, her heart thumped against her chest. Her palms were sweating. A quick check through the peephole brought a rush of warmth.

She opened the door slowly, seeing what she hoped would be in his eyes, his parted lips, hearing him moan with need as he took her into his strong arms, surrounded her with his familiar scent, and backed her inside. With a shove of his foot, the door closed on the outside world.

THE END

About the Author

Laura Elvebak sometimes feels she has led several lives, but throughout the years, her passion for reading and writing has never faltered. Before the twenty-something years, she worked for lawyers and oil and gas executives, she had a variety of occupations, including working as waitress and even as a go-go dancer in the late sixties in Philadelphia. Born in North Dakota and raised in Los Angeles and San Francisco, she settled in Houston after living in parts of New York, New Jersey, Philadelphia, and Florida. She is happily unmarried after six attempts with men who would make fascinating characters in books but didn't succeed as husband material.

Elvebak studied writing at UCLA, USC, Rice University, and Beyond Baroque in Venice, California. After taking a directing class in Houston, she co-wrote, directed, and acted in a one-act play. She optioned three screenplays to a local production company and co-wrote a script for the 48 Hour Film Project. She is the author of the *Niki Alexander Mysteries*. Her novel, *The Flawed Dance* (Black Opal Books, 2015) takes place in Philadelphia in the late sixties. She is a member of MWA, Sisters-In-Crime, The International Thriller Writers, and The Final Twist Writers and has a presence on Facebook, Twitter, LinkedIn, Good Reads, and Amazon Author Central.